A NIKKI EASTON MYSTERY

DAZZLED

MAXINE NUNES

FIVE STAR
A part of Gale, Cengage Learning

GALE
CENGAGE Learning

Detroit • New York • San Francisco • New Haven, Conn • Waterville, Maine • London

LIBRARY OF CONGRESS CATALOGING-IN-PUBLICATION DATA

Nunes, Maxine.
Dazzled : a Nikki Easton mystery / Maxine Nunes. — First edition.
pages cm
ISBN 978-1-4328-2730-4 (hardcover) — ISBN 1-4328-2730-8 (hardcover)
1. Actresses—Fiction 2. Murder—Investigation—Fiction. 3. Los Angeles (Calif.)—Fiction. 4. Mystery fiction. 5. Romantic suspense fiction. I. Title.
PS3614.U8645D39 2013
813'.6—dc23 2013019270

First Edition. First Printing: October 2013
Find us on Facebook– https://www.facebook.com/FiveStarCengage
Visit our website– http://www.gale.cengage.com/fivestar/
Contact Five Star™ Publishing at FiveStar@cengage.com

Printed in Mexico
1 2 3 4 5 6 7 17 16 15 14 13

For my mother and father, in tender memory and gratitude.

ACKNOWLEDGMENTS

I owe thanks beyond words to Zen Chang for his unerring critical instinct and incredible generosity. Also, for their invaluable input and inspiration, huge thanks to Ian Demsky, Victoria Golden, Linda Gunnarson, Lynda Hansen, Virginia Johnson, Jim Krusoe, Dylan Landis, Matt Maranian, Darien Morea, Chuck Rosenberg, Eva Wilson, Ada Bird Wolfe, and Joan Wood. And much appreciation to the wonderful team at Five Star: Erin Bealmear, Deni Dietz, Nivette Jackaway, Tracey Matthews, Tiffany Schofield, and Deirdre Wait.

CHAPTER 1

What's real? Darla used to ask me. *How do you know what's real?* I never understood the question. But then I didn't have platinum hair and cheekbones that could cut glass, and no one ever offered to buy me a Rolls if I spent one night naked in his bed. Darla was a brilliant neon sign flashing pure escape. You almost didn't notice that those lovely green eyes didn't blaze like the rest of her. She was both main attraction and sad observer at the carnival. Something had damaged her at a very young age. We never talked much about it, but we recognized this in each other from the start. Isn't that what friendship is?

The week she disappeared was as extreme as she was. Triple-digit heat in late August and wavy layers of smog suffocating the city. By ten in the morning, it was brutal everywhere, and on the sidewalks in front of the homeless shelter, with the sun bouncing off the film crew trailers and the odor of unwashed bodies and general decay, it was a very special episode of hell. Beneath an archway, a tall man with a filthy blanket draped over his head rolled his eyes heavenward like a biblical prophet. Or a *Star Trek* castaway waiting to be beamed up.

In one of those trailers, where air conditioning brought the temperature down to the high nineties, I was being stuffed into a fitted leather jacket two sizes too small. Perspiration had already ruined my makeup and the dark circles under my eyes were starting to show through.

Heat keeping you up, hon? the makeup girl had asked. I'd nodded. Half the truth.

Mykel Z, the costume designer, was trying to zip me into the jacket, but his fingers were sweating and frustrating his attempts. "If you'd get yourself boobs, Nikki," he said, "we wouldn't have to squeeze you into size zero to work up a little cleavage."

"Bigger boobs for you, smaller nose for my agent. Average it out and I'm perfect."

"Almost. Legs from here to eternity, long dark hair to die for. But the nose *is* a bit roller derby, darling. Did you break it?"

"When I was a kid."

"I'll give you the name of a marvelous doctor, a genius with noses. And his lifts for my older ladies . . . I swear the seams don't even show."

"I'm not sure I want to wake up one morning and see someone else in the mirror."

"An idealist. Good luck, honey."

I was used to this. At my first Hollywood party, a guy asked me what I did. When I told him, he looked bewildered. Then he brightened. "Oh," he said, "I guess you could play a real person."

Outside, a prop guy was spraying a couple of shopping carts to dull down their newness, and a wardrobe assistant walked a few extras onto the set.

"No, no, no!" Mykel cried, running out the door, letting in a flush of hot air. "Layers! They need layers!" With a broad motion of his arm, he pointed to some people in the little park on the corner. "Use your eyes! The homeless *totally* invented layering!"

I took advantage of the break, managed to find my phone in the junk shop that is my shoulder bag, and called Darla's cell again. It flipped straight over to her voice mail. Like it had for three days, since this shoot had begun. No point leaving another message.

Mykel flew back into the trailer and stared at me for a few

seconds, blinked like he was fighting back tears, and began to tackle the zipper again. It moved up an inch, before it caught on the leather.

He dropped his arms, his lips trembled, then he opened the trailer door again and stuck his head out.

"Benito!" he hollered, with an edge of real panic in his voice. When Benito, his "shlepper," did not appear, Mykel flopped down on a chair and blotted his face with a tissue.

"Where the hell has *he* gone?"

"You sent him for a Frappucino," I said.

"Ten minutes ago!"

"It's hard to find a decent barista on Skid Row, Mykel."

"Maybe that's why these people look so depressed."

"You know what," I said, "let's forget the jacket for a while. They're nowhere near ready to shoot. I'm gonna grab some water from the fridge. Want a bottle?"

"Thank you, sweetie." Mykel placed the jacket back on its hanger with all the tenderness due a garment that cost more than I was being paid for a week's work.

Beneath my tank top, a trickle of sweat from my bra reminded me I was still padded with chicken cutlets—the silicone inserts the director wanted for every female in the cast over the age of twelve—and when I removed them, I felt almost human again.

Outside, an assistant was trying to wrangle the extras—a task that had turned chaotic, since real street people kept slipping past security to get to the bagel table. But even from this distance, it was easy to tell them apart. You only had to look at their faces. On some, the flesh itself was infused with misery, the eyes dazed with hopelessness. The rest, in the same soiled layers, were radiant and eager to be noticed.

I'd had a taste of both, but a year on the streets at fifteen had been enough. I got a false ID, found jobs, and managed to take care of myself. But there was something restless in me and I never stayed in one place too long. Somehow, more than a decade slipped by. And what had seemed like freedom began to close in on me.

Then I wound up in L.A. and started picking up rent money working as an extra. A crime show was shooting a Manhattan street scene in downtown Los Angeles, and I got pulled out of the crowd because of my "New York face" for a line they had added: *Ain't seen her in a long time, mistah.* That amazing stroke of luck—and the three-thousand dollar initiation fee I was still paying off—got me my union card.

Now I had pictures and an agent and classes, and that was what really hooked me. Acting may be make-believe, but class was where the truth beneath the face you showed the world was not only welcome but demanded.

Only that wasn't exactly what working as an actor was like.

This job was for a midseason pilot called *Street,* a "fish out of water" comedy about three girls from Beverly Hills who start a gourmet soup kitchen for the homeless. "*Clueless* meets *Pursuit of Happyness*" is how my agent described it. My role—two days' work that could "go to semi-recurring"—was as a homeless person who gets a makeover.

A wave of hot air blew into the trailer, followed by the production assistant, who looked at me and let out a shriek.

"*Mykel!* Why isn't she in costume? They're *ready* for her."

And they were.

Four hours later.

By the time they released me it was past ten, and as the crew struck the lights and equipment, the homeless began crawling into makeshift tents of newspapers and old blankets and cartons, or gathering in doorways, palming small packets that would get them through the night.

Hot stale air still hung over the city as I walked to my car, an ancient MGB that looked right at home here in its own version of layers—black over Haight-Ashbury psychedelic over the original British racing green. The standard joke about MGs is that you share custody with your mechanic, but someone had replaced the temperamental English parts with American ones, and it actually started up every time I turned the ignition key.

With the top down, the hot Santa Anas were better than no breeze at all as I passed the rolling lawns and swaying palms of MacArthur Park, moonlight dusting the lake and the silhouetted figures of dealers and users.

A half hour later, I turned onto La Cienega and headed north past the cool stone facades of restaurant row, past Beverly Center whose colored lights bounced off gleaming Mercedes, Lexus SUVs and the occasional virtuous Prius, past the mansard-roofed Sofitel, past the crowds milling outside a few nightspots.

My little cottage still held all the heat of the day. I stripped down to panties, then finished off a pint of Chunky Monkey—ate it from the carton in a current of cold air from the open fridge door—and dragged myself into the bedroom.

I used up all the cool spots on the sheet in about five minutes and picked up a mystery from the night table. But no matter how hunky the hero, an old paperback cannot fill the other side of the bed, and I started to think about the man who'd occupied that space until a couple of weeks ago. Dan Ackerman. A good, solid guy, and I left him . . . why? Maybe because he was a good, solid guy.

The only other person in my life who mattered was Darla, and she hadn't returned my calls, which really wasn't like her at all. Even when she was on location, she'd phone and talk about anything—what they had for lunch, how filthy the honey wagons got—just to keep from feeling lonely.

I wondered if she was mad at me, if maybe I shouldn't have

been so blunt about her ex-boyfriend Jimmy. It was past midnight and too late to call. But I sent a quick text, then found myself listening in the silence for the phone to chime with her answer.

I turned on the TV. Fourteen dead in the Middle East and four dead in a murder in the Hollywood Hills. But no worries. Just wait for election day. Mike Ryle, TV Land western star/turned senate candidate, was saying, "Let's return to the America I grew up in." He sounded so earnest, you could almost forget that he'd grown up in the America of Vietnam and segregation and backstreet abortions.

When the infomercials started, I flicked the TV off and watched the minutes and the hours on the clock change. As the city was waking up, I fell asleep.

Chapter 2

Cool air drifted through the window and I opened my eyes to a crisp, clear morning that made the heat wave seem like a fevered dream.

I showered, had a cup of coffee with cream and plenty of honey, put on yoga pants and the disintegrating *Misfits* T-shirt I'd owned since I was twelve, and went out for a run.

It felt good to use my body again. I took the steep hill on La Cienega at a decent clip and when I hit the Strip, the uneasy undertow from yesterday caught up with me.

I pulled out my cell and was about to dial Darla again, when it rang.

"Nikki? Thank god!"

"Sari?"

"Yes. You've got to come over here."

"What is it?"

"I just called the police, but I—"

"The police! What's going on?"

"I can't wait for them. I have an audition!"

"Sari, what happened?"

"Darla's apartment. It's just awful. Someone must have broken in and—"

"Where's Darla?"

"I don't know. *Please* come."

I took Holloway back down, running all the way, trying to convince myself Sari was overreacting. She was always in a panic about something. The three of us led precarious lives, but she didn't have Darla's ambition or my need for freedom, and after her divorce she spent the better part of a year barely able to get out of bed.

Sari had been married to a lawyer who got the house, the pool, and the pool boy. Now, she had somewhat put herself back together and was trying her hand at acting. But what she really longed for was another man to take care of her. She spent most of her nights at private clubs, dancing with old guys in young clothes or nursing drinks at the bar, waiting for her future to show up.

Darla and Sari both lived in one of those apartment houses built for glamour in the fifties, with birds of paradise, browned at the edges, surviving among the wild aloe and yucca. Darla's living room blinds were closed, but water from the air conditioner dripped into a spreading stain.

Sari came running toward me as soon as I walked through the glass doors.

"Omigod, Nikki!" She gripped my hand and led me up the hallway to Darla's door. "I was on my way out and needed to ask her something. The door was open a crack so I knocked to see if she was home and then it opened a little wider and . . . look!"

Darla's living room had been assaulted. The sofa—cushions, back, arms—had been slashed open. The floors and tables were covered with down as if some giant bird had been slaughtered. Everything in the room had been destroyed. Every picture had been pulled from the walls, every vase and every lamp lay shattered on the floor.

"I kept calling her name," Sari said, "but she didn't answer."

"You didn't go in?"

"No." She looked pale and terrified under her makeup.

"Do you want to come in with me?"

She shook her head, looking, with her soft round face and pale curls, like a little girl.

I was no less frightened than Sari, but who knew how long the police would take to get here?

Inside the apartment, there wasn't a sound, except for the hum of the air conditioner. I glanced down the hallway that led to the bedroom. The photos that had lined its walls lay all over the floor. I made my way between the broken frames, steeling myself for what I might find.

Through the open door, I could see the explosion of clothing. Her closet, her dressing table, the night tables had been emptied. Hangers and drawers had been flung at odd angles everywhere. The mattress had been ripped open and pulled half off the brass bed.

Then, praying I would not uncover what I most dreaded finding, I began pulling aside piles and piles of clothes. To my enormous relief, she wasn't there.

"Nikki," Sari called from the doorway, stretching my name into three syllables, each with its own need: *I'm scared. Is Darla in there? I have to leave soon.*

I started back toward the living room, then froze.

I saw a thin stream of watery red trickling out onto the floor. I froze, and had to force myself closer to the archway that opened onto the kitchen.

It too had been ransacked, the fridge and cabinets completely emptied. Rice, sugar, flour, cornflakes blanketed every surface. Puddles of ice cream oozed from containers. It took a minute before I could make out where the red liquid had come from—slabs of frozen steak thawing and leaking blood onto the floor. *Thank god.*

I went out to the hallway.

"She's not there," I said to Sari, who took what must have been her first full breath since she'd opened Darla's door. "But

I haven't heard from her in days. When's the last time you saw her?"

"I don't know. It's been a while, I guess. Who could move during that heat wave? I had to drag myself—"

"Sari, has Jimmy been coming around?"

She stopped dead and stared at me. "Oh, no, you don't think—"

But she was thinking the same thing, and what I had feared all along finally took on the hard edges of reality.

"You know how he's always driving up and down our street," she said. "And what good is a restraining order if she never calls the police when he shows up?"

A few weeks earlier, the three of us were walking home from a movie together when Jimmy came up behind us. Despite Darla's large-than-life sensuality on film, she was slender and fine-boned, almost petite. He lifted her effortlessly off the sidewalk and shoved her into his car. As they drove off, she turned to look at me from the window and mouthed the words "It's okay." I hadn't called the police. Now I regretted it.

Sari grabbed my hand. "Nikki, I'm sorry."

"About what?"

"Please don't hate me, but I have to leave. The audition. It's a *national* spot!"

"Go ahead. I'll wait for the police."

She hesitated, then blurted out, "I needed to ask Darla if this outfit works. Does it?"

She was wearing a plaid shirt and mom jeans.

"What kind of commercial?"

"Floor mop."

"You're fine."

"Let me know what happens. Please, Nikki. I'm worried sick."

I shut the door to the apartment and walked out to the street with her. As she headed toward her car, I noticed Darla's bright yellow Beetle parked a few doors down, a ticket flapping from the windshield wiper. I walked over and took a closer look. The paper didn't look smooth enough to be fresh. I flattened it with my palm. Alternate side parking. Three days ago.

I sat on the steps outside the building, my arms circled around my knees, waiting for the police. An orange-blossom breeze riffled the trees. A girl too pretty for any other town jogged past, and a city garbage truck emptied three cans and dropped them right smack in front of a driveway. It wasn't long before the black-and-white pulled up.

Deputy L. Flutie, clipboard in his beefy fist, followed me into the apartment and let out a long, low whistle.

"Someone really did a job here," he said as he took a sheet of paper from under the clip and handed it to me with a pen. "Here ya go. Just write down what they got, then you can file a claim with your insurance company."

"It's my friend's apartment."

"So where is she?"

"I don't know. I—"

"Write her name in and she can fill out the rest later."

When I handed him the paper, he took one look at it and broke into a wide grin.

"Darla Ward? Miss April? From *Bachelor Pad*? No kidding!" He glanced around the apartment as if he hadn't seen it before, then started down the hallway. I saw him stop, glance at the floor, and with uncanny instinct, turn over the large picture frame of her centerfold. I'd never really looked at it, though I'd passed it hundreds of times on that wall—three feet long and a foot and a half high. More of your best friend than you really need to see.

Officer Flutie took his time in the bedroom, occasionally lifting, for closer examination, silky underwear that threaded through the piles of clothes. When he came back to the living room, his face was a little pink.

"So where is your friend?" he said.

"I don't know. I haven't been able to get in touch with her and her car's got a three-day-old ticket. Something's wrong."

He looked amused. "Maybe the lady hasn't been sleeping at home. Looks like some thief took advantage of it."

I wanted to tell him to take his fat head out of the gutter and open his eyes, but I said, "Does a thief usually slash the sofa, pull all the food from the fridge—"

"You're lucky he didn't take a dump on the floor. These crackheads and meth freaks, they can get pretty nuts."

"So could her ex-boyfriend," I said. "She had a restraining order out on him."

Flutie found that less amusing. "What's his name?" he said, pulling a notepad from his pocket.

"Jimmy Van Druten."

He jotted the name down. "Okay, got it." He turned to leave.

"That's it?" I said. "That's the investigation? Nothing else? No fingerprints? Just a good long look at her *Bachelor Pad* shot and a stroll through her lingerie?"

"You know, nothing makes my life tougher than these cop shows. Everyone expects a whole damn forensics team to show up for every punk thief. Well, my world is a reality series and it's called *Backlog.* Murders, armed robbery, five thousand rape kits rotting on the shelf and no manpower to deal with them." He gave a tired shrug. "So, as much as I'd love to find the creep who did this, there's not much I can do."

"And Jimmy?"

"Yeah. We'll check him out."

Then I was alone again in what remained of the home Darla had made for herself. The overstuffed furniture, the overstuffed fridge, the vases full of silk flowers, and paintings of more flowers and fluffy kittens—none of which had ever quite erased the deprivation in her eyes—all destroyed. The photographs that marked her small successes—the centerfold the deputy had gawked at, the stills from films and shows she'd had small parts in, the pictures taken with celebrities and any number of men in well-tailored suits who leaned toward her like plants bending to the sun—all strewn amidst the broken glass on the hallway floor.

The sliding door to the patio was open. Outside, a dozen large geranium planters had been overturned, their contents emptied. The flowers were wilted, some of them already brown and withered.

I didn't much like geraniums, trite flowers with hairy stems and the odor of mildew, but Darla loved them because they were survivors. She even brought me some to plant in the four-foot patch of dirt I called my backyard. Break a stem off, she told me, stick it back in the ground, and it'll keep growing. I scooped the soil back into the containers, replanted the flowers, and watered them.

When I came back inside, I took one more look around. Beneath the coffee table lay pieces of an ashtray that had been shaped like a daisy, and two gold-tipped cigarette stubs, thin and brown, the ones that boasted no preservatives. Like that made them some sort of health food. Darla didn't smoke. They could have been anybody's.

Then I noticed her cordless handset on the floor, the voice-mail light blinking. I wondered about violating her privacy. But not for long. I pushed PLAY.

There were several calls from me, others from people I knew and some I didn't.

Her brother Kyle had phoned a few times. I knew his voice. A whine. With an edge. Saying he needed a favor. Money, of course. Always money. To pay for his habit. No matter how often he lied or stole from her, she never turned her back on him.

He was the only clue I had to the childhood she never talked about. She didn't like being asked about her family. All she had ever told me was that her mother had died and her father ran off before she was born.

I wondered when Kyle had last heard from her and dialed his number. He didn't pick up and I left a message.

The next voice on Darla's phone was a woman. Older. No name. Clipped diction, every syllable enunciated. "My dear, if you are under the illusion that I will allow you to ruin my husband's life, then you are not only a cheap little whore, but a terribly stupid one."

I had no idea who she was. Jimmy didn't have a wife. It was the one good thing you could say about him.

Chapter 3

When I pulled into my driveway, I saw my landlord, Billy Hoyle, walk diagonally across the road and head right toward me. Six skinny feet tall, a white crewcut, and a muscle shirt baring his sixty-year-old arms. Cadaverous, but bursting with energy.

His own house across the street was purple. Very purple. At least once a day, for a couple of hours, he'd blast classical music from his open windows. You could hear it from one end of the block to the other, but his speakers were first rate and the music sounded almost live. The neighbors were always complaining, but I kind of liked the way he shared his passion instead of living in his own little iPod universe. And I liked the way he kept an eye on all of us.

"Who's the new beau?" he shouted as he approached.

"The who?"

"Or should I say *beau-laid*?"

"The what?"

"French, my dear, for someone who's so ugly he's beautiful. The man was quite eager to see you—paced and waited and pressed his large and rather pulpy nose against the window."

Jimmy.

"No friend of mine," I said. "But thanks for the heads-up."

Billy knew me well enough to see I didn't feel like chatting. He gave a little salute and took off.

Renting my cottage from Billy had been an amazing stroke of luck. Not only was it West Hollywood rent controlled, it had a decent-sized living room, a bedroom, a tiny kitchenette, and so many windows that the place was always full of light.

It was sparsely furnished, although for the first time in my life I owned a few things you couldn't pack into the back of a car. An overstuffed armchair, a Tuxedo sofa covered in an almost-worn-smooth corduroy, garage sale bookcases, and a dining table. Well, not exactly a *dining* table. More like a narrow piece of glass and a couple of sawhorses, real saw horses with Jackson Pollack–like splashes of paint I'd found in the shed out back. One side of the table was pushed against the back wall and on the other three sides were director chairs in bright Crayola colors. There was also a laptop, an ancient TV I'd found online, and a *Shoot the Piano Player* poster I loved almost as much as the books that overflowed their shelves. It was in every way the opposite of Darla's place. Everyone's childhood exacts a different price.

I hadn't heard my cell ring, but now it was yipping for attention like an anxious puppy. Sari had left a worried message. I called her back first to let her know that the police didn't do much but were going to talk to Jimmy.

Dan Ackerman, my ex, had also phoned. "Miss you. Just wanted to say hi." It was good to hear his voice, but not the way it's good to hear someone you're in love with. He was such a decent guy, and the only person I knew who didn't live on dreams. I thought about how nice it would be if he could wrap his arms around me and create the brief illusion that the world was good. No harm in returning the call. I let it ring one-and-a-half times before I hung up.

Then I called back Phil Levitt, my agent.

"So how'd it go on *Street*?" he said.

The memory of yesterday's shoot, as if buried under the debris of Darla's apartment, took a minute to retrieve. "I think it went okay," I said.

"Wrong." He let me squirm a minute before he said, "You did great! They love your 'scrappy' quality."

"That's good," I said, but I was so drained, it came out flat.

"What, you're not excited?"

"Yeah, I am. It's been a strange day."

"Look, here's the thing, Nikki. They want to know, if it goes to series, are you willing to get a little work done on the nose?"

"You know I'm not."

"I'll take that as a maybe. Meantime, there's a little *Case Closed* thing I think you're right for. Goes back to World War II. Singers. Like the Andrews Sisters. The one who gets bumped off will be a semi-name. But the other two have to lip-synch 'Boogie Woogie Bugle Boy.' So go find a track. And dress for the audition. A WAC uniform, shoes, and do some forties thing with your hair."

I wrote down the details. It was almost a week away.

I leaned back on the couch. As my body began to relax, I realized I hadn't eaten all day. But when I went to the fridge, there was only a pint of cream, a fossilized lemon, and a container of leftover Thai. I opened it. Something blue and fuzzy had gotten there first.

Carlito's Cantina was right around the corner. As soon as I walked in, Carlito set his straw cowboy hat on the counter, gave me a big gap-toothed grin, and said, "What is it, kid? You look like hell."

"You really know how to flatter a girl."

"*Ay, mi flaquita.* You gotta put a little fat on the hook to catch husband."

I was five-seven and a size six. To Carlos that was scrawny. To Hollywood it verged on plump.

I ordered a couple of tacos, but he had his own ideas about what I needed to eat. A few minutes later he handed me the

Butch Cassidy special, a burrito big enough to saddle up and ride into the sunset, surrounded with multicolored "fiesta" chips as cheery as a plastic bouquet.

I took my tray out to a table on the terrace, people chatting and laughing, the normal world whirling on. The cold Dos Equis was good, but I barely made a dent in the mountain of food.

By the time I left, the boys in cutoffs and muscle shirts were already out cruising, and the nightly parade of cars up and down the street had begun. Someone had written this side street into a gay travel guide. Every night it was busy, the sellers on foot, the buyers driving slowly by. But their transactions must have been made in whispers because, except for the hum of traffic, it was always quiet.

Back home, I clicked on the TV. Middle-aged men in expensive suits assured us that the war was "winding down." At every break, there was Mike Ryle, with rugged, six-shooter resolve, promising that when he got to the senate, he'd "clean up the Middle East and get rid of all these darn fanatics and troublemakers once and for all." At his side, his wife Dolly gazed up at him the way saints in paintings gazed heavenward.

The big local story was still the multiple drug murder in the Hollywood Hills. One of the victims was Johnny Rambla, king of the late-night used-car ads. Two of the others were alleged drug dealers. The fourth victim had not yet been identified. She was female. She was blonde. She was in her twenties.

For a minute, I thought I was going to be sick. Only it couldn't be Darla. She wouldn't touch drugs and, except for her brother Kyle, she couldn't bear to be around anyone who used them.

I remembered a date she'd had with a superstar producer who invited her to his estate for dinner. He served Oreo cookies and cocaine. Another ambitious girl might have stayed, let him indulge, even taken a taste. But Darla called and was waiting for me at the gates, shivering in a thin summer dress.

I dozed off, awoke to someone banging at my door and my heart banging against my chest. I walked into the living room and glanced out the window.

The stark porch light wasn't kind to Jimmy. A tall man, maybe six-four, he had a long face with a wide, fleshy nose and deeply pockmarked skin. The only person I'd ever seen who was uglier than Jimmy was an old forties actor named Rondo Hatton. He'd suffered from a disfiguring disease, and Hollywood cast him as The Creeper in a couple of horror movies. But Rondo Hatton, even playing a killer, evoked empathy. Jimmy was just unpleasant. Still, it wasn't hard to see that in a weird way he was a match for Darla's extreme beauty.

"Open the goddamned door, Nikki!"

"What do you want, Jimmy?"

"Come on, please," he said, changing his tone to a harmless nice guy's. "I just wanna talk to you."

I opened the door part way. His eyes were red from crying or from drinking or both.

"Where is she?" he said.

"You tell me."

"You think maybe I sliced her up in pieces and buried her in my backyard? Is that why you sicced the cops on me? You're a real bitch, aren't you?" He shoved past me into the room.

I tried to keep my voice even. "I told the cops about you, Jimmy, because the last time I saw you, you grabbed her right off the sidewalk."

His eyes couldn't meet mine, but he let out a dry laugh. "You know, for a smart girl, you know fucking squat about love."

"Just tell me where she is."

"Maybe she's on vacation. Maybe she found a new sucker to throw money at her. Say Cancun and her thighs spread like butter."

I'd had enough of him. I opened the door. "Leave," I said.

He looked at me like I'd slapped his face.

"Come on, Nikki. You gotta understand. I'm worried sick. I don't know what's happened to her. You know I didn't mean what I said. Okay? You gonna accept my apology?"

He seemed so bereft, I believed him.

"Sure, Jimmy."

He tried a smile, but it was more like an animal baring its teeth. Yet there was something touching about it, too, as if he knew what it was like to be human, wanted badly to experience it, but never had.

"Man," he said, "I could use a drink."

I poured him a shot of brandy. He tipped back his head and downed it all.

That seemed to do the job. He set the glass on the coffee table and looked around, a man who had swum to shore from a wild sea of emotion. He took in the room, appraised its value, and dismissed it all with a half sneer. Then he appraised me.

"You got a tight little body," he said, leaning back on the couch like he owned the place, his knees wide apart. There was a nasty grin on his face and the wounded look in his eyes had been replaced by something mean. That was the Jimmy I knew.

Enough of being the good hostess.

"All right," I said, "closing time."

As I picked up his empty glass, he grabbed my wrist and tried to twist me down next to him. I shoved him away hard with both hands.

"Get out of here now," I said.

"Hey, I can take it or leave it, baby."

I held the door open. He sauntered over to me, a cruel smile on his face. Then he pushed the door shut so hard, my fingers stung as it snapped out of my hand.

"And I guess I'll just have to take it," he said.

He grabbed my shirt in his fist and shoved me against the wall. The fishy stink of metabolized alcohol was nauseating. I looked him in the eye, but he was somewhere else, unreachable.

In that instant I was fifteen again, a runaway hitching a ride. An old guy driving a big black car stopped at the side of the road. Caught me by surprise. Pulled me into the car and pinned me down. He smelled like medicine, crushing me with his fat belly so I couldn't breathe. I punched his face and when he reared back, I rammed my foot into his stomach. He looked at me like he wanted to kill me, then bent over double and spit blood. I ran.

Now the same fear and rage formed a blazing red ball in my chest as Jimmy's rawboned hands pressed against my shoulders.

"You ever had the pleasure of a big man, Nikki?"

He leaned in closer. His misshapen nose was right in my face. I bit it, hard. He howled and his hands flew to his face and I shoved him, still wailing, out the door.

A few minutes later I heard an engine turn over, saw headlights flash on and dissolve into the night.

Then I began to shake.

Chapter 4

I slept lightly, the smell of Jimmy's liquor breath weaving through my dreams, and I woke up too fast, all raw nerves.

After a long strong shower to get him off my skin and two cups of hot sweet coffee, I drove down to the Sheriff's station.

It was barely eight, and there were a few other distressed souls on the narrow wooden bench who also looked like they hadn't slept much. When it was my turn, I told the old cop at the desk about Jimmy's visit and what had prompted it.

"You wanna press attempted rape charges?" he asked in a beleaguered voice, like I was a troublesome customer at a department store. "Your word against his."

"No," I said, "I just want you to find out what's happened to Darla."

"Whatever you say. I'm here to serve." He grabbed a Missing Persons form, asked a few questions, wrote a few answers, then looked past my shoulder and said, "Next."

I did what I often do when I feel up against a wall. I got in my car and drove out to the ocean and up the Coast Highway, my foot heavy on the gas, as if speed could push through this feeling of helplessness. I was stopped at a light when my cell rang.

"Thanks a lot, Nikki."

"Joey?" We'd worked on a scene and I'd completely forgotten that class was today.

"Where the hell are you?" he said.

"On my way."

Joey's anger was tinny and distant. "Thanks for totally hanging me up."

"I'll be there in twenty minutes," I said, then grabbed at a question that could turn everything normal again. "Listen, did Darla show up today?"

But the screen said CALL ENDED.

I turned around and headed back without breaking fifty. The MG took the lush curves of Sunset through the chain of wealthy towns from the Palisades to Beverly Hills, an emerald necklace of manicured lawns and neatly clipped hedges fronting amazing feats of undigested architecture: an oversize ranch house with Greek pillars, a giant white amoeba with French balconies, and a mansion twice the size of a football field. Darla once told me that when she was a kid, it had been the charred remains of a Saudi sheik's home, surrounded by nude statues painted in glorious lifelike detail right down to the black curlicues of their pubes.

I didn't slow down till I neared the radar trap west of Doheny. Billboards loomed over both sides of the Strip, neon and video signs flashed from the clubs and shops, and a painted rap star twenty stories tall toasted oncoming traffic with a giant vodka bottle in his bejeweled fist. But once I crossed Fairfax, it was all ramshackle shops with faded signs that looked like ads for failure. Even the palm trees here were thin and wasted, like the skinny straw-haired hustlers who shuffled along the sidewalks.

The Derek Provisor Studio was on a side street in Hollywood. Inside, it had the rank odor of rancid scenery paint and ripe emotions. The walls and floor were black, and in the light coming from the stage I could make out the risers where about twenty actors sat on folding chairs. I saw five heads of tousled, blonde hair, none of them Darla's.

Derek was on his faux leather chair, his legs on the footrest.

He threw me an annoyed glance as I made my way to a seat.

Joey, in pressed jeans and royal blue sneakers, was onstage working with a man I'd never seen before, who was so bald he looked like a human lightbulb. Cool and a little arrogant, he was making Joey uncomfortable.

"You're wearing blue shoes," Lightbulb said.

"I'm wearing blue shoes," Joey answered.

"You're wearing blue shoes."

Repeats. Meaningless words, but you take the ride on whatever emotion is running through you. You don't need writers to get a hell of a drama going this way.

"I'm wearing blue shoes!"

"YOU'RE WEARING BLUE SHOES!"

"I'M WEARING BLUE SHOES!" Joey was trying too hard.

Lightbulb started to laugh. "You're wearing blue shoes."

Joey leaned back in his chair, his arms folded across his chest. You could see he felt humiliated, but he put a smirk on his face and shrugged. "I'm wearing blue shoes."

"Take the losing beat!" Derek cried.

Joey looked down and mumbled the line.

"You're *acting.*" Derek's voice was full of disgust.

Joey's head lifted up, jerked back, fell. At that moment I saw—I think we all saw—the exact way his father must have cuffed him when he was a child.

"That's it!" Derek dyed his hair and played tyrant from his fake-leather chair, but he had a perfect eye for what was true. "We're done." He cocked his head to Lightbulb and mouthed the words "Good work."

Then Joey was alone on stage.

"How do you feel?" Derek asked.

Joey blinked into the lights. "How do I feel? Fuck you, Derek! That's how I feel."

"You're an angry guy," Derek said. "All you five-and-under

guys are angry." Five lines and under was one step up from an extra. "No wonder Nikki ditched you."

Joey looked down and muttered something.

"What did you say? I'm a son of a bitch?"

"Yeah. You're a son of a bitch."

"Go on, let it out, Joey."

"Son of a bitch!" Joey yelled, still trying too hard.

"Impotent little faggot. And the operative word is *little.*"

Joey grabbed a padded stick lying near the wall and smashed it down on a cushion.

"Go on, I'm a son of a bitch, kill me, kill the son of a bitch!" Derek cried.

Joey attacked the cushion with the stick, again and again, his face red, the veins on his arms popping, the rage pushing up through him and driving him, until finally, exhausted, he sank to his knees and looked up at Derek.

"Good," said Derek, "good clean work. How do you feel now?"

Joey took a deep, ragged breath. His eyes were remarkably clear. "Good."

"That's what sells tickets, my friends. Okay, Nikki, you're up."

I hadn't expected to work and Joey's explosive violence had opened up what was still raw in me from Jimmy's visit, but Derek couldn't abide excuses. I stepped onto the riser.

"Okay," he said, "Do a check-in."

I took a minute to feel the heat of the lights on my skin, the ungrounded lightness in my legs, a quivery feeling in my solar plexus. I tried breathing into it, but the tension was way too strong to dissolve. I looked out into the audience, at the eyes floating out there in the dark like fish in a tank, at Derek's face in the shadows and his pale hands in his lap.

"You here now?" he said.

I nodded.

"You and Joey were supposed to do *Streetcar,* right. How were you doing with Blanche?"

"I don't get her at all," I said.

Derek could sense a strong emotion like an animal smelling blood.

"You sure? You never felt helpless?"

Damn him.

"Go on, Nikki. Do helpless."

I turned to him, blinking out at the lights. "I can't, Derek. Not today."

"There's no excuses when you walk onto a set. You deliver what the scene demands. Just say the line, Nikki."

Bitterness tugged at my mouth. My throat was tight. The words came out squeezed and angry. "I'm helpless."

"Work from where you tremble. Again."

"I'm helpless." It felt like a scream inside, but my throat was so tight it came out barely a whisper.

"Better. Who are you seeing now?"

It wasn't Derek. It wasn't Jimmy, either. It was the man I always saw when everything in me quieted down enough to feel the aching knot in my heart that never really eased up. My skin felt cold. I could hardly breathe.

"Let it go, Nikki. You've been running from this all your life."

Something in me went rigid. I looked away for a minute and felt myself starting to surface. When I looked back at the chair, all I saw was Derek looking at me, disappointed.

"You went right to the edge," he said, "and then you cut your feelings dead."

I nodded.

"You'll get there, kid."

Derek got up from his chair and took a little bow. "Okay, people, that's it for today."

A few seconds later, the room filled with the sound of cell chimes as everyone turned their phones back on, anxious to check for messages.

A couple of people came over to me, patted my shoulder or squeezed my hand, and said reassuring things in that voice you use with very small children and the terminally ill.

I wanted to apologize to Joey, but couldn't get near him. He was the star of the day and everyone wanted a piece of him.

Chapter 5

I had one missed call. Darla's brother. I hit the number and rang him back.

"Yeah?" The voice was lazy and tight at the same time.

"Kyle?"

"Who wants to know?"

"It's Nikki. I've been trying to get hold of you."

"Yeah, so . . . here I am."

"Listen, someone broke into Darla's apartment. And I haven't seen her for days. Do you have any idea where she is?"

"Maybe."

"Is she okay?"

I heard him draw hard on a cigarette. "Not on the phone."

"What's going on?"

"Meet me somewhere."

"You know Benny Binks up on Sunset?"

"Yeah," he said again with all the charm of a man whose closest friend was a needle.

Benny Binks' rocket marquee towered over the Strip, a relic of the space-age fifties. As soon as I walked through the thick glass door, Lydia, one of the waitresses, greeted me with: "Hey, honey girl!" It wasn't a term of affection, it was what she called me because I always bothered her for honey for my coffee. Lydia had to be past sixty, but the management still made her wear the regulation miniskirt and fishnet hose. I don't think she minded. She had a great pair of legs.

Kyle was slumped in a red leather booth near the window, scraping a fingernail against the skin of his thumb with such agitation that a cracked line of blood had opened up. A cup of black coffee sat in front of him, untouched. He could have had Junkie written across his baseball cap.

Lydia came by with a carafe, one disapproving eyebrow raised at my choice of companion. The coffee was extra fresh and extra hot. She set a saucer piled high with honey packets down on the table, but I didn't touch them.

Kyle grunted a hello, then stared out the window, squinting against the late afternoon sun. If you didn't look too closely at his delicate features, you could take him for a kid. But in this light, he looked ancient.

"Where is she?" I said. "Where's Darla?"

He raked his fingers through his hair. It wasn't a casual gesture—the cords raised up on the backs of his hands.

"It's maybe, like, bad," he said.

A shot of cold fear ran through me.

He clenched his teeth while his glance shifted from his hands to the window to the door. "See, I fixed her up on this date a couple of weeks ago. This guy'd been bugging me."

"What guy?"

"And I kind of owed him."

"Owed him?"

"A couple of grand."

"What are you saying? That you used Darla to pay for some smack?"

"Gimme a break, Nikki. It was just dinner, no strings."

"This guy gave up a few grand for a dinner date?"

"I still had to pay him. He was just gonna wait a little bit is all."

"Pay who, Kyle?"

He needed both hands to support his head while he stared down at the table. "She saw him a few times after."

"To buy you more time?"

He looked up at me, indignant. "No. She got involved with him on her own."

"With *who*?"

His voice was so low I could barely hear him. "Johnny Rambla."

My brain didn't want to hook it all together, my friend and the grim scenes I'd seen on TV. Then it hit me in the stomach and knocked the breath out of me. It was a minute before I could speak.

"Kyle, are you saying she's the fourth victim?"

He nodded.

"You didn't go to the police?"

"Look," he said, "I can't deal with the fuckin' cops. Okay?"

"I'll go," I said, "but you won't be able to avoid them."

He pulled a cigarette from a crumpled pack. There was so much tension in his fingers, the cigarette broke in half.

Chapter 6

The LAPD operator connected me with a homicide detective named Adder. I told him that the unidentified Ivarene victim might be a friend of mine, and he gave me directions to an address on North Mission Road.

A soot-darkened bridge with fairy-tale minarets carried me over the concrete sluice that is the L.A. River to the other side of dreamtown, a cinderblock wasteland of auto salvage shops, junk yards, and the County Coroner. Man or machine, this is where you wound up when you were beyond repair.

The Coroner's building was at the top of the hill, fifties modern, big chrome letters glistening in the sun, and a panoramic view of the city the customers would never get to enjoy.

I gave the receptionist my name, then waited in one of the worn leather chairs. There was a faint but distinct odor: disinfectant with a trace of zoo.

I tried not to think about what I would soon have to face and watched a woman sweep the floor with a wide broom. She had man-short orange hair, a square body, and oxfords with rubber soles so thick, they made you wonder what she might have to slosh through in other parts of the building. She swept the entire floor methodically from one end to the other, and when she finished, she started all over again, though there wasn't a speck of dirt anywhere. Maybe this was how she stopped herself from thinking.

"Ms. Easton?"

A hefty fellow, with eyes that peered out over fleshy cheeks, extended a dry, weightless hand, tilted his head to one side, and smiled at me, a professional greeter of the grieving.

"Bart Bridgeman," he said.

He stood with his hands clasped together like a salesman about to show a property. His hair, combed straight back from his forehead, looked like it had been slicked down with polyurethane. Everything about him had been wrestled into rectitude, except his eyes, which peered out from the prison of his discipline, fluid and mute.

"Detective Adder is running a little late," he said. "I'm the Coroner's investigator, and I can show you the photograph."

That was a small relief. "So I don't have to actually look at the—"

"Body?" He gave a practiced chuckle. "No, no. We don't do that."

He led me down a hallway to a conference room where another smell, like fish, hit me hard. I put my hand to my nose.

"This is awful," I said. "How do you ever get used to it?"

Bridgeman looked annoyed. At first I thought it was my question, but then he pointed to something on the table—a brown paper bag, and lying on top of it, a half-eaten tuna salad sandwich. He walked over, scooped it up, and dumped it in a hallway trashcan.

"Nothing," he said, "makes me sicker than someone's leftover mayonnaise."

The irony was lost on him, and at any other time I might have been amused.

He asked me to sit down, then set an envelope on the table. "I should tell you," he said, "that it may be, uh, difficult. The face has been pretty badly battered."

The picture he handed me looked like an aerial map of

unknown territory. One side was a dark, swollen hill, and the other side flattened out where bones had been smashed. The nose was dented across the center, the lips caved in where teeth had been, the eyes were swollen shut. Above them, the forehead had collapsed. I wanted to look away, but I couldn't stop staring.

Bridgeman said, "Is it her?"

The hair could have been platinum, but it was filthy and matted down with dried blood. I looked for something familiar, tried to find some hint of Darla in that mess. But I saw nothing. I felt nothing. Only the shock of seeing the damage wrought by such brutal force.

"I don't know," I said.

"Why don't you take a look at these, please."

He slid three more pictures across the table. The same face at different angles.

I shook my head. "I don't think that's her."

He sighed as if I were a poor student who'd flunked an easy test.

"All right then, come with me," he said, "I want to show you a few of the victim's possessions."

He led me back through the reception area to another room where he put on plastic gloves, took a box from a wire cage, and removed some bloodstained clothing.

The metallic smell of dried blood rose from them. From the powder blue cami with white lace trim. The corksole sandals. The jeans and belt she'd bought at Kitson when we'd gone for a walk on Robertson one afternoon. At the bottom of the box, with her wallet and two lipsticks, was her key ring with my own key next to hers.

"Did these belong to her?'

"Yes, but . . ." Maybe it was too much for me to accept, but I still couldn't believe it was Darla in those awful photographs.

"But you're still not sure." He sighed theatrically.

As we walked back to the reception area, Bridgeman, with all the relief of a hostess whose guest of honor arrives late, called out to a man coming through the door, "Detective Adder!"

He appeared to be in his late thirties and his face was lined, especially around the eyes. I thought they were too blue for a cop, as if everything he'd seen should have faded them. He wore an ill-fitting gray suit, but it couldn't hide the well-made man underneath. As he introduced himself to me, I could feel him take in every detail, making a cop's assessment.

He turned to Bridgeman. "We get a positive?"

"Only the clothing."

"She see the pictures?"

Bridgeman nodded.

"Then let's take her down to the morgue."

"Detective Adder, with all due respect, that is completely against regulations."

Ignoring Bridgeman, Adder turned to me and his eyes surprised me with their warmth. "It'll be tough," he said. "Can you handle it?"

"Yes," I said and hoped it was true.

"Okay, Bart, let's take her down."

Bridgeman's whole body tensed, but he didn't argue with Adder.

As soon as the elevator doors opened on the basement, the smell hit me hard. A mixture of Formaldehyde and decomposing flesh and something to disguise it that was worse than what it was supposed to cover.

Bridgeman led the way to a busy room that looked like the hub of a hospital floor. A hospital where the patients were never demanding and never in pain. Workers in scrubs were joking, complaining, flirting like anywhere else. On the wall was a big board, the kind you see in railway stations, with numbers and names to track the arrivals and departures of the dead. The odor was more than I could stand. I groped around in my bag for a tissue and held it over my nose.

One of the workers handed me a mask. I put it on. It didn't help much.

"Why don't you wait out in the hallway," Adder said, "while we set this up. It might be a little better out there."

It wasn't.

To distract myself, I wandered down the corridor, still trying not to think. But I kept flashing on Ivarene and what it would have been like for Darla—the sudden horror of it. And every time my imagination was pulled there, it would leap back as if it had been scorched.

The hallway ended at a door with a window. On the other side were the shells of what had been people. Discarded, encased in plastic, waiting to be disposed of. Never in my life had I such a clear feeling that we were more than a body, that a corpse was something we have cast off, no sadder than an empty cocoon suspended from a tree.

Suddenly I heard someone cry out, "No! No! No!"

At first I thought it was a cry of mourning, but when I turned around I saw Bart Bridgeman trotting down the hallway toward me. "No! You're not allowed here."

Detective Adder, several feet behind, wasn't trying very hard to hide his amusement.

Bridgeman fussily hustled me into a room with a steel sink, a gurney, and a body covered with a sheet, except for the face and neck.

It was somehow less dreadful than the pictures. Now there was a person in front of me, and even in that damaged landscape of purples and reds, I could imagine a face that had been pretty. But was it Darla? Maybe I was searching for some trace of her spirit in that corpse. But the more I looked, the more I was certain it was someone else.

"What about the hands?" I said. "Can I see the hands?"

Adder lifted the edge of the sheet to reveal the left hand. I'm not sure why it was harder to look at than the face, but it was. Bloated like a clown hand.

"You want to see the other?" he said.

I shook my head. "Was there a ring?"

Adder glanced at Bridgeman, who shrugged and said, "No ring."

"Darla had a garnet ring. She never took it off."

Bridgeman looked at me and shrugged. "Maybe she pawned it."

"She would never have done that."

"My dear," he said, "she was a junkie."

"This girl might be," I said, "but it's not Darla."

Adder followed me into the elevator, and when it let us out on the main floor, he held open the glass door and I took huge gulps of fresh air.

Chapter 7

The sun had never felt so good on my skin.

Adder took off his jacket. His white shirt was freshly pressed and you could still smell a trace of bleach.

"First time's always tough," he said. "I've seen hotshot rookies lose it down there."

"I don't think I'll know how tough until I close my eyes tonight."

"You did all right. You took a good long look. Most people turn away after a second or two."

"I couldn't stop looking," I said. "I'm not sure I like what that means."

"Doesn't matter what you like. Won't change who you are."

The terrace we stood on looked out on the city below, at the traffic coursing along freeway bridges, swirling down curved ramps, streaming into the streets.

"All that speed," he said, "It's just fear, you know. That's what drives the whole show. Everyone trying to forget they're scared. We can't run fast enough. Sooner or later the machine goes *Tilt.* Game over."

"What kind of fear makes someone beat a girl to death?" I said.

He shook his head. "According to the coroner, she was already dead from gunshot wounds. Someone beat up a corpse."

That gave the brutality a strange numbness that made it seem even worse.

"Were all of the Ivarene victims battered like that?"

"Two of the others weren't. But someone stabbed Rambla thirty-seven times."

Adder turned his face to the sun and closed his eyes like he could burn away whatever movies ran behind a cop's lids. But when he turned back, those eyes were cool, taking my measure as he had when Bridgeman first introduced us.

"So you smoke a little weed from time to time?"

"Not since I was a kid."

"What about your friend?"

"Darla? She didn't even like wine."

"Wine wasn't her problem. It was drugs. She was shooting where it wouldn't be seen. Between the toes."

"You're talking about the girl on the gurney. But she's not Darla."

He popped a cigarette out of the pack in his pocket and lit it against the breeze. He had good hands, long strong fingers, broad flat nails.

"Listen," he said, "maybe that's not your friend down there. I hope not for your sake. But I know one thing. You don't always know what the people you care about have to do to make life bearable."

In the distance was a thrift shop with a rack of clothes outside, dispirited castoffs, slacks with the impression of knees sagging in the fabric, Hawaiian shirts, ancient cardigans. A barefoot child in a limp dress watched her mother pick through the rack. It occurred to me that twenty years ago, that child could have been Darla. Or the girl on a gurney who nobody missed.

I felt my throat tighten, then the tears came up suddenly. I didn't want to be this naked. Not here. Not in front of this cop with shoulders as broad as a bed.

He handed me a handkerchief. Pressed, folded, immaculate.

And he waited until I was okay again. Then he said, "I'm sorry. I know how it is to lose a friend."

His eyes were full of understanding, only he didn't understand.

"I don't know who that poor girl down there is. But something *has* happened to my friend and no one's trying to find out what."

He studied me for a good long moment, his eyes so steady in that broad, solid face. "I'll see what I can do."

He smiled, or at least his mouth went a little lopsided. It was an interesting mouth, a thin top lip that was all business and a full bottom lip that wasn't.

"Thank you," I said.

"If I learn anything more," he said, "I'll call you."

He didn't say it like a cop. He said it like a guy smoking a cigarette in the sun.

CHAPTER 8

I drove back over the bridge to a different world. Everyone I saw, no matter what their age, already resembled the waxy corpses we were all on our way to becoming. It was entertaining in a way. A fresh perspective, if you will.

What kept running through my head was the question Darla always asked. "What's real?" It would be easy to say that reality was the corpse on the gurney. But that afternoon it seemed to me that we moved through the world in these suits of flesh, driven by longing and need, a little burdened by the weight of our human costumes, like kids on Halloween. Trick or treat.

I'd only been gone a couple of hours, but my house had the same distorted strangeness it gets when you've been away on a long trip. I poured myself a shot of brandy and swished it around in my mouth to drive away the taste of the morgue. It worked and did one better. It burned the chill out of my soul. Then I stood under the shower for a good half hour and let the hot water beat down on me. When I got out, I took the clothes I'd worn to the morgue, threw them in the trash bin out back, and put on clean jeans and a T-shirt.

Bougainvillea brushed against the windows and gray clouds moved against the sky like a slow train. Across the street my landlord, Billy Hoyle, played a dark symphony. The light outside turned gold, then peach. The houses across the street became silhouettes, and street lamps came on, glowing softly against a black sky.

I caught the scent first—part raw male, part good, clean soap. Then I saw him squinting through the mesh of the screen door. Detective Adder.

"I hope I'm not disturbing you," he said.

He was, but not in the way he meant. Those shoulders took up a lot of space in that small room, and the pulse in my neck beat a little too hard. I knew what it was, this ravenous edge to being alive. I'd felt it when my father died. I was nineteen, married to a man I didn't love anymore. But I'd wanted him that night with a crazy fierceness.

Adder took the large armchair by the window, pulled out a pack of Marlboros, and offered me one. I shook my head.

"Mind if I smoke?"

"It's fine."

He lit a cigarette, then held the match up between two fingers with a question on his face.

I knew no one who smoked, but I did own an ashtray, a giant blob of a triangle that said Cinzano. It was on my dresser holding safety pins, a couple of pesos, and god knows what else. I dumped out the contents and brought it to him.

He took it with a surprised smile that said he'd been expecting a chipped saucer, dropped the match in, set his cigarette in the ample groove, and said, "You doing okay?" He smiled, but the set of his jaw told me he wasn't here with good news.

"What's wrong?" I said.

His eyes were direct, but softened when they met mine. "I just wanted you to know," he said, "we've got a little more information."

"Go ahead."

"First, we ran the prints against the DMV records. They found maybe five points of similarity."

"Maybe five? What does that mean?"

"Just that the guy who took the DMV prints had his eyes on

your friend instead of his work."

"Five points doesn't sound like a lot."

"Look, ten or twelve would be better, but—"

"So it's not definitive."

"Very little ever is. But we've got more."

"More?"

"Rambla's bookkeeper says your friend was at the car lot the night of the murders. She told us her boss drove off with Darla around nine. The Ivarene four were killed about an hour later."

"I told you she'd been seeing him."

"I'm not quite finished."

"Go ahead."

"A couple of other people gave us a positive I.D."

"Who?"

"Her brother, for one."

I thought about how scared Kyle was of the police and the way he hadn't met my eyes once at the coffee shop.

"How good a look did he take? A couple of seconds?"

"That's all he needed. It was a clean I.D. Not a moment's hesitation."

"Just the photographs?"

"That's how we do it."

"Was he high?"

"Not so it would make a difference. But like I said, he wasn't the only one. We brought her mother in, too.

"Her mother?"

He saw my shock. "You okay? Want to talk about it?"

I reached for the brandy glass, something to hold onto while the ground beneath me slipped away. "She told me her mother was dead."

He leaned toward me, forearms resting on his thighs. "I know this is hard," he said, "but maybe now it will be easier for you to accept what happened."

For a moment, the scent of blood on her clothes came back to me and an oppressive sadness overwhelmed me. But when I saw the dead girl in my mind, I still couldn't believe it.

"Look, I know it all fits together perfectly. But I don't think that girl was Darla."

"You strike me as pretty down-to-earth," he said, "And I don't want to dismiss what you're saying, but everyone from the family to the D.A. is satisfied."

"What about a DNA test?"

"They'll never okay it unless you give me something more concrete than a feeling. Is there something you know that you're holding back?"

"No. I've told you everything I can think of."

"Listen," he said, "can I ask you one more question?"

"Sure."

The tiniest taste of a grin appeared on one side of his lips. "How long are you gonna sit there nursing that empty glass?"

"Not a minute longer." I got up and headed to the kitchen.

"And if it's not too much trouble, I wouldn't mind some myself."

"Aren't you on duty?"

He looked at his watch. "What do you know, quitting time."

I got another glass from the kitchen and poured us a couple of drinks.

He tasted his and said, "That's good."

"Just ordinary brandy."

"I'm just an ordinary guy."

Neither of us said anything for a while and the ease with which he sat there, not intruding, not needing to make conversation, gave me a chance to absorb all that he'd told me.

"Truth's tough," he said, "especially when you don't want to see it."

I wondered about the truths he'd endured, a daily grind of homicide. His weathered face was a story it would take years to understand.

"What about her father?" I asked, wondering if Darla had lied about that, too.

"What'd she tell you?"

"That he left before she was born."

"The birth certificate says 'father unknown.' "

"At least that much is true," I said. "It had to be."

"What do you mean?"

"As different as we look, as different as we are, when I first met Darla, it was like we recognized something in each other. But it wasn't anything we ever talked about."

"Your father left you?"

"No," I said. "It wasn't like that."

He was smart enough not to pry. Instead, he picked up his brandy glass. The round bowl rested on his palm. Warming the brandy. I began to envy that glass nestled so perfectly in his hand. I spoke partly so I'd stop thinking about it.

"What's she like, Darla's mother?"

"I'd have to say she's a bit strange."

"Strange how?"

"Too old and too alone, maybe."

"I'd like to see her," I said.

"And you want me to give you her number."

"That would be nice."

"I'm afraid it's against the rules," he said, even as he pulled out his pad and copied it down for me.

Then he set his glass on the table and gave me a surprisingly shy smile. "Well, guess I'd better go," he said.

I didn't want him to leave, even as I opened the door and watched him walk to his car.

Chapter 9

DAZZLE, DRUGS AND DEATH:
FOURTH VICTIM WAS NUDE MODEL

If you read past the headlines to the bottom of the story, you would have learned that the nude model had just completed a film called *Hometown* and that the director had called her a young actress of extraordinary dimension.

On the cable news networks, it was wall-to-wall Darla, head-shots and publicity stills of her, sequined and lip-glossed, along with the *Bachelor Pad* centerfold, black rectangles covering her breasts like they were guilty of some unspeakable crime.

Interspersed with the pictures were the talking heads—a former district attorney in dapper pinstripes, glossily groomed lady lawyers, and every breed of political animal. Mike Ryle, the senate candidate, was getting plenty of mileage out of it, too. Ryle's voice trembled when he talked about "this lovely young girl with her whole future ahead of her." His eyes seemed to plead for a saner world. You wouldn't have known it from his movies, but he was a hell of a good actor.

It was the kind of spectacle Darla deplored. She once told me how upset she'd been when Michael Jackson died and reporters tore apart his life like ants swarming over the remains of a beetle.

Now it was Darla's life on display, and coverage of the Ivarene murders, endlessly repeated. When the phone rang—which it did all evening—it was not only friends but reporters. I told the first few I wasn't sure Darla was the fourth victim, that maybe the police should still be looking for her. They weren't interested. They wanted to write the story they'd been assigned. After a while I turned the ringer off.

The funeral took place at the Hollywood Forever Cemetery, which is set between the back lot of Paramount and a strip of Santa Monica Boulevard. Gordy Hewitt, the publisher of *Bachelor Pad,* had taken care of all the arrangements. There were uniformed city police everywhere and Gordy had stationed his own security guards at the entrance to keep the swarm of reporters and news vans out.

Several cars ahead of me drove straight through, but one of Gordy's guards took a look at my beat-up MG and stopped me. I told him where I was going. He glanced down at a clipboard with the guest list, found my name, then stared at my chest and said, "I guess you're not one of those centerfolds."

"I am," I said. "They use a body double."

"And Photoshop the nose, right?"

"Guess you know all the trade secrets," I said. "Can I go now?"

"It's interesting," he said, "I hear they've got another Darla buried here. Darla Hood. You know who that was? Pretty little girl from them *Our Gang* movies. Lotsa famous murder victims here, too. Y'ever hear of Bugsy Segal? He's over there in the Jewish section. Weird thing is, if he'd had a tattoo, they couldn't have put him there. But a cold-blooded killer, that's okay. Go figure."

"Yeah, go figure." I stepped on the clutch and shifted into first.

But he wasn't done. He got a look in his eye I knew well. When you saw that look hitchhiking, you got out of the car no matter how fast it was going. "Your friend's grave is right near Virginia Rappe," he said. "Ever hear of her?"

I knew who she was. The girl Fatty Arbuckle allegedly killed back in the twenties during a wild party in San Francisco. I could see how badly the guard wanted to give me the lurid details.

"Tuck it back in," I said and stepped on the gas.

The chapel was already full. Friends, actors, Gordy and his entourage. Notably absent were several famous faces Darla knew well but who probably did not want their names linked to the Ivarene murders.

As I came in, Detective Adder was standing near the doors. He introduced me to his partner, Herb Lefrak, an older man who was trying to get a Tums out of the bottom of the tube. Adder took me aside to tell me they were working day and night on the case, but were still pretty much in the dark.

The ceremony was brief. Gordy's minister said Darla had been given God's most gracious gifts and that her brief life had been a gift to all of us. He went on to say that the Lord created us nude and the true sin in Eden was not taking pleasure in the forbidden apple, but shame of our God-given beauty. And no one in the chapel that day was more pious than Gordy's girls, their limbs barely covered by tiny black dresses.

Most people left after the service. Those of us who remained walked down the winding path to the lakeside grave in The Garden of Legends. A coffin was suspended above the freshly dug earth, and gathered around it were Gordy and Lindsay, his number one blonde of the moment; Derek Provisor; Jimmy, eyes moist above his sunken cheeks; and Kyle with a heavy woman in a black dress and shapeless cloth hat whose brim shaded her face. Sari stood next to me, gripping my hand tightly until the minister finished his prayer and the coffin completed its slow descent into the ground.

Each of us took a handful of dirt and scattered it over the wooden lid. The thin hollow sound seemed to underscore the scant connection I felt with the girl they were burying and the emptiness of this meaningless goodbye.

Sari, whose perfect makeup couldn't hide eyes swollen from crying, said she was going home to freshen up and would pick me up later for the memorial at Gordy's. I headed toward Kyle and the woman I assumed was Darla's mother, but he was already leading her away. I called out to him. His shoulders said he'd heard me, but he didn't stop.

Joey and some others from class were going for coffee, but I didn't join them. I walked across the grass, the ground disturbingly soft, the sun glinting on the marble tombs of old-time stars from that black-and-white world of satin gowns and tuxedos. Here, as in life, the wealthy and powerful had waterfront property and the most impressive houses. Only now, the wives had equal billing: Mr. and Mrs. Cecil B. DeMille, Mr. and Mrs. Harry Cohn.

I sat on a marble bench that marked the grave of Tyrone Power and watched the breeze ripple the blue-green blades of grass. It was so peaceful here, the brassy glory and vicious struggles of Hollywood tamed and muted.

I sensed someone looking at me, turned around, and saw Derek. During class he sat in the shadows while we stood in the surgical glare of the stage lights. Now, in this manicured graveyard beneath the unforgiving L.A. sun, his face was soft and the dyed blond hair made his aging skin look too thin, time slowly reclaiming him.

"You looked pretty upset back there," he said, walking up to me. "This is a tough one."

"Even when you don't know who you're burying."

"What's that supposed to mean?"

"Derek," I said, "does it make sense to you that Darla started doing drugs out of the blue?"

He shrugged. "I've seen it happen to other people."

"But everything was going right for her. Everyone was saying *Hometown* would make her a star. People were finally taking her work seriously and she was getting the kinds of auditions she never had before."

"Darla wouldn't be the first one to break when she got what she wanted. You push hard against something all your life, and when it gives, there's nothing there to hold you up."

"But it's not like she'd already made it. She was still down here among us mortals, not swept off in some weird neverland of fame."

"That's not the dream that would have broken her."

"What are you talking about?"

He chewed his bottom lip. "I can't talk about what goes on in private sessions."

"Derek, if you know something, please tell me."

He gazed up at the sky as if he were waiting for the heavens to tell him it was okay to reveal something confidential. God must have given him the high sign because he turned back to me and said, "I suppose it doesn't matter anymore, and I can see how you're trying to process all this. The thing is, you know how fearless she always was in her work, right?"

True. It shocked people, how much depth there was under the gleaming surface.

"A few weeks ago, she came in for a private," Derek continued. "Never saw her so blocked. She'd always been willing to get down to the pain, but this time she wouldn't go near it. It must have been new. And raw. Jimmy could never get to her like that. That's what made him safe. Maybe he got a little rough with her sometimes, but—"

"Maybe he got a little rough? Like it's a small quirk of his?"

"Nikki, what I'm trying to say is that Jimmy couldn't wound her emotionally. Couldn't reach her heart. But someone did."

The clarity and intensity of his eyes always took me a little by surprise. "Did she ever tell you," he said, "that she was looking for her father?"

"She never said a word. But I'm beginning to find out how much she didn't tell me."

Derek couldn't quite hide his pride at being the insider. "Well, she started looking for him months ago, before shooting on *Hometown* began. She brought in that scene with the father so we could work on it. And she was great. Jeez. She was incredible. That beauty with that depth, and that willingness to go to the edge. Nothing like it since Angelina. You ever see her in *Gia*?"

I nodded. It was an amazing performance.

"Anyway, when the scene was done, Darla couldn't pull herself together. I stayed with her for more than an hour until she was herself again. And just before she left, she turned around and said with absolute conviction, 'Derek, I'm going to find my father.' I wished her luck and tried to warn her that if she ever found the son of a bitch who'd abandoned her, he sure as hell wasn't gonna be the dream daddy she was looking for. But the heart never hears advice."

The sun was lower on the horizon and the air was turning cool. We walked silently across the lawn to the parking lot. When we reached my car, Derek opened the door for me, then draped his hands over the top of the window.

"Nikki," he said, "that cop you were talking to, is he getting anywhere with the investigation?"

I shrugged. "I only know what's in the papers. Just like you."

"He doesn't whisper private little morsels of information into your lovely ear?"

I could feel my face flush, and Derek gave me that sly grin I knew so well from class.

"Who are you kidding, Nikki? The way that man looks at you, the way you look back at him. Anyone who walked between you would get zapped by the current."

I laughed, half embarrassed, half pleased. "All I know is that they're looking at the drug angle."

"Yeah. And how does that theory explain why she was beaten after she was dead?"

"They figure drugs make people go a little crazy."

"You saw her, didn't you?" he said.

"Yes. It didn't look like her."

"Of course it didn't. Whoever did it wanted to obliterate her."

He closed his eyes and took a few long beats before he said, "You ever think about the pain that drives that bastard Jimmy? You don't know what that girl did to a guy just walking past him on the street. He'd look at her and he'd *hurt.* She'd make him feel everything in life he'd never have."

It was interesting that Derek used those words. Because they were exactly the words he had used when, a few months ago, he'd called Darla into his office after class and "shared."

I didn't say anything, but he was practiced in observing us all. He looked at me, boyish, a little shy. "She told you, huh? Yeah, of course she did. Well, I never said I wasn't a man."

He shut the door of my car and turned away, but as the engine revved up he turned back to me. "Nikki," he said, "take it slow with your cop. He's deep waters, and you're not ready for a big plunge yet."

It sounded more like payback than insight. At least that's what I wanted to believe.

Chapter 10

In L.A., money flows uphill, and Gordy Hewitt lived at the very top of Beverly Hills.

Sari and I drove to the memorial in her old Lexus, another spoil of marriage. We both wore basic black dresses, but hers offered such a breathtaking expanse of décolletage that no one would ever notice that our outfits were almost identical.

An iron gate anchored between two granite nudes marked the entrance to Gordy's Bachelor Pad. From the navel of one stone lady came a voice that asked us to identify ourselves. Sari gave our names, the gates opened slowly, and the car wound uphill to a circular driveway.

Gordy's house could have been a mansion in a British movie, only instead of a line of dour servants to greet us, Mexican valets in little red jackets spirited the cars away.

A memorial at Gordy's wasn't much different from any other party at the Bachelor Pad. The men gathered in the entry hall and talked mostly with each other, while their gazes slid from time to time to the girls huddled together in colorful little clusters like bouquets, and butlers circulated with drinks and hors d'oeuvres. You'd think girls would be doing the serving up here, but I guess they don't because they are, in fact, what is being served.

When Darla took me up here, she'd often say, "Isn't it magical?" I guess it was, because only magic could make you completely invisible, which is what I always became in the glare of all that platinum hair and megawatt celebrity.

Sari gave a little wave to Gordy who made his way toward us. Tonight, his trademark turtleneck was black, and instead of perfectly faded jeans with a pressed crease, he wore black dress pants that slouched over black velvet loafers. He took my hand between both of his and I could feel how genuine his sympathy was. "How are you girls holding up?"

Before either of us could answer, one of Gordy's minions—a man who evidently thought a strip of chest hair would do for a dark tie—took Gordy's arm and began to steer him toward some people who had just arrived.

Gordy shrugged as if to say his life was not in his control. "We'll talk later, Nikki. Promise."

I lost Sari in the crowd, and for a while my only company was a silver bowl of M&Ms on a side table. I watched the famous faces, the people who hadn't shown up at the cemetery, stars from every era and every movie on my greatest hits list—from *The Godfather* and *Chinatown* to *Good Night and Good Luck.* I'd been in L.A. for a while, but it still startled me to see people walk right off the screen and nibble chicken wings and blot grease off their chins.

I looked around the room for Sari. She leaned against a hall table and talked to a gnome with drooping jowls and two or three hairs combed flat across his scalp. She smiled at him, tilting her head like she was trying to read a bank balance stamped on his forehead.

I made my excuses to the M&Ms and walked over.

"Nikki!" she exclaimed as if she hadn't seen me for years. "This is Leo. He was telling me how he created that ad for Johnny Rambla. You know, the one where he has the chair and the whip and the lion and he's saying, 'Bring me your wild car prices and I will tame them!' "

"I'm so sorry," I said, "it must have been quite a shock, the way he died."

Leo waved his hand like he was brushing away a fly. "Yeah, but he died a *somebody,* thanks to me."

He handed me his card. THE AURIOLE AGENCY, LEO AURIOLE, 800-POUND GORILLA. "Advertising," he said. "Life is all advertising. Look at your friend here. A walking personal ad with some first-class packaging." He slipped a finger into her top, pulled it away, and peered down. "Nice product, too." At least he didn't check for the expiration date.

Sari giggled, which only encouraged him. "Now lookit you," he said to me. "The message is not at all clear what you're selling here."

"Not for sale," I said. "That's the message."

"Everything's for sale. People, pleasures, and every goddamn politician in Washington, D.C." He examined me as if he hadn't seen me before. "Who did you say you were?"

"Nikki's an actress," Sari offered.

"Not if no one's paying her, doll. A word to the wise, sweetheart. You want to make it in this town, you got to sell your soul to the devil."

"Whatever he paid for yours, Leo, he got the raw end of the deal."

As I walked away I heard him say, "*Ahhh,* another nobody."

The main floor was packed with people now, men who knew how to fill the air with their voices and women who laughed musically when nothing amusing had been said.

A mahogany staircase led from the foyer to Gordy's private quarters. At the end of an evening, Darla always made sure we left as soon as guests began drifting up there. The Gordy I knew was always kind, intelligent, and vulnerable in a way that never seemed calculated and never failed to charm. Yet the upstairs always seemed to loom above us as if it held his darker side.

I didn't think anyone noticed me making my way to the

second floor, where I found myself in a long hallway with mahogany molding and red-flocked wallpaper that made the place feel like a gloomy brothel. There were several closed doors along the corridor, but one was slightly ajar.

Inside, a man was sitting on a velvet sofa, his head in his hands. For a minute I thought he might be crying, but when he looked up he seemed only drained. I recognized the face and those famous black curls instantly—Anthony Scott.

"Sorry," I said and started to move away.

"Don't go." He picked up a glass of scotch and took a sip. "What's your name?"

"Nikki."

"Didn't I play someone with that name?"

I knew the answer. They used to run his old films on a local channel when I was a kid. "Nicky Rocco. *City of Darkness.*"

"That's right, that's right. Come on in here, sweetheart, and sit yourself down."

"Thanks," I said.

Up close, his skin had the sick shine of a chemical peel and the black curly hair was a rug. He patted it, like a beloved pet, and leaned toward me with some intensity.

"You like poems?" Without waiting for an answer, he pulled a piece of paper from his pocket. "My own personal *homage* to the tragic death we're here to honor." He unfolded the paper, stared at it like he was trying to memorize what was written there, and looked at me. Then he stood up, walked to the window, looked out, looked back at me, looked at the paper again, put it down, fixed me with his eyes, and gravely intoned, "Tinsel has strangled the fleshy petals of a rose."

I waited for the rest of the poem, but he just stared at me.

"Okay, let me try something else here," he said.

He looked down at his feet and they must have made him very sad, because when he looked up there were tears in his eyes. And when he spoke, his voice trembled with emotion.

"Tinsel has strangled the fleshy petals of . . . a rose." The last two words were whispered and held. He gave it time to sink in. Then he said, "What do you think?"

"Go on."

He shook his head. "You don't know shit about poetry, do you?"

"Not really."

"There is no *go on.* That was the poem, dollface. Short. Powerful. True."

He waited for me to praise it. "Short is good," I said.

"Damn straight." Now he seemed relaxed and happy. "I don't know where this stuff comes from. Just flies into my head and I write it down. Who did you say you were?"

I told him my name again.

"Yeah, but like, who *are* you?"

"It would probably take a poem to answer that," I said.

"In other words, nobody."

"That seems to be the consensus."

"So who's the somebody that got you in here?"

"I'm a friend of Darla's."

His pulled his face into a perfect mask of profound sympathy. "What a tragic, tragic, *tragic* thing," he said. And paused. Waiting, perhaps, for applause. When none was forthcoming, he said again, with great finality, "Tragic."

He refilled his glass, took a good long sip, and said, "You know, everyone looked at that girl—but I *saw* her. That's what they call the eye of the poet. She looked like a little French pastry. But she was no creampuff. She was that pastry the French call *mille feuilles,* a thousand layers. Sweet but very complicated. Of course, an onion's got the layers thing going on, too. But it wouldn't be the right image. That's the gift of the poet."

"You knew her pretty well?" I said.

"She never talked about me?" He looked quite shaken by this possibility—and I was about to utter an assuring lie when he turned his attention to the doorway.

Gordy was standing there, though for how long I couldn't say. "There you are, Nikki. Someone told me you were up here."

"You were looking for me?" I said, more than a little surprised.

"I didn't mean to interrupt."

"She's a cute kid," Scott said, "but if you have dibs, I wouldn't think of jumping her lovely bones."

"He's all gentleman," Gordy said. "My apologies." From a wide flat packet, he extracted a long brown cigarette with a gold tip.

He saw my reaction immediately. "Something the matter?"

"No," I said in as ordinary a tone as I could muster. "Just an unusual cigarette."

"Pure tobacco. It's the additives that kill you, you know."

"Life," Anthony Scott piped up. "Life itself ultimately strangles the flesh."

"I thought tinsel did," I said.

"You got a tin ear for poetry, kid."

"Gordy," I said, trying to sound casual and not quite succeeding. "When did you last see Darla?"

He patted his pockets like he was looking for matches, buying time. Scott picked up a silver lighter from the table and Gordy bent over to catch the flame.

"Anthony," Gordy said, "you ready with that thing you're writing?"

"I could use a few more minutes."

"Why don't we leave you alone then?"

Gordy took my arm and led me into the hallway, closing the door behind him.

"Sorry, Nikki, he's an old friend and his charm may be an

acquired taste," he said as we headed down the stairs. "We were interrupted before and I just wanted to finish our conversation. I know Darla always thought of you as her closest friend. She had a lot of respect for you. For your independence."

The crowd had abandoned the foyer for the dining room, where they were filling their plates from buffet tables. Except for a couple of butlers cleaning away glasses and soiled napkins, we were almost alone.

"Gordy," I said, "you never answered my question. But you saw Darla just before she died, didn't you? At her apartment."

"She told you about it?"

"No. You left a couple of fancy cigarettes behind."

He looked amused, but not at all thrown. "You don't miss much."

"I thought you almost never leave this place," I said as offhandedly as I could.

"I rarely do," he said, "but some things require a bit of discretion."

He caught my surprise at the implication. "No, no, nothing like that," he said, "though I'd certainly made the offer. Many times. I went to see her because she needed a favor and was very adamant about not coming up here. As soon as I saw her, I knew why."

He gave a quick nervous shake of the head, as if to shake off the thought. "I was an idiot," he said. "I should have known she was in trouble. I could have done something. Gotten her some help."

"How could you have known?"

"It was so obvious. I didn't want to see it, but she had that look. Half scared, half not giving a damn. Look, I'm no choir boy. I know when someone's got a habit. But I always had her on such a pedestal, I couldn't admit it to myself. So I didn't do a damn thing. I told myself I was being a friend by lending her a few bucks."

The minion had appeared again at Gordy's side. "A few bucks," he piped in. "More like ten grand."

Gordy shot him a look and the minion tried to make up for having talked too freely. "Lookit this guy. Heart of gold. People don't know this about him."

Another cold look from his boss and he backed away as discreetly as a Downton Abbey valet.

Gordy gave me his full attention again. "I want you to know," he said, "that asking for money wasn't Darla's style. She had a way of making you *want* to do things for her. We all gave her gifts from time to time. But she'd never asked me for anything before. Never."

I can't say this was a surprise. Neither of us earned enough to rise above the official U.S. poverty level, but her life overflowed with expensive things. Gifts. From Jimmy and perhaps from others, who may also have helped with her rent from time to time. I had seen shopkeepers hand her stuff for free in the hopes that they might get to know her better. I have to admit, it bothered me sometimes, this barter for beauty. I asked her once how she felt about it, trading on her looks so that she could live well. She took it as a reproach—I guess it was—and for a split second, all her fluid motion stopped. Froze. Then she forced a laugh and said, "Live well! Oh, Nikki. Look at me. In a rented apartment with cottage cheese ceilings!"

Heels clattered across the parquet floors and Lindsay, Gordy's girl of the moment, took his arm. "Honey, Warren's at your table?" She was a girl who ended every sentence like a question. "And he's, like, a little put out you're not there?"

Gordy sighed. "I'm sorry, Nikki. You were so kind to listen. I guess I needed to unburden myself a bit." He gave my hand an affectionate squeeze then let Lindsay haul him away.

In the dining room I found Sari, who'd saved a seat for me at a table with a few other stray girls, a plastic surgeon and his taut wife, who rested a well-manicured hand on my arm and said, "She's in a better place now," as if Darla had simply moved to a condo in Brentwood.

After dinner Gordy rose. His voice broke several times as he made a little speech that seemed unrehearsed and heartfelt. When he'd finished, several others stood to say a few words, including Anthony Scott, who pulled the slip of paper from his pocket and recited his poem about tinsel and the rose. Whispers of *brilliant, simply brilliant,* fluttered through the room. What did I know about poetry?

Afterward, Sari went outside to request her car from the valet and, as we were getting in, Leo Auriole came trotting out.

"Girls, girls, no goodbye?" He took Sari's hand and pressed his card into it. "Give me a call sometime, sweetheart. You look like you could use a friend, am I right?"

I've seen men with desire in their eyes, but in Leo it was polluted with a heavy dose of something so malignant, I understood for the first time why lust could be called a sin.

Chapter 11

The morning had a gleaming surface full of promise. Outside, under a brilliant sky, neighbors walked their dogs, watered their gardens, went off to work in crisp outfits and shined shoes. A girl on a gurney had been buried and life trampled hopefully, relentlessly, remorselessly on.

I made a pot of coffee, poured myself a cup, and added a fat tablespoon of honey and enough cream to turn it a rich shade of tan. As I sipped the sweet, heavy brew, I noticed that the light on my muted landline had stopped blinking and was glaring accusingly at me.

There were messages from people I knew and people I barely knew and people I hadn't heard from since elementary school. There were reporters wanting "insight into the real Darla Ward" and someone named Manny Roberson, who claimed to be a private investigator. On my cell were calls from Sari, Derek, Joey, and my ex ("If you need to talk, you know I'm always here").

I was just about to get into the shower when someone knocked at the door. I threw on a robe and had the misfortune to pass a mirror. With Cabbage Patch hair and a sleep crease slowly fading from my cheek, I hoped I would not find Detective Adder on my front steps.

But it was only my landlord, Billy Hoyle. His face was as grave as a child's as he handed me a bouquet from his garden—coral and white and yellow roses.

"A little beauty to chase the sadness away," he said.

"They're lovely. Thank you."

Billy's roses were so fragrant, you didn't have to bend to them to catch their gorgeous scent. For a moment it was enough to make life seem pretty good again.

I found something about the size of a vase and filled it with water. As I was putting the flowers in it, Billy looked in the mirror and touched his pinky between his eyebrows. "What do you think, Nikki? A little Botox? Or has that train left the station?" He turned to me so I could study his face. The entire surface was a roadmap of lines. I didn't know quite what to say and when he saw me with my mouth hanging open, he roared with laughter and I couldn't help laughing with him.

Then he noticed my flower arrangement, picked it up, and examined the container, which he held by the rim with two fingers, his long pinky elegantly extended. "What a charming vase. Lovely striped motif. With an inscription, no less. *Slurpee.*"

"Original Warhol," I said.

"Indeed."

He began to rearrange the flowers I'd so unceremoniously stuck in the supersized cup, until each was perfectly set off by the others. Then he stepped back, stared at his composition, moved one yellow rose, and, after contemplating the effect for a few seconds, put it back where it had been.

I watched him, thinking about the care he took with everything but his own purple home, which was so crowded with junk, it spilled out onto the porch. I thought about the way he looked after me and about how generous he always was. Then I remembered the rent. Three months overdue and he still hadn't said a word.

"Billy," I said, "that residual finally came." It wasn't true, but I wrote him a check to cover one month, which left me barely enough to feed a parking meter.

When he left, I showered and threw on some clothes just in time to answer another knock at the door.

I expected to see Billy again, but it was a black man in a dark suit and crisp white shirt. He looked like he was about to hand me a church pamphlet.

I said, "Sorry, I don't need any religion today. Bought a brand new one last week."

"I hope you didn't pay too much," he said. "Because we got a recession special going."

The grin that threatened to break out all over his face told me my first impression was way off.

"Not selling salvation, huh?"

"Uh, no. My name is Manny Roberson. I'm a private investigator. You don't return calls, so here I am."

He held an I.D. card against the screen door. It bore his name and an official-looking seal. For all I knew, he'd made it at home.

"I'd just like to talk to you for a few minutes. About Darla Ward."

"What about her?"

"You were her closest friend. I just want to get a better sense of what she was—"

"What she was really like? What are you, a reporter?"

"No. I really am a PI. Not the most genteel way to make a living, but I've got a kid to put through college in about ten years."

Manny Roberson had a broad open face, a slight paunch, and a voice that could soothe a baby. I'd already misjudged him once, but maybe because men in suits didn't often show up at my door.

I let him in and offered him the chair by the window. He sat forward, his hands in his lap—a man who knew people did not open up to the overconfident. He would have looked positively meek if you didn't notice the bulge of a shoulder holster under his jacket.

"I understand," he said, "that when you went to identify the body, you said it wasn't her."

"That didn't make the news."

"No, it didn't. Bridgeman down at the Coroner's is an old acquaintance of mine. And I have a client who hopes you're right."

After feeling for too long like I was in one of those dreams where you try to talk and no one can hear you, it should have come as a relief that someone had finally paid attention. But I wasn't entirely comfortable with a stranger showing up and asking questions.

"This client of yours, who is he?"

"Did I say he?"

There's usually a very subtle difference in a person's voice when they talk about someone of the opposite sex. I hadn't heard that when Manny mentioned his client. "Your client is a woman?"

He shook his head as if I were too cagey for him. "You know I can't give you that information. All I can tell you is this person doesn't want to believe your friend is dead."

"A wife? Or a guy with a wife," I said, remembering the venomous message on Darla's voicemail.

"You have someone in mind?"

"You want to get information without giving any?"

He chuckled. More charm than amusement. "Anyone else paying attention to you? What do you have to lose?"

He had a point.

"Someone's wife left a threatening message on Darla's phone," I said.

"She didn't leave her name?"

I shook my head.

"Did you recognize the voice?"

"No."

"People get a picture in their mind when they hear a voice. What kind of person did you see?"

"A piece of work. Tightly wound. Definitely not young. I kind of imagined one of those scarecrow wives with accessories that weigh more than they do."

I saw a glint of recognition in his eyes.

"You know who she is," I said.

"No. Darla Ward probably made a lot of wives angry. Simply by walking into a room."

"Manny, I've been straight with you. Who came to mind?"

"No one." For a moment I glimpsed the toughness beneath that gentle, pleasant face. It disappeared the instant he saw I'd caught it. "Look, we're both on the same side here. Both trying to find out what really happened to your friend. Tell me why you think the girl they buried wasn't Darla?"

I didn't really trust Manny. How clean could a guy in his business be? But like he said, no one else was listening.

"I've been asking myself the same question, but I can't pinpoint it. Except for the ring. A garnet. The girl I saw didn't have one. And Darla told me she would never take that ring off."

"Did she ever say why it meant so much to her?"

I shook my head. It still stung. How much of her life she'd kept hidden from me.

He gave me his card before he left. "We can help each other," he said. "Call me anytime."

A while later, I did make a call. But not to Manny Roberson.

CHAPTER 12

The house on Poinsettia was no shabbier than any of its neighbors. The garden featured lush clumps of crabgrass, abloom with colorful bits of trash. A cat with one torn ear was sizing me up, but when I knocked on the door, he humped his back, hissed, and ran off.

The face of the woman who opened the door shocked me. It was like looking at an ink drawing of Darla floating in a pool, its lines smudged and feathered. She wore a chenille robe that might once have been peach. In one hand she clutched something I couldn't see.

"What're you?" she said. "Another one of them LAPD Blue?"

"No. I'm Nikki Easton. I called you earlier. Darla's friend."

She squinted against the sun to get a better look at me and seemed disappointed. "Oh, sure. I just thought you'd be more . . . actressy lookin' . . . you know."

I knew.

"I hope I'm not intruding," I said. "I can only imagine how hard this must be for you."

"Hard ain't the half of it. I don't know what I'm gonna do with my baby dead."

If there were words to soothe this kind of pain, I didn't know them. "I'm so sorry."

"She took good care of her mama. Always gave me a little extra. And the Social Security don't come till next week."

She couldn't quite hide the tiny glint in her eye that told me

I was being played, but it was the least I could do. There were a few bills in my wallet. Not much, but I handed them to her.

She opened her fist to take the money and seemed surprised to see a half dozen pistachio nuts in her palm, which had turned bright red. She cracked one open with her teeth, sucked out the meat, and spit the shell past me onto the lawn.

"Here, have some," she said.

"That's okay."

She shrugged and spilled the nuts into her pocket, where she also tucked the money. I hadn't been invited to follow her back inside, but she didn't seem to stand on formalities.

Jasmine and gardenia wafted through the window and mingled with a bouquet of rotten fruit, toothpaste, and liniment, subtle yet permeating the room, as if the odors had been absorbed by every pore of the walls and floorboards.

The cat, now settled in the armchair and licking his belly, paid little attention to our arrival. Darla's mother walked over to the chair and began to stroke his back.

"Mama's handsome boy," she cooed into his ragged ear. "Be a good kitty and let the nice lady sit here. Okay?" She paused and cocked her head as if he might answer. He didn't. "I'm asking you nice, my little honey bunny."

The cat opened its small, fierce mouth and yawned.

She gave a deep, disappointed sigh. Then she looked at me and shrugged. "Well, I tried."

I was about to say it was okay, I could sit anywhere, when she raised her arm in the air and knocked the cat off the seat. He hit the floor with an indignant howl, then jumped quickly to his feet and beat a hasty retreat.

"Now," she said, "you just make yourself comfortable."

Right.

I took the cat's place and, with more grace than I would have imagined, she sat down on the sofa and crossed her legs. As her robe parted, I was astonished at the milky smoothness of her skin and the delicate curve of calf into ankle.

"Mrs. Ward, I know this must be—"

"Mrs. Ward! Hah! Who's she? Never been no Mrs. to nobody. Just call me Dottie."

Dottie, I thought, and then some.

"So what is it you want, Missy? I hope you don't expect no handout from me. I got hard times, you know."

"I don't want money. I want to talk to you."

She tilted her head to one side and gave me a girlish, flirtatious smile. "Could you spare a couple of bucks, then?"

"I pretty much gave you what I had."

She grinned and patted her pocket. "Oh, yeah. You're a real angel girl, aren't you? Just like my baby was. I used to be one a long time ago. But now I'm all red and black inside and got terrible jaggedy edges."

Was she completely crazy or just poetic?

"A long time ago," she went on, "I had a friend, too. Lenore was her name. Lenore Lerner." The dreamy look on her face turned mean. "You know what kind she turned out to be—jealous. I had my beautiful Darla, and Lenore, she was barren."

I hadn't heard anyone use that term since I'd left home. My own mother always liked old-fashioned phrases. She thought they sounded refined.

"That Lenore, she pretended to be oh so sweet, but I knew she was trying to take Darla away from me, always coming over here, bringing all kinds of gifts, showing me up, making it so that she was the one my little girl confided in instead of me. And her telling me, all sweet as you please, 'Dottie, you've changed, you need help, you need to see a shrink.' Thought she was better than me 'cause she got married. That husband of hers must have whispered in her ear about me, too, 'cause after awhile she didn't come 'round no more. But who needed her? I had plenty of boyfriends. I was prettier, and I got lots of parts. You ever seen me on *Rockford* or *Barnaby Jones*?"

Before she could drift too far away into the past, I put my hand on her arm to draw her focus back. As soon as she felt my touch, she released a little sigh and her face softened.

"Dottie, I need to ask you something."

"What's that, sweetie?"

"About when you went to make the identification."

She blinked her eyes hard two or three times and then smiled at me. It was the kind of smile a child gives a stranger who's frightening her.

"Dottie, I'm sorry. But it's really important. When you went down there, were you really sure the girl you saw was Darla?"

The question killed whatever connection I'd managed to make with her.

"You calling me a liar?"

"No. It's just that I saw the battered girl too, and I didn't think it was Darla."

"Well, that don't surprise me. What they did to her. Just like *Dawn of the Dead*. They put all that makeup on us and you couldn't even recognize your own self."

"We're not talking about a movie, Dottie. This is real."

"You think I don't know that? I seen them horrible pictures they showed me." Her eyes grew wet, but no tears fell. "My baby was always so beautiful." She glanced over at two framed photos on the drum table next to the sofa. They might have been high school yearbook pictures. Darla's face was much fuller but very pretty, and her hair was a dark honey-blonde. Kyle looked frail beneath shaggy Kurt Cobain hair.

Dottie leaned toward me and grasped my hand as if it were all in the world she had to hold onto. "She was a special one, just like her daddy."

"Dottie, who was Darla's father?"

"Ain't that the $64,000 question!"

"You don't know who he was?"

"Erased him a long time ago." She made a wiping motion with the flat of her hand. "Washed my blackboard clean."

"You mean you don't even remember his name?"

Dottie pulled her hand back from mine. "You tryin' to trick me? You think I don't know he watches me right out of the TV? He's got his people that come right out of the tube. They'll grab you just like that." She reached out her hand and twisted it with a violent jerk. "They can do that, you know. Come right into your living room. One of them sat right where you are the other day. Told me if he wanted he could kill me, too. Just like my little girl."

"Someone came here and threatened you?"

"Oh, yeah. But the really bad ones come when I go to bed. They live in the walls. And they whisper all night."

What was real and what wasn't? The question Darla always asked.

As I stood up to leave, she gave me the coquettish smile I'd seen before. "Say, Missy," she said, "You couldn't spare a couple of bucks, could you?"

Chapter 13

It was late afternoon, the painter's hour, when I pulled up in front of Darla's building. The street was illuminated in a wash of golden light—ragtag gardens overrun with giant aloe and gaudy canna, elegant Spanish duplexes, boarded up or reduced to rubble to make way for new condos—the past, slowly collapsing in silence above the shifting tectonic plates beneath the city. I wondered how anyone ever felt at home here, where there was nothing you could trust to hold on to, not even the ground beneath your feet.

Her apartment looked the same as it had the day of the break-in. I cleared some debris from the couch and sat there across from the counter that separated the kitchen from the living room. I remembered how she would stand there, tossing strawberries into the blender, making something as healthy and pink as her cheeks, excited to show me the rhinestone-covered sunglasses she'd found at a vintage shop, excited about the herb garden she thought she'd start out on the terrace next to the geraniums, excited about the word-of-mouth on her work in *Hometown.*

What had happened to her?

I found myself remembering the first time she had taken me to a Beverly Hills party. I was new in town and owned nothing but a backpack with some jeans and T-shirts. She'd loaned me a Versace dress and a pair of Jimmy Choos, then spent an hour styling my hair. I felt like a stray dog being groomed for Westminster. All this fussing would never be my thing. But I don't think I'd ever been treated with such care.

It was around Christmas, my first year in L.A. The host of the party had trucked in real snow from the Sierras to pack against the house. I'd never been around people like this before—the hungry smiles, the cool edge to the laughter, the hard eyes of men assessing flesh, of women taking in the details of a man's tailoring and totaling up his net worth. In the middle of that crowd, yet never a part of it, Darla radiated exactly that light the other women, with their sequins and their glitter, tried to evoke. One of the people drawn to her light had been Johnny Rambla. He was a horrible little man, reeking of hair gel and shave lotion, and the loud clothes that made him funny on TV were kind of creepy in the flesh. He kept coming around Darla. Wouldn't keep his hands off her. The few times she couldn't avoid dancing with him, her body had stiffly leaned away from his. It was still hard to believe she would have spent five minutes with him, much less let those squat fingers touch her. How had she wound up with him? Even if she'd been trying to help Kyle, she knew better than anyone how to keep men happy without giving too much. How had she let herself be drawn down into his world? *More in front, more behind,* Derek liked to say. The stronger the personality, the more it hid. Darla's brilliant smile, her never-ending stream of cheerful conversation, her almost aggressive vitality had been more than strong. I began to wonder if I'd been as blinded by her dazzle as everyone else.

Sometimes, in a certain light or in certain rare moments of stillness, she would remind me of a girl I went to school with, a girl who'd worn the same thin dress every day and had seemed more shadow than child. There were traces of a child like that in Darla's face, like pale tracks of tears that had never completely disappeared.

I walked down the long hallway, stepping between the broken

glass and framed photos on the floor. It was hard to look at Darla smiling up from them with such hope and confidence. I stood in the bedroom for a long time, staring at the piles of belongings that had once been part of her beauty, wondering what I was even doing here, what I was looking for.

"Nikki, how'd you get in?" The voice had a slight edge of resentment.

I turned to see Sari standing behind me.

"I had a key."

"Well, don't let the landlady catch you here. She's telling everyone that whatever's here will barely pay for the cleanup crew she has to hire. *Pu-leez.* Do you know what the cashmeres alone are worth?"

Sari sat down on the bed and looked around. Then, like someone too used to losing, she said, "I guess you've already gotten everything worth taking."

"I just got here," I said. "And I don't really want anything."

"Well, I'm going to look, okay?"

"Sure."

I left Sari assessing the piles of clothing strewn everywhere and wandered through the apartment one more time. Whoever had been here had torn the place apart. But I didn't think they'd found what they were looking for because they would have stopped if they had, and there wasn't an inch of the apartment that hadn't been touched. Even the top of the toilet tank lay shattered on the bathroom floor.

When I came back into the bedroom, Sari had set aside a little pile of cashmere sweaters and a few beautifully cut dresses. Some had never been worn and still had tags. She slipped her tiny feet into a pair of red-soled Christian Louboutins, but they made her look like a little girl in mommy's shoes. "Nikki, these would fit you."

I shook my head, repelled by the way she was picking over

Darla's belongings. Sari saw my expression and looked hurt. I felt bad. "You know I'd break my ankles trying to walk in those things," I said.

She looked down at my ancient Chucks, rolled her eyes exactly the way my mother used to, and set the shoes regretfully down on the floor near the night table. Its drawers, with all the private things everyone keeps there—birth control pills, feminine hygiene paraphernalia, a vibrator—had been dumped on the floor. I nudged some clothing over them with my toe, then noticed, half concealed under the bed, a small box. I pulled it out. It was covered with lacquered pictures.

"Look at this," I said. "Darla and her découpage, always dragging us into junk shops to look for old pictures and magazines."

"She made me a box once for my birthday. Puppies and vintage Valentines. To bring me faithful love. As if it even existed." Sari sounded like a child who'd learned there was no Santa, but deep down still longed to believe.

This box was covered with antique pictures, some Victorian, others from the fifties or earlier. It took me a moment to realize what the theme was. Fathers and daughters: a little girl being tucked in at bedtime, or cuddled with daddy in an armchair reading a book, or fishing with him in cutely patched jeans.

I opened the box. Inside were several old snapshots, the colors faded.

We sat on the bed, Sari and I, and looked at the pictures. In one, a little girl and boy squinted into the sun. The boy looked forlorn, but the girl's smile was heartbreakingly eager. They were standing in a backyard of scraggly grass and wilting weeds. Some people are easier to recognize as children than others, and this towheaded pair were clearly Kyle and Darla. I picked up the next picture and saw the house where her mother still lived. The paint was peeling even then, and overgrown yucca threatened to swallow up the porch where Darla nestled against her mother's chest. Dottie, in a flowered halter dress, could not have been much older than thirty. She looked straight ahead at the camera with a smile that seemed like a loose invitation. There was also a snapshot of Dottie and another woman, both with bell-bottom jeans, platform shoes, and long, feathered Farrah Fawcett hair.

Two of the pictures in Darla's box had been torn in half, but, judging by the worn, soiled edges, not recently. In one, Dottie, her eyes alive, her smile soft and happy, was seated on a banquette, a disco mirror ball glittering behind her. In the other, she was on a beach, and you could still see a man's hand on her shoulder. I wondered if the person who had been ripped out was Darla's father, the one she'd never known.

There was also a studio portrait of Darla at about age five in front of a white trellis. Another photo showed her in a prom dress, again with that bravely cheerful smile. It occurred to me that these might have been pictures she had been saving for the father she never knew—until I saw the last few photos in the box: Darla at perhaps fifteen, perched on a rock in a bikini, and a few nude stills from her *Bachelor Pad* shoot.

At the bottom of the box was an old leather address book and a few scraps of paper with names and numbers scribbled in Darla's round hand. As I looked through them, I recognized one. Lenore Lerner, the friend Dottie had talked about.

I asked Sari if Darla had ever mentioned that name to her.

"Lenore Lerner? No, I don't think so. Who is she?"

"Someone Darla knew when she was a kid. Do you mind if I take this box?"

"Thank god you're taking something." She looked at me, then tried to say casually, "What about her emerald choker? And the diamond studs? Do you think whoever broke in here got them?"

I had no idea, but I rummaged through the clothes until I found the old jacket Darla never wore, the one with zippered pockets. The jewelry was still there, tucked away where it had always been.

"Oh, let me see!"

I handed the necklace and earrings to Sari and she gazed at them sparkling in her palm.

"You can't take those," I said.

"Oh, sure. You turn down a few sweaters and a pair of shoes, so now you think this is yours."

"Sari—"

"I only meant we should share them, Nikki."

"They should go to Darla's mother."

"That weird old lady at the funeral? What would she do with jewelry like this?"

"She needs the money they'd bring."

Sari dropped down onto the bed and her eyes got watery like she was going to cry. "Oh, god, I'm so sorry. You must think I'm the greediest person on earth."

"If that was true," I told her, "you wouldn't be picking through these clothes now. You'd be sitting pretty in a big house with some rich slob you didn't give a damn about."

"Nikki, I hate it. I feel so *pinched* inside, always counting pennies like those poor old ladies dipping into their little purses at the supermarket. Sometimes," she said, "I think anything would be better than this."

CHAPTER 14

The phone was ringing as I walked into my house.

"This is Detective Adder. I hope I'm not calling at a bad time."

"No . . . it's fine. What is it?"

Everything in me quickened at the possibility of new information—or maybe it was the sound of that soft, rough voice.

"Nothing really to report yet. I just wanted to make sure you were doing okay. I know this has been tough for you."

"It's nice of you to call."

"Look, if it's any help, I have an idea what you're going through." His voice had dropped to a softer register, maybe almost tender, and it vibrated through me like a slow temblor. "I did three tours of duty. I know what it's like to lose a friend. And I know what it's like not to know who a torn-up body once was."

I think I had seen that in him, seen the war in his eyes. I'd noticed one or two other things about him, too. The ramrod straight spine, those crisp pressed shirts.

"You were a marine," I said.

"*Semper fi.* I didn't know you were paying that much attention."

"Yes you did."

He laughed. "Yeah, I did."

Somehow, we'd eased ourselves over the line into territory that was clearly personal. There was a goofy smile on my face I was glad he couldn't see.

Then my call waiting beeped. I looked at the number and knew I had to take it. "My agent is on the other line," I said. "I'd better pick up."

"I'll call you again sometime, okay?"

"Very okay," I said. The words weren't much, but our voices said a whole lot more.

I pressed the flash button, and before I could finish saying hi, Phil exploded.

"What the hell is wrong with you, Nikki? *Case Closed* was yesterday!"

Damn! I'd completely forgotten. "I'm really sorry, Phil. Yesterday was the funeral, and with everything that's—"

"I know. Death's a biggie. I hurt for you. Sincerely, kid. I do. But you should take a lesson from the former Governator. Right before the Mr. Universe finals, his own father up and dies. You think he flies home to Austria for the funeral? Hell, no. He goes out there and takes the championship."

"That's really warm and fuzzy, Phil."

"Bunny rabbits are warm and fuzzy. And you know what they get? Eaten. I think I can reschedule, but don't do this to me again."

CHAPTER 15

The next day I searched the vintage stores in West Hollywood for a forties costume, but found only disco-era polyester and the occasional bowling shirt. I knew Western Costume in the Valley would have a WAC uniform, probably a real one, possibly even one an Andrews Sister had actually worn. Renting from them would cost a lot, but what the heck. It would be an investment in my career, a career that had, so far, cost way more than I had earned.

As I headed toward the Cahuenga Pass, I felt compelled to take a little detour.

I wasn't sure exactly where Ivarene Street was, but a quaint sign welcomed me to the Hollywood Dell. I went through an old stone tunnel where overgrown foliage tumbled down from the freeway with astonishing grace. On the other side, I got tangled up in the web of streets that cover the foothills until, by sheer accident, I found the house.

Shreds of crime-scene tape fluttered from a tree and skittered in the breeze across the sidewalk. The house had once been a pretty cottage with an ample front yard and a picket fence, peeling now and protecting a few scraggly rose bushes with one or two starving blossoms. I tried the door. Locked. The front curtains were closed. They had an abstract brown pattern. At least that's what I thought at first, until I realized I was looking at dried blood that had spattered and soaked into the cloth.

The blinds in the side windows were shut. The slats were

damaged and bent, and I peered into the living room. The place had been cleaned and looked like any empty rental filled with secondhand furniture—except for the darkened areas on the rug and upholstery and walls that could have been shadows but weren't.

I went around to the back door. Through its window, I could see the kitchen. The walls here were stained too, blood mixing with the kind of filth that coats old paint and seeps through cracked linoleum and can be covered but never cleaned.

Behind the house, a yard ended abruptly at a steep hillside. I looked around as if I might actually find something that had eluded an entire team of police experts, but all I saw was weeds.

I noticed a narrow path through the brush. Curious, I started down, the fleshy leaves of jade plants brushing against my ankles.

The hill bottomed out at a culvert, the weeds flattened out on either side. I didn't know if I was retracing a path the cops had already taken, but I started to follow it uphill. The sun was warm and the air heavy with eucalyptus, and the exertion of a steep hike felt good. After a long climb, the brush opened into a huge wooded area that could have been a park or part of someone's estate.

I sat down on a flat rock to rest, and when I looked up, I saw, half hidden behind the fronds of a eucalyptus, a woman no taller than a ten-year-old child. She grinned at me, her round face stretched wide by a smile like a kid's drawing of the sun—too bright and a little cockeyed.

"Sorry," I said. "I guess I've stumbled onto your property."

She stared at me and that smile got even wider. Finally, she said, very slowly as if the words were emerging from some vast and distant space inside her large head, "My . . . property."

I knew that smile. I'd been there myself one crazy drugged-out year in high school before I left home. I remembered what it was like, soaring so high you broke free of all the painful threads that bound you to your life.

"Property!" she cried out again and, as if it had been the punch line to the best joke on earth, she laughed. She laughed so hard her skin turned pink and moist. Then she looked at me through gone eyes and, holding her stomach and staring as if I were the most bizarre and hilarious creature, she wheezed out the words, "How could a person own a piece of a planet?"

She fell to the ground laughing, then turned over on her belly and lifted a handful of soil to her face. "Smell the earth," she said, her eyes glowing through a face now streaked with dirt. "That's the whole thing!"

The smell the breeze carried to me was of her body and filthy clothes, yet it was more the outdoor scent of someone camping than the fetid odor of the homeless who sleep in doorways.

"The whole thing?" I said.

She looked like she was lost in concepts that her mind couldn't pull into sentences. "The senses. They pull us back down from the light."

The sight of her stained face brought back memories of the battered face in the morgue. She saw the shift in me and her balloon face crumpled. She was older than I had thought, with fine lines around her mouth and below her eyes. Her hand went to her chest, and she began to play with some sort of pendant under her sweater, but she let go of it abruptly when she saw the man walking toward us through the woods.

Bare chested, weighing maybe a hundred and twenty, he had a Mohawk four inches high and streaked purple. When he reached us, he enfolded the tiny woman in his arms. But his eyes were on me.

"Go on, Callie." He gave her a pat on the butt. "Get home now."

He stepped back and she looked bereft at the loss of his body in her arms. But she wandered off and hadn't gotten very far when she stooped to talk to a lizard, who cocked his head as if he were actually listening.

"Chick's plugged right into the juice," the man said, "but her wheels ain't running on the tracks."

"What's she on?"

"What're you, a cop?"

"Just out for a hike."

"Yeah, right. Hikers take Runyon Canyon. You some kind of reporter? Looking for some Hollywood Hills *color* so you can keep your murders on the front page? Write some story about the weirdoes up in the hills and bring the heat up here in a New York minute?"

"I'm not a reporter."

"You came up from around Ivarene."

"That's right. They say my friend was killed there."

This statement seemed to have touched him deeply. He took a deep breath and his head bobbed slowly up and down like he was considering just how to express himself.

Finally, he rolled out one heartfelt word. *"Dude."*

Then he gave me a half-lidded appraisal. "Bet it was the pretty one, right? The model?"

"Yes," I said.

"Listen, they call me ZuZu. What's your name?"

"Nikki."

"Nikki." He purred my name out from deep in his belly. "I like your eyes."

"Can't have 'em."

He grinned. A couple of teeth were missing. "Come smoke a little weed with me, girl."

"Sorry, dude. Not interested."

"Not interested in Ivarene?"

"What do you know about it?"

"Nuh uh, sugarface. First show me you're good people."

I really didn't want to get stoned. I'd once lost a year of days that way. But I followed him through the woods to a clearing that was like nothing I'd ever seen before.

A huge tarp had been lashed to a circle of trees. Beneath it was an almost fully furnished living room. Worn rugs covered the ground and on top of them were a couple of beat-up sofas and a coffee table strewn with magazines, ashtrays, rolling papers and other assorted paraphernalia. A porcelain sink, overflowing with filthy dishes, had a black rubber hose where the faucet should have been.

Most remarkable was the television, whose wires ran out to a tree and from there must have tapped into power and cable lines, because the TV was on, tuned to a courtroom reality show.

A deep voice oozed from one of the couches. "Bet that judge shits rusty nails, dude."

The tarp and foliage blocked out most of the sunlight. All I could make out at first was about a yard of heavy blonde hair hanging off the edge of the sofa. Then I saw it belonged to a man who was more or less melted into the furniture like a used-up candle. He had an ashtray on his bare chest and a pair of jeans skimming the sharp bones of his hips.

"Dude," said ZuZu, "that TV is one fuckin' energy drain."

"Keepin' occupied till Hollywood knocks at my door."

From somewhere, a girl said, "You have no door, Flowertop." She was leaning against a tree, tall and gaunt. If her low-slung jeans hadn't been stiff with grime, they would have slid right off her narrow frame. She shuffled over to the couch and lay down alongside him.

ZuZu sprinkled some dope into a rolling paper and flicked his tongue along the edge. He took a hit and passed me the joint. The smoke burned my lungs. It had been a long time.

"How'd your friend get tangled up in that Ivarene scene?" He held the pot in his lungs and squeezed out his words.

"Smack, man. Fuckin' death trip."

"Life's a death trip," Flowertop said. "Eat sprouts or smoke crack. We're all headin' to the same final destination."

"But burnin' someone on a heroin deal, man, that's a first-class ticket on the *adios* express," ZuZu said.

"That's pretty much what the cops think," I said.

"Cops don't know shit. They're saying Johnny Rambla was a victim of, dig this, *recreational* drug abuse. *Re-creation.* Oh, man. Dig it! *Re-creation.* Story of the cosmos. Our cells, man, our molecules, every little proton in the universe." His glance took in the room and his friends lying inert on the couch. "We're all re-*creatin'* ourselves . . . *non-stop.* Whew." He rolled his eyes, looked up, and went wandering through the winding corridors of his mind. It took him a while to get back. "Where was I?"

"Johnny Rambla," I said and knew I was high because my own voice sounded like it belonged to someone else.

"Right! They're saying the dude just needed a little *rehab.*" He took a long drag on what was left of the joint, burned his fingers, and put it out fast. "Cat was buying wholesale from the Taliban. Flyin' it in on his own fuckin' plane."

"Ain't the Taliban," Flowertop said. "Taliban wiped out the opium trade. CIA put them poppy farmers back in business."

ZuZu grinned. "Conspiracy freak."

"You don't believe me? Check it out on the Web, man."

Flowertop nodded toward the upturned milk crates that served as a coffee table. Peeking out from under a discarded shirt and a drift of dead leaves was the shiny aluminum corner of a laptop.

"You figure out that passcode yet for the wi-fi?" Flowertop said.

"Don't need no pass codes," said ZuZu. "We've all got brain-to-brain wi-fi. Just gotta stay high." He laughed and got lost again.

"Rambla was flying heroin out of Afghanistan?" I asked, pulling him back.

ZuZu made a soft landing and refocused. "Huh?"

"Rambla. Heroin. Afghanistan."

"Yep. Some heavy player was fronting the bread. Big-time straight-world cat. Smart money ain't on Wall Street anymore."

"ZuZu, you talk way too fuckin' much," the girl said, her hand massaging the length of Flowertop's thigh.

"Dude's dead, Jaycee," said Flowertop. "Can't bust him now."

"Asshole," she muttered. But she couldn't have minded too much because a few minutes later I heard the hiss of Flowertop's zipper. It was definitely time for me to leave.

As I walked back down the culvert, I found myself looking for Callie, the moon-faced lady. I felt a pang of dope-heightened disappointment when I didn't find her. I needed to see her again. It was really important. I just couldn't remember why.

CHAPTER 16

On the oldies station, Gloria Gaynor was trying to convince me she'd survive. But I knew I wouldn't unless I got something to eat, like *now.* I screeched to a stop in front of Pink's. So what if the curb was painted red. I was *hungry.* I ordered two chili dogs with fries. Flavor exploded on my tongue. I threw my head back and merrily popped ketchup-soaked fries into my mouth. It was unbearably good, and I remembered what had been great about getting high. I ordered two more chili dogs—with bacon this time—and a cream soda to wash it all down.

When I finished, I had an almost overwhelming urge to lie down on Pink's patio and doze off like a cat with the sun warming my belly, but a little shred of propriety remained. I went back out to the street, yanked the ticket off my windshield, pretended to myself that it didn't hurt, got into the car, and headed home.

I drove past squat buildings whose facades looked like the flattened faces of sad old men. There were sallow boys walking the streets with bare concave chests, graying T-shirts hanging from their back pockets. Street hustlers, slouching toward nowhere. I thought of Kyle and his scared eyes. I flashed on how our ties to things we love will sooner or later pull us down. I saw all those ties like so many sticky spider webs trapping us at every turn. Those threads turned hard inside me, dark, sharp, broken connections, a barbed-wire network of memory. What a fucked-up world when love kills and you can't live without love.

I felt brilliant for seeing this with such astonishing clarity. Then I thought about Detective Adder and how maybe there was something between us, and maybe we might even love each other for a while. He would leave me or I would leave him. There would be other men and other loves. And I would always, finally, be alone.

I sank into a tepid pool of self-pity, then thought, *What the hell, I'd be free!* My spirits lifted, then sank again because freedom's just another word for nothing left to lose. My mind went on and on like that, and it wasn't until I pulled into my driveway that I realized it was simply the weed working its way through my brain. And then I remembered why I'd stopped smoking this stuff a long time ago.

I opened the door and fell onto the couch. A sumo wrestler sat on my stomach. I wasn't so stoned anymore, but I couldn't handle anything more strenuous than breathing.

I dozed off and when I woke up I was thinking about Callie. About that moment when ZuZu came by and interrupted us. About how scared she looked when she first saw him. About how she'd been playing with something under her sweater and then dropped her hands too suddenly. About the way he had sent her off like he didn't want her talking to me, then asked straight away if I was a cop.

I drove back to the hills and wound my way up the labyrinthine streets, not sure exactly how to find the encampment by car. At every fork, I took the road that led uphill, only sometimes it would hairpin down again. When I found myself back on Ivarene, I was almost ready to give up. *One more try,* I thought, and was about to turn around when I saw her.

She was sitting on the porch steps of the murder house, toying with a piece of crime-scene tape and talking to herself. As I approached, I could hear her repeating something over and over again, faster and faster, the way little kids do to make a word lose its meaning. *"Blood, blood, blood, blood, blood."*

My footsteps startled her. She stopped her chant and stared up at me for a moment, then whispered, "Too much blood."

"Oh my god," I said. "You were there!"

Like a child who knows she's in trouble, she smiled coyly. But her hand went straight to the little object under her sweater.

"What is that?" I said.

"Nothing."

"Show it to me."

From inside her sweater, she pulled out a chain with a garnet ring on it. The last time I had seen the ring, it was on Darla's finger.

"How did you get that?"

"I found it."

"Where?"

She looked at me like a kid unjustly accused. "She didn't need it anymore. She was free."

"Free? What do you mean free?"

"Freed from her body."

"You mean she was dead?"

She nodded. "Someone beat her up real bad. But now she's where there is no pain."

"The girl with the battered face? She was wearing this ring?"

"It was so sparkly—"

I gripped her bony shoulders with both hands. "You killed them?"

"No! We found them after. We just took the freebies."

"You and ZuZu and the others killed them! You killed them and then you beat that girl. You beat a dead girl."

A dead girl. But it wasn't a dead girl anymore. It was Darla. I had been wrong, like everyone had tried to tell me. I'd simply refused to see what was right in front of my eyes that day at the morgue. The pride I had in my ability to *see,* without which I never would have survived the streets or the road, had become blind stubbornness. The anger drained out of me. For a minute I couldn't breathe.

Callie's trusting smile had returned. "You won't tell ZuZu I told, will you?"

I could barely get the words out. "No. I won't tell ZuZu."

As soon as my car turned the corner, I called Detective Adder.

That evening, the arrest of the "Ivarene Cult Killers" was all over the news. Every station had live coverage. As helicopters circled and officers armed with assault weapons surrounded the encampment, pretty girl and boy reporters talked excitedly into the cameras, speculating on whether there would be a violent standoff.

But there was no shootout, no conflagration, and the news people couldn't hide their disappointment when four dazed dopers shuffled out of the woods and were led away. Callie looked like she was still smiling, but she was only squinting into the barrage of flashbulbs and TV lights. And there was Adder, one big hand circling ZuZu's arm, the other pushing that Mohawked head down into a squad car.

I sat for hours in front of the TV screen, jumping from one news network to the other, hypnotized by the repetitive footage. The police had found plenty of evidence. Bloodstained clothes, two guns of the same caliber as the ones used at Ivarene, and—in the sink with all the unwashed dishes—a knife that matched Johnny Rambla's stab wounds.

That night I dreamed that Darla's face wasn't battered. Her skin was gray and her eyes were empty and her mouth was forming a silent "Help," the same way it had formed "It's okay" from the back of Jimmy's car.

I woke up with a jolt, and the full weight of what had happened finally hit me. My sobs were choked at first, then the tears tore out of me. After a while they came easier, and it was good, the childlike comfort of crying against a damp pillow.

Chapter 17

Detective Adder called a few times. He was easy to talk to. He listened to all the thoughts I needed to get out of my head. He listened to my silences without needing to fill them. He knew when I began to feel like myself again, and that's when he asked me if I wanted to have dinner.

He made reservations at the Palm, where everything was supersized, from the monster lobsters to the basketball stars devouring them.

I took more care than usual getting dressed—a spaghetti-strap silk top, kicky skirt, and heels that would get me from a car through a restaurant door and not much further.

He showed up right on time in a sports jacket and gray slacks with a razor crease. We exchanged a few words, but all I could see were his eyes. Clear blue with a direct line to the very core of me. His arms circled my waist, and I felt the back of his neck, smooth and taut against my fingers. My heart pounded against his and his mouth found my mouth and the swelling between his legs pressed against the hunger between mine, raw at first, then subtle and full of grace.

By the time we began to regain a separate sense of ourselves, the sky was vulgar with stars. The window was open and the breeze on my damp skin made me shiver.

"That was pretty nice, Adder."

"I think," he said, "you can call me Jack."

A grandpa name. It didn't fit him at all. "Okay, Adder," I said.

We were both wide awake in the moonlight, side by side, our thighs still touching, like one organism in the last stage of mitosis. I didn't want to think about anything. I just wanted to breathe in the blossomy L.A. night and the musk of the man next to me.

"I like the night," Adder said after a while. "All the static disappears."

He felt for his shirt on the floor, extracted a pack of cigarettes from the pocket, and lit one with his free hand, still holding me close with the other.

"When I was over there in the desert, with flames bursting way off at the horizon and the explosions so soft and far way," he said, "I felt like I could hear the heart of the universe . . . animals, insects, every creature on a battlefield, as fierce and driven as we are."

"Part of you is still over there, isn't it?"

The look on his face was the look of a man remembering the lost love of his life, a look that shifted between terrible beauty and exquisite pain.

"There's no way to imagine it," he said, "until you're in it. Sometimes it's only that big open desert and the beauty of it, the mystery. But sometimes that vast emptiness feels like a cell with tin walls, everything reverberating back at you too strong—the blood, the stench, the noise, the boredom, the bullshit." There was tension in his jaw and something bitter in the tightness of his lips. "The fear that never lets up, not even when you sleep. But all of it—every goddamn moment—is unbelievably vivid. Then you come back, buckle up your seatbelt, and everything kind of flatlines."

He leaned in and placed his lips softly on mine, and a sharp current ran right through me. "Baby," he said, "I sure don't feel that way now." He turned away and I heard his quick exhale as he ground out the cigarette, heard my own breath catch because I wanted him again.

After we made love, I drifted into sleep.

Three loud cries—one right after the other—woke me. Adder's eyes were open, and he sought comfort in my body, but I wasn't sure he knew whose stomach he rested his head on, whose hand stroked his hair, whose feelings were deeper and more complicated than they should have been for a man who was a stranger a couple of weeks ago.

It was after three when he fell back to sleep, but I was restless. I got out of bed and went into the living room. The cruisers were gone and the street was quiet. Only darkened windows and empty cars, except for an old hatchback parked across the street. The man in the driver's seat was eating chips. I couldn't see his features clearly but he had a thick, fleshy face. He must have sensed someone staring because he turned and looked straight at me. Then he tossed the bag of chips down, started up the engine, and sped off.

Maybe just a lonely guy looking for a pickup.

When I slipped back into bed, Adder, still asleep, turned toward me and wrapped me in the strong cushion of his arms.

The sound of the shower woke me around six, but I didn't open my eyes until he was standing in the doorway with a towel around his shoulders. It was definitely nice watching his easy stride as he walked across the room, and the way he pulled his jeans on over his long-muscled thighs.

But those jeans never quite made it all the way up.

When he took his second shower, I fell back asleep.

Adder was gone the next time I woke up. A pot of coffee was warming for me, and his rinsed cup sat all by itself in the dish drain.

On the counter was a paper napkin. On it he had written one word. "Wow."

In the warm, sunlit morning with a slightly smoggy orange-blossom breeze stirring the curtains and the scent of Adder still on my skin, I put *American Beauty* on the turntable and listened to the lazy riffs of "Sugar Magnolia" while I sipped hot, sweet coffee.

I listened a lot to old sixties music. After I left home, I was occasionally befriended by aging longhairs who saw in me their own lost freedom. One thing I learned early was that a desiccated old doper was a safer bet on the road than those nervous family men or lonely bachelors who started battling repressed fantasies the minute you got into the car. You could always trust aging hippies. All you had to do was develop a tolerance for patchouli. They often offered me a place to stay for a while and usually asked nothing of me but that I read their books and listen to the licorice-colored LPs they held so delicately at the edges.

Now, even with the sweet sounds of "Sugar Magnolia," I could feel the unease coming awake beneath the sultry morning lassitude. It pushed up through the memory of light glinting off a brandy glass resting on Adder's surprisingly smooth chest, and of Adder waking from his feverish dream and laying his head across my belly with a tenderness that rippled through me like an evening lake.

Yet underneath it all were the last two weeks and everything that had happened. Not just the loss, but the image I couldn't shake of the brutally battered girl on the gurney who had been my friend.

The phone rang as I was pouring my second cup of coffee.

"Hey," he said, "I was thinking about you."

"Adder, a new girl deserves a new line." I aimed for cool, but my voice was so heavy with wanting him it broke.

"I'd like to see you."

"Me, too," I said.

"Are you doing okay?"

"It's a little tough."

"I know."

"The bad moments kind of come in waves."

"Baby, would you like to get out of town for a few days? Clear away the past. Give ourselves a fresh start."

Exactly what I needed. I'd put down fragile roots, but there was still nothing like that feeling of getting on the road and watching the past disappear in the rearview mirror.

He arranged some time off and we drove up to Big Sur. Of all the places I'd been, I've never loved one better—its raw, wild beauty, the jagged cliffs, the roar of the ocean, the wind in the pines.

We stayed in a cabin near the river and hiked through silent redwood forests. We took a dirt trail to the ocean and found ourselves on a deserted beach where we made love like we were the only two people on earth. They say Big Sur used to be a sacred Indian healing ground. Whatever it was, it's a place that puts a lot of peace in you.

But as we headed back to the city and the narrow Coast Highway became a six-lane freeway, bright lights obliterated the starry sky, and everything we'd left behind came rushing back at me.

Chapter 18

There had been no cell phone reception up in Big Sur, and when I finally retrieved my messages, there was a text from Phil.

2 strikes, u r out

I'd completely forgotten the new audition he'd set up.

He wouldn't take my call, so I drove straight to his office with a heart so full of remorse he couldn't possibly stay mad. His assistant said he wasn't in. Said, with genuine sympathy, that for me he would not be in—ever.

I didn't have too much time to feel crummy about it, because on the way home I saw a Chevy hatchback in the rearview mirror, a man with a fleshy face at the wheel. The same car that had been parked in front of my house. I pulled abruptly into the first parking space I saw and watched him shoot past. The license number was covered in mud, so completely unreadable it had to be intentional.

Rattled, I threw a few coins in the meter and walked across the street to Jerry's Deli, into the reassuring buzz of people and the busy clatter of plates.

I ordered an egg cream and kept my gaze on the entrance. The only men who came in wore shoes that cost more than the hatchback. But when I got up to leave, I realized my mistake. There was a back door.

He was a few booths behind me with his face half-buried in a sandwich, but I recognized him immediately. He came up for air and looked over at the empty table where I'd been sitting.

"Hi," I said. "Thought you lost me?"

He was so startled he almost choked, but he didn't say anything, couldn't say anything with a lump of pastrami and rye working its way down his gullet.

When he was finally able to speak, he said, "Huh?"

"I want to know why you've been following me."

"Following you?" He stared down at the sandwich on his plate. I think he would have liked to ostrich his face in it and disappear. "What are you talking about?"

"You've been watching my house. And you followed me here."

"You got the wrong guy, lady."

"No, I don't." I looked him straight in the eye. He glanced away.

Then he reached into his jacket and I went cold. Sure, the restaurant was full, but could I really count on one of the patrons to risk a bullet hole in his designer sweats?

But the man merely withdrew a wrinkled white handkerchief and wiped the mustard from the corner of his lips, then the dampness from his forehead, all the while running his tongue across his teeth, clearing away clinging bits of food like a windshield wiper scraping off flattened mosquitoes.

Whoever he was, I was pretty sure he wasn't doing anything on his own. He had the dull eyes of a man who'd taken orders every day of his life and had never stopped resenting it.

"I don't hold it against you. A guy's got to make a living," I said.

"That's right. I'm just doing a job, lady."

"I understand. What's your name?"

He hesitated and I could almost see the slow wheels of his brain working to come up with a false one. I said, "Don't even think about lying. You're not good at it."

He lowered is head to his food like a dog and mumbled, "Raymond," before taking another chunk out of his sandwich.

"Who are you working for, Raymond?"

He moved his mouth around like it didn't know what direction to go in, then he started chewing the inside of his cheek.

"This guy hired me. A private detective. With a license and all. Ain't done nothing against the law."

I remembered the nice, friendly man who'd knocked on my door, but it took a beat for the name to click in. "You work for Manny Roberson?" I said.

I saw at once he knew the name, but he tried to cover his reaction by tearing into that sandwich again, except the crust of rye wanted to play tug-of-war. I almost felt sorry for him.

"I know Manny," I said. "He told me he'd been hired to find out if Darla Ward was really dead. Well, she is. So why is he still interested in me?"

"How should I know? Ten bucks an hour, no one tells me shit."

Chapter 19

I found the card Manny had left with me. *Emanuel Roberson—Discreet Surveillance, Process Service.*

Back in the day, when the Hollywood swells still dined at the Brown Derby, Manny's building must have been a class act. The entrance was framed with an ornate design of palm leaves and cherubs with empty stone eyes.

The only person in the lobby was a man standing still but weaving slightly. He looked like someone who had been on a long and difficult space voyage and was stunned to find himself back on earth, exactly where he started, with nothing to show for his travels but a warm can of beer in his hand.

A board with plastic type stuck into grooves listed the tenants. "Ema el R ber on" occupied "Siute 304."

The elevator ride was unbearably slow. Gears wheezed and the door rattled. In the fluorescent light you could see blotches of old gum on the floor and the tarnished brass wheel some sad soul must once have captained.

I stepped out on the third floor into a long narrow hallway of closed doors.

Through the rippled glass window of 304, Manny at his desk appeared to be underwater. A small sign on the wall said PLEASE RING BELL. I did. It sounded like a fire alarm, but he acted like he didn't hear it. So I knocked. The door swung open.

Manny was sitting straight up in his chair. Blood drenched

his white shirt. His eyes were wide open and so was his mouth. I guess there's no bigger surprise than death walking in your front door.

I didn't scream. I didn't run. I just stood there as the door slowly closed itself behind me. Below on the boulevard, I could hear the dense hum of traffic, rap music pounding from a passing car, a burst of reckless laughter. But here in this room, its walls bare except for a few ancient stains and a bank calendar stranded in a grimy green sea, it was a world apart. Here it was silent, and I found myself encapsulated in the illusion that life was standing still.

Then the tinny sweet smell of blood cut through the stillness and brought with it a raw animal fear.

I was digging through my bag for my phone when I heard the elevator door open, heard an odd pattern of footsteps in the hallway, one longer, one short. A heavy step. A man with a limp.

He stopped in front of the door but didn't knock. I could hear one side of a whispered conversation but couldn't make out what he was saying. Then the knob turned.

There was only one place to hide.

I ducked down behind the desk and pushed against Manny's legs to wedge myself under it. A wave of nausea ran through me as I crouched there, with the weight of his legs pressing into my shoulder. The gag reflex lurched in my throat and I bit my fist until it passed.

Then the door opened and I stopped breathing.

The whisper was more intense now. "You just said do 'im. This is nuts! Yeah, yeah, okay, okay."

Snap. A flip phone closing.

I could see nothing from where I hid, but heard everything with startling clarity. A file cabinet drawer creaked open. His fingers flicked over folders. Files swooshed as he removed them. The drawer slid shut.

I waited, my breath so shallow I was afraid it might explode out of me.

He came closer to the desk. Stopped inches away from me, so close I caught the sour smell of him. Manny was the only thing that kept me out of sight.

The man opened the side drawers. Then he let out a long, discouraged sigh.

A minute later I heard the squeak of wheels—Manny's chair rolling back from the desk. I was trapped. In another second he'd see me.

I heard a loud thud above me. The sound of Manny's skull hitting wood.

Then, a harsh whisper. "Oh, fuckin' heavenly Father forgive me." And the smell of the man got thicker.

I saw his fingers—wide, flat fingers—reach beneath the desk and open the middle drawer. It rattled above me as he felt around inside. He whispered a curse. Whatever he was looking for, he hadn't found it.

He stood there, his weight shifting from foot to foot, his breath thick and anxious. Finally, he turned away from the desk. I listened as he walked toward the door, stopped there for several seconds, then closed it softly behind him. I heard the odd rhythm of his footsteps as he headed up the hallway, and when the elevator gate opened and banged shut, I came out from under the desk.

The man had left all the drawers open. In one was a change of clothes that looked home-pressed and a photo in a cheap frame of a woman with a lovely smile and worried eyes, one hand resting on the shoulder of a young boy. In the other drawer were a few loose staples, a hardened spill of glue and one thing that told me more than I wanted to know about Emanuel Roberson—an enormous and almost empty pink bottle of Pepto-Bismol.

I noticed something sticking out of Manny's jacket pocket. Gingerly, with two fingers, I lifted out a small notebook with an imitation leather cover, the kind they sell at drugstores.

I threw it in my purse, then beat it the hell out of there. I took the stairs back down, took them two at a time. When I got to the lobby, I opened the stairwell door a crack. The man with the can of beer was teaching himself how to walk, one careful step at a time, but otherwise the lobby was still deserted.

Out on the Boulevard, I hurried past men with lust-sick eyes, feral street punks, and a family of tourists, the wife's arms billowing out of a short-sleeve blouse like soufflés.

As I headed for my car, I heard a long, sharp wolf-whistle.

I quickened my pace.

Then someone called my name.

CHAPTER 20

Dan Ackerman, my ex, was walking toward me, all lit up with a tense, excited smile. When he saw my face, his own face drained of color.

"Nikki! What's wrong?"

He was a bear of a man, and when his arms went around me I felt such deep comfort, I could have stayed there for days.

"You're shaking," he said.

I wanted nothing more than to tell him everything, to pour it all out so I wouldn't have to carry it alone. But how could I drag him into this?

"An audition," I said. "All those emotions are still running through me."

Dan shook his head as if this whole "acting thing," as he used to call it, was beyond him.

"Listen," he said, "I was going to get a bite at Musso's. You look like you could use a drink."

I wanted to get home and see what was in Manny's notebook, but I really did need a shot of something. Dan took my hand as we walked up the Boulevard. I realized I needed that too, his calm bulk absorbing all the jangled energy in me.

Musso & Frank had been our place. We had gone there many times to soothe the wounds we'd inflicted on each other. I loved the old restaurant with its wood paneling so elegantly worn, so warmly indifferent to fame, to scandal, to tragedy. Peg Entwistle, Johnny Stompanato, even the Black Dahlia might have dined in these leather booths and looked up into the impassive face of a red-jacketed waiter. Maybe even the same one who stood at our table now, with a pad and pen in his ancient hand.

We ordered Remy and rib steaks, and we both smiled too much—Dan because the two of us were here together again, and me because I was trying to hide the dead man behind my eyes.

"I'm sorry about Darla," he said. "I guess you got my messages."

I nodded and cupped the snifter between my hands and fought the desire to unburden myself. There was no one in the world I trusted more than Dan. No one I was more fond of. Of course, *fond* was the word he took like a kick in the belly the day we broke up.

"I liked her," he said. "She was one of those people you don't get right away. You see the hair and the dazzling smile and the tight, bright clothes. But when you finally noticed her eyes, she was one lonely girl."

The cognac went down like smoke and cast a mellow amber haze over Darla's lonely eyes. It expanded into a bubble of happiness. I wasn't alone, not one bit. Dan was my friend. Good old Dan. Big old heart. The cognac drew a loopy smile on my face. And when I got tired of listening to the voice in my own head, I realized Dan was talking.

"So I've been doing a lot of thinking, Nikki. I realize I was pushing too hard. But if you gave it another chance—" He laughed. "See? I'm doing it right now. But I caught myself."

He got that grateful-to-be-here look on his face, and his hand did a jumpy dance on the table, as if resisting the impulse to take mine.

I took his. It was almost as familiar as my own. The alcohol heated up the affection I felt for him, and I couldn't help myself. The words bubbled over and slipped out.

"I love you."

He took a deep breath. "You mean Remy Martin loves me."

That sobered me up for a moment.

"I meant—"

"I know what you meant." He gave my hand an affectionate squeeze and we both reached for our drinks.

I finished off the cognac and floated up, up, and away where reality couldn't touch me, not through the wood paneling and the soft clink of dishes and the low hum of conversation, not with Dan's warmth enveloping me, not with the ancient waiter watching over us like a gargoyle.

Except the Manny Roberson movie kept flickering through my thoughts. To keep it at bay, I tried to focus on Dan.

"How's campus life, Professor?"

"Well, to my many skills, I can now add pulling knives out of my back at the end of every day."

"You're kidding. I thought you were the golden boy. What's going on?"

"The chairman is not pleased with the book I'm working on."

Even sober, I could never remember the name of it. "The Empirical Whatchamacallit?"

"*Empirical Neopatrimonialism: An Historical Analysis of Political Funding and its Impact on the Federal Government from Post–World War II America through the Present.*"

"Maybe you need a catchier title. How 'bout *Grease*?"

Granted, it wasn't all that funny, but Dan didn't even crack a smile.

"It's not bribery, Nikki, it's more like ownership. The whole thing is a hall of mirrors. Lobbies, campaign funds, and so much money coming from shell companies, it's almost impossible to trace."

"You must have stumbled onto something, Dan, or you

wouldn't be worried about your job."

He looked, with some anxiety, around the restaurant, then leaned across the table and lowered his voice. "I did, Nikki. But you can't mention this to a soul."

"No, of course not." His anxiety amplified my own. I took another sip of brandy.

"There's one overseas bank that seems to own more than its share of these companies, and one board member whose name keeps cropping up, a guy named Lyn Fourray. Apparently, he made a few phone calls to some major donors, and the university put the screws to the department head."

"What are you going to do?"

He didn't have to answer. I knew that set of his lips. Dan was big-hearted, gentle, full of integrity, and stubborn as they come.

"If I back off from the truth, Nikki, then I'm one more dope who sold his soul for a paycheck."

We finished our drinks and he walked me back to my car. The scent of night jasmine drifted down from the hills, mingling with the general odor of soot and despair.

"So," Dan said, and there was a universe of hope and history in that little syllable.

"So," I said.

He put his arms around me, but the alcohol was wearing off. Even in the warmth of Dan's hug, all I could feel was the chill of Manny Roberson's murder.

CHAPTER 21

Whatever relief Dan had provided disappeared the minute I turned the corner onto my street and saw spinning red lights and two Sheriff's cars in front of my house. My first thought was that they'd come for me.

Only why were the deputies, four of them, standing in a circle staring down at something? From between columns of khakis, I saw a red-and-white shoe. It took a moment to grasp that it was actually a white sneaker swirled with blood.

At the sound of my car in the driveway, two of the cops stepped back. Billy Hoyle, my landlord, was lying on the sidewalk, his eyes closed.

"Oh my god! What happened?" I rushed toward him, but a deputy blocked my way.

"You'll have to stand back, Miss."

Billy's eyes opened. "Nikki," he said in barely a whisper, "I stopped him."

"Sir," said a snub-nosed, boyish cop, "you shouldn't try to talk."

Billy struggled to prop himself up on his elbows, then ran a hand along his calf and stared at the blood smeared across his palm. He looked bewildered. "It doesn't hurt."

"It's shock, sir. The body kills the pain for a short time. But that bullet went in quite a ways."

"Bullet?" I said. "What bullet?"

An older cop, with a suggestion of jowls that matched the

pooch beginning to peek over his belt, turned to look at me. Before he could explain what had happened, an ambulance screeched around the corner. Its siren abruptly cut off as it pulled to a stop.

The paramedics lifted Billy onto a stretcher. His eyes closed again. The skin was thin and loose over his bones. He was always in motion, so you never really thought about it. He was old.

"I'll go with him," I said to one of the men from the ambulance.

"Who are you?" the older cop said.

"I live here."

"Then you better stay for now."

That's when I noticed the shattered glass in my driveway and the trail of blood from the open front door. I started toward the steps.

One of the cops blocked my way.

"It's okay, let her go in," the older one said and followed me through the front door into the living room.

It was nowhere near as bad as the destruction I had seen at Darla's. But it hurt just as much. It was mine. My cozy old sofa had been slashed, exposing cotton batting and yellowed foam rubber. Every book had been dumped from the shelves. A bit dazed, I walked into the bedroom. Nothing had been touched there. The kitchen, too, was as I'd left it.

"You can thank your neighbor for that," the cop said. "He saw the guy break in and decided to play hero."

I thought about the man in the hatchback, about Manny, and felt sick. I was responsible for what happened to Billy.

"How bad is his wound?"

"They'll patch him up fine over at Cedars."

"Do you have any idea who—"

"We'll talk to him when he gets settled at the hospital.

Meantime, my guys are on the street. We'll see what they turn up."

He walked over to the broken window, examined the sill, went out the back door, and paced around my few square feet of yard, eyeing the ground like a man who'd lost a quarter.

When he came back in he said, "Another damn junkie. You seen those Mike Ryle ads?"

How could you miss them? "The cowboy who wants to be senator."

"He's got the right idea. This ain't the America I grew up in. Get rid of the creeps and sleazebags. They ought to invent a spray for 'em, like cockroaches."

I stopped myself from suggesting there were some ovens in Germany he could probably get cheap, and said instead, "I'm not sure this is a simple break-in."

"Talk to me."

I tried to calculate how much I could tell him, especially with Manny's notebook burning a hole in my bag.

"Darla Ward was my friend," I said. "I think this might have something to do with the Ivarene murders.

"Where you been? We got the doers locked up tight downtown."

Before he could question me further, we heard a cry from outside, almost a whimper.

We both looked out the window.

A brown-skinned man crouched near the curb, the three deputies surrounding him. One struck his back with a baton. The young wholesome cop gave him a kick. Not the kind of kick that could do a lot of damage. More like you'd give a soccer ball.

They seemed to be enjoying themselves. "Talk, amigo!" one of them said, then twisted the man's arm behind his back.

"Hey!" I cried, running out the door. "Stop it! He's not fighting you."

The old cop trotted out behind me and one of the deputies pulled the man to his feet. "We found him up at the end of the street."

"Doing what?" I said.

"Looking damn suspicious."

"What does that mean?"

"He was lurking, ma'am. In your neighbor's bushes."

A woman ran toward us. "Let him go!" she cried. "That's my gardener!"

She spoke a few words to the man in fractured Spanish, talking very loudly as if upping the volume would help him understand her. He mumbled what seemed like an elaborately polite apology, but what I saw in his face was shame, with anger burning just below.

"The mayor is a personal friend of my husband," she told the deputies, "and believe me, he will hear about this. Police brutality and pure racism. For goodness sakes! These people are as gentle as children."

Certain of the virtue of her upscale brand of racism, she took her gardener's arm as if he were, indeed, a child, and led him back up the street.

"Okay, let's wrap it up here," the old cop said, and they got into their cars and drove away.

When they were gone, the street looked as peaceful as it always did, except for the pool of Billy Hoyle's blood drying on the concrete.

CHAPTER 22

I looked around at the chaos of my living room, at the floor strewn with books I'd been lugging from place to place for half my life. When I was lost and confused, I searched these books, thinking I would find answers. It was only when I realized there were no answers that I really fell in love with books.

I was sitting in the midst of them, feeling overwhelmed by all that had happened, when Adder showed up.

He looked at the room, then at me and said, "Jesus! You okay, baby?"

"I guess."

"Why didn't you call me?"

Uh, because I stole evidence from a crime scene? Because even though we're crazy about each other, maybe you won't be able to overlook a felony?

"I was going to," I said.

He sensed this new distance between us and nodded in that way he had of adjusting to whatever the world threw at him.

I told him most of what I knew about the break-in. He listened without interrupting, without asking questions. Then he walked through the house, examining everything, a cop at a crime scene, while I wondered if I could tell him about the rest.

He came back into the living room, sat down beside me, and chucked me under the chin. "So, let's get this place cleaned up. Okay?"

We started with the books. From time to time, Adder would

pick one up and stare at the cover with a deliberately befuddled expression. He'd read aloud, mocking the gravitas of those two-ton titles—*Man's Fate, War and Peace, The Sound and the Fury*—trying to coax a laugh from me. But he couldn't. The day had razed me inside.

"Whoever broke in here," he said, "must have stolen your sense of humor."

He picked up a small clothbound book and gave me a cold cop stare. "*Cubism*? What are you doing with Fidel Castro's manifesto?"

I threw him a look like he'd turned into a frog.

"Come on, give it up, girl. You gotta admit *that* was funny." He scrunched his face into a silly wink that finally did make me laugh and I began to feel a little like myself again.

It didn't take much more than an hour to straighten up. Adder found some boards in the shed out back to close off the broken window. I patched up the sofa with duct tape. Silver, a sales clerk once assured me, went with everything.

We got cozy on the bandaged sofa. He put his arm around my shoulder and leaned in to kiss me. It was sweet, unhurried and undemanding. Everything slowed down, and my insides stopped feeling like sirens. This was a different kind of calm than with Dan. It didn't feel like permanent, unconditional shelter. It was a stillness waiting to ignite.

Adder lit a cigarette.

"I *love* my job," he said.

"This was a professional visit?"

"Got a call from the sheriff's station. They said you mentioned Ivarene, thought I might be interested."

"Maybe you should have Miranda'd me before we fell into bed."

"If you had remained silent, darlin', it wouldn't have been

half as good."

He kissed me softly, then propped himself up on one elbow and looked at me. "You read books," he said. "I read people. I'm good at it. Because the day I'm wrong could be the day I die. You're holding something back, baby. I need to know what."

I tried to sidestep the question. "Isn't there some LAPD bylaw about interrogating people with your pants off?"

It got a grudging smile out of him before he asked me again what I was hiding. And I knew that if I didn't confide in him, it would slowly poison everything that was good between us.

"Are you asking as a man or a cop, Adder?"

He took his time before he answered. "I understand it's hard to trust me. To trust anyone. But if we don't take that leap sometimes, Nikki, we're just prisoners inside our own skin."

We sat across from each other on the bed, half covered by blankets, and I wanted to trust him. I told him about the hatchback and Manny and the limping man who had killed him, then had come back looking for something.

"He took papers from the file cabinet, then left," I said. And stopped there. I couldn't tell him the rest.

Adder looked me straight in the eye. "He didn't find everything, did he?"

His gaze went straight to my bag and I had a sudden sensation of free-fall. I must have telegraphed it a dozen ways, all those little tells a cop is trained to look for.

I got up, took out the notebook, and handed it to him. He ran his hands over the cover, the back, the spine, and the edges, taking Manny's measure in the cheap but immaculate binding. Then he said, "Come on, let's find out what we've got here."

The way he said "we," I was sure, as much as you can be sure about anything, that we were in this together. Lying on our stomachs, with the book propped up on a pillow between us, we began to read.

Manny had a careful round handwriting. His notes were abbreviated but clear. He detailed his expenses to the nearest penny and noted his time to the quarter hour. Clients and quarry were recorded with initials or nicknames. Manny liked to amuse himself. Early in the year there was Yogi and Urkel, to name two. But nothing we read meant anything to us until we hit July when someone called Birdman hired Manny to tail a Mr. Smith.

Smith spent a great deal of time at home (no address) visited by people denoted with initials that meant nothing to me, or dining out with these initials and others at the stuffy restaurants where an older generation took their power lunches. There were a lot of parties, too, in Bel-Air, Hancock Park, Trousdale Estates.

After the Trousdale party, Manny tailed Smith up to Mulholland, where he parked and sat. After about ten minutes, a Volkswagen convertible pulled up alongside Smith's car.

That was what Darla drove. Adder glanced at me and we read on. At the wheel was someone Manny called April. The little hairs on my forearms stood straight up. I said, "Her centerfold month." Smith entered the convertible and Manny followed it back down to an address in West Hollywood. Darla's address.

My heart was pinballing around inside me as we read on without saying a word. Manny detailed many more assignations between Smith and Darla, every one of which involved changing cars in out-of-the-way places and going back to her apartment.

The journal ended the last day in July, weeks before Darla's disappearance, before Ivarene, and as far as I knew, before Manny and the man in the hatchback began tailing me.

When we turned the last page and closed the book, neither Adder nor I said a word. Cars hummed silently down the street. A breeze brushed the willow leaves against the window.

"Smith," Adder said, "is probably not his real name."

"Ya think?"

Adder rolled his eyes at my sarcasm and said, "The guy was involved with Darla. Could be Johnny Rambla."

"Johnny at the country club? Playing golf in a satin shirt? I don't think so."

Adder's face relaxed into a smile, but his eyes didn't. "The question is, who hired Manny to follow them? A jealous lover? Jimmy?"

"What would that have to do with someone breaking into my place? What are they looking for?"

"Same thing they were looking for when they tossed her apartment. It's got to be connected to Ivarene. Drugs. Or drug money."

Adder seemed to pull into himself, absorbed in thought, more distant than I'd ever seen him.

"Tomorrow," he said, setting the journal aside, "this gets mailed to Homicide."

He took both my hands and looked directly at me. "Listen to me, Nikki. We're a lot alike, you and me. We don't like rules. We like taking action. But you've got to stop sticking your neck out. Manny's dead and someone may have you in their crosshairs."

That phrase raised a cold sweat on my skin. "What am I supposed to do? Sit here like a waiting target?"

Instead of answering, he got out of bed, pulled on his pants and walked out of the room. When I heard him leave the house, heard his car door open then close again, I thought: *You really blew it this time.*

A few minutes later, he appeared in the bedroom doorway, holding a leather case about the size of a book.

"A little gift," he said.

He sat down on the bed and put the case on the sheet between us.

"If you can't keep away from trouble," he said, "you'd better know how to take care of yourself."

It opened like a jewel box. Inside, nestled in a bed of faded red velvet, was a small, sleek gun.

"Baby," he said, "meet Baby Browning."

Chapter 23

The gun came with one condition—I had to learn its proper use. So the next morning, we sped south toward the desert, Adder at the wheel of my MG. He wasn't a man who was comfortable in the passenger seat.

With the top down and the wind beating against our faces, we discovered something else we had in common. Adder shared my passion for vintage rock, as well as my complete inability to carry a tune. We sang all the way down to the desert, everything from *Break on Through* to *Piece of My Heart* to *Ohio.* We were passing the flock of white windmills that power the low desert when I heard myself singing John Lennon's *Imagine.* I thought about the Baby Browning in my bag and wondered who I was on my way to becoming.

The thought must have been loud enough for Adder to hear, because he said, "You don't believe in violence? Well, violence doesn't give a damn what anyone believes."

He turned off the highway and took back roads through the dunes and brush. About a quarter-mile up a dirt road we stopped at a sign whose ghosted letters read SHOOTING RANGE. Set back from the road was a windowless shack, its sign riddled with bullet holes. Behind it was an open stretch of desert, with dozens of wooden frames, collapsed or half buried in the sand. Spent casings littered the ground like peanut shells.

On a card table with rusted legs, we laid down the Baby and a box of bullets.

"Ready?" Adder smiled. His face was open, easy, as if some part of him that the city compressed could finally expand out here, as if his spirit were too large for the constraints of a job or anything else that wanted to shape him to its own form. With the warm breeze tossing his lank hair, he had never looked better.

"Ready," I said. I wanted to be good at this, told myself it was simply a skill to master.

The Baby was not much bigger than Adder's palm, but no one would have mistaken it for a toy. He named the parts for me, holding it up like a slicer-dicer pitchman. He took a couple of rounds from the box and deftly slipped them into the magazine. "You try," he said.

It was tougher than it looked. The springload mechanism was tight. I pushed a shell in at the wrong angle and it stuck. He popped it out and I tried again. It was hard for me to relax with a gun in my hand, so it took awhile before I had six tiny missiles neatly tucked in place. I smiled up at Adder. He deadpanned like the Marine sergeant he'd been and showed me how to push the magazine into the grip.

That was a piece of cake, but pulling back the slide was another matter. I'm pretty strong, but the spring was really tight. After a few attempts, out of sheer frustration, I switched hands and pulled it back with my right.

"Are you kidding? You can't change hands."

"Adder, I'll be dead before I even get this thing cocked."

"I'm glad you understand that," he said. "And don't get all bent out of shape when I tell you that a woman is better off with a revolver. But this is what we have, so you gotta get that slide back, fast and smooth with your left hand."

I tried again. The slide stuck. A bullet wobbled out of a hole on the side.

"Semiautomatics jam. Try it again. Don't limp-wrist it."

It was tedious repeating the simplest maneuver. But Adder kept at me. Patient, like a good dad, until I finally managed to pull the slide back smoothly seven or eight times.

"Again," Adder said.

I did another dozen.

"You nailed it, baby." He planted a kiss square on my lips. I loved the smell of him outdoors, sweet like wheat.

I'd been concentrating so hard, I barely felt the sun on my arms or noticed the desert flowers sprouting up behind the target posts. It was a world of luscious, warm color, except for the cool blue steel in my hand. And a knot in my stomach that would not let go.

Adder walked over to the car, brought back the paper targets he'd swiped from the police range, and tacked one up to a frame. A torso in silhouette. Armless. Legless. Couldn't run, couldn't shoot. The ideal perp.

Then he pulled a pair of earplugs from his pocket. "Here, use these."

"Okay," I said, "But let me get this straight. Some guy's about to shoot me, I pull back the slide, then stick these in my ears?"

Not even a flicker of a smile. All marine.

"Look down the sight and aim," he said.

I raised the gun.

"Not like that," Adder said. "Both hands."

He stood at my back, circled his arms around me, placed his hands over mine, and moved them, thumb over thumb, into the right position. Then he stepped away.

I looked down the sight, centered it on the target, held on tight, and fired.

The gun jumped to the right. I gripped it harder, fired, and missed again.

The sun was high now and the desert heat pressed down on us. My skin felt sticky, my arms were getting tired. But I didn't complain, not to a man who'd trekked through the deserts of Al-Anbar with a fifty-pound pack on his back.

The third bullet hit the target in the shoulder. I looked at Adder and grinned. He frowned. "Here's the other problem with the Baby," he said. "It's a .25-caliber firearm. Hit a man where you hit that target, all you'll do is piss him off."

"Adder," I said, "maybe I need a better gun."

"A better gun?" *That* made him laugh. "The Baby Browning is the best small pistol ever made, but you need to know how to use it. Always aim for the heart. When you shoot, shoot to kill."

Shoot to kill. The knot in my belly clenched even tighter.

"This isn't going to work," I said.

"You're giving up?"

"It's one thing to defend myself. But I'm not okay with killing."

"What you're not okay with," he said, "is the way it feels to have all that power in the palm of your hand."

He was right. I wanted to hate it, but I didn't.

So I kept at it. The sun got hotter and my arms got heavier. But I went through a dozen magazines, and five of the last six bullets tore holes in the black paper chest.

"Not bad. I knew you'd get it." Adder grinned.

I couldn't grin back.

The power of death in a forefinger. One split-second decision. One quick and irrevocable motion. All that power was inside my body, locked down tight.

"Why don't you take a break," he said. "I'll go a couple of rounds."

I set the Baby down on the table, and he took out his own gun. I'd seen it before, of course, in its holster, draped over the chair in my bedroom, peeking out from under his shirt like some weird underwear. A nine-millimeter Beretta.

I was struck by the unexpected contrast between the unfettered side of Adder I had glimpsed earlier and the Adder I could see in that gun and its leather holster, deadly but worn, like a city cop. I understood the choice he would sooner or later have to face—to break free and shape his own life or to slowly diminish into an old cop, smaller each year in his ill-fitting suits. I watched him take a few shots, easy but careful. Then he showed off, fired with just one hand, then the other, twirled around like a back-lot cowboy, and fired again. When he finished, the bullets made a ragged circle in the center of the target.

He reloaded the magazine and slipped it back in.

"You try," he said.

His gun was a lot heavier than the Baby and when I fired, it recoiled hard to the right and the bullet hit a Joshua tree. I gripped the gun tighter, fired again, and hit the target frame. But the next four bullets hit paper, the last one dead center in the chest.

"How does that feel?" he said.

"Fine."

He raised one eyebrow. "You're a good shot, but a lousy liar."

I loaded up the Baby again, but this time he wanted me moving. Walking. Turning. Crouching. Running. It was a workout. I wasted a lot of ammunition shooting dunes and shrubbery. But after a while I managed to put a couple of holes in the paper man.

It was a wild kind of high, all that firepower coursing through me. Only it came to a dead stop somewhere in my gut. I tried to relax, took a deep breath, and it stabbed me with a cramp so fierce I bent over double.

"What is it?" Adder asked.

He put his arms around me, and that was all it took. Everything jammed up inside me broke loose. I could feel the voltage shooting off me, and Adder felt it too. He said, "Sweet

Jesus." But whatever was happening in me, he matched it. I could feel him in a way I hadn't before. Or maybe he was showing me what I hadn't been willing to see—his war, his cop's life, the harsh desperation and nasty beauty of it.

He grabbed my lip in his teeth till we both tasted blood, and I bit hard into the strong muscles of his neck, and we rode through his dark movies, or maybe mine. A desert night, the horizon in flames, our rhythm driven by echoes of helicopter blades and distant explosions until this inner landscape was punctured by fierce, raw cries that were coming from us. Our eyes were open. His were brilliant and full of fear. Then it finished, not in half a dozen pistol shots, but in a machine gun chain that went on and on until our bodies gave out.

We rolled apart, flat on our backs on the sand, with spent shells all around us, glinting and shooting fire in the last rays of the orange sun.

We didn't go back to L.A. that night. Instead, we drove to Palm Springs and checked into an aging stucco motel. The Astroturf strip between our door and the pool was wide enough for a handful of lounge chairs, some with broken straps that trailed the ground like slatternly sunbathers. The room's carpet had a few cigarette burns. The bedspread and curtains were frayed, but definitely not from too many washings. And a small family of crickets had moved in before us. They stayed up late and got a little raucous, but had good enough manners to keep to themselves in a corner.

The night was warm, and we lay out by the pool under an almost full moon. The mountains were a soft, dark purple, and the air was a mix of desert flowers and chlorine. We were silent with all that beauty, but I didn't feel peaceful.

I kept wondering what it would be like if I ever had to pull the trigger and take a life, to cross yet one more line that divided the world into those who knew and those who didn't.

Adder laid his hand over mine.

"Stop thinking," he said. "Just be here with me."

CHAPTER 24

We spent the next night together, too, at my place. Around three, a thunderstorm woke us and we lay awake listening and watching the lightning flash across the sky. When I got up the next morning, he had already left for work. A steady but gentle rain still fell.

So dramatic was the loss of sunny skies in southern California that it was the lead story on the local news. I finished straightening up, called a handyman to fix the boarded-up window, and found a Tijuana blanket to throw over the sofa to hide its bandaged wounds.

In the late afternoon I walked over to Cedars to see Billy. He was on painkillers and barely coherent and fell asleep before I left. I asked the nurse how he was doing and she said they'd know in a few days. I asked her what happened, said the police told me the gunshot wound hadn't been that serious. But she was "not at liberty to say." Her smile sliced like a paper cut.

On the way home I stopped at the Cantina and happily let Carlito foist on me a couple of tons of steaming, lard-saturated food and garishly dyed chips. I'd earned it. As I sat on the terrace in the rain-sweet evening air, feeling like I'd reclaimed a small piece of normal life, my cell rang.

"How ya doin'?" The voice was lazy but tight, tension fighting with cool, or maybe junk wrestling with cocaine. Kyle.

"Listen," he said, "I wanna talk to you. Meet me at Benny Binks."

The restaurant's lights glared against night-black windows while musicians ate breakfast and hookers rested their wares on the counter stools. The one next to me was wearing a drugstore perfume that said everything about sex I had known at thirteen. And said it loud.

I had three cups of coffee and watched the minute hand deduct thirty ticks from my lifespan before I was sure Kyle wouldn't show. I tried his number, but voice mail picked up. I didn't leave a message.

Maybe he'd needed a handout and found money elsewhere, or maybe meant to meet me but got high instead. Either way, I was pissed enough to go looking for him.

Kyle lived in a four-story walk-up near Hollywood Boulevard. Darla and I had dropped him off a few times, but I'd never been inside. There was a row of rusted-out name plates, all of them empty, and holes where the bells once were. But you didn't have to ring to get in. There was a broken pane of glass right next to the door handle.

I stepped into the hallway. A single bulb cast a dim yellow light. On a staircase to the right sat a man with his head against the wall and his eyes closed.

"Excuse me," I said. The eyes opened, but nothing else on his face moved.

I asked him if he knew Kyle. He pointed up the stairs and turned his hand once, which I took to mean up one flight. The hand came down slowly and landed softly in his lap like a sick bird. He licked his dry lips and said, "Two-oh-one." Then he asked if I had any spare change.

I pulled out a dollar. He could not stir himself to take it, so I set it in his palm.

Upstairs, I found 201 and knocked. No answer. Through the door I heard the phone ring. Then it stopped and the apartment was silent again. Only I had the feeling someone was in there. I called Kyle's name. Waited. Nothing.

Downstairs, the man on the steps hadn't moved, but the dollar had disappeared. Out of the corner of my eye, I saw a small boy running down the hall, the bill fluttering in his hand.

On a slow news day, the murder of a junkie in Hollywood might get a few lines in the local section, but this one made the front page because he was Darla Ward's brother. Kyle was found, literally, in a gutter on Gower.

I don't know why it hit me so hard. I can't even say I liked him. Maybe it was the bleakness of his death and his life as I imagined it—with never a win or a tiny triumph or even a momentary window of joy, except for the rush of a drug hitting his bloodstream.

I thought about Kyle's mother, Dottie, and wondered if her madness was enough protection from the loss of both her children. I phoned her, but no one answered and no voicemail picked up. So I drove over to her house. She was sitting on the porch, talking to a man with a notepad in his hand. I recognized him. Adder's partner, Lefrak. She smiled and flirted with him. Even at a distance, you could see the disconnect from reality. Maybe it was better that way.

I drove off without disturbing her.

The first leg of the hiking trail in Laurel Canyon was way harder to run than usual. My thighs burned and my breath came short. I hadn't been doing my daily run and had to push myself at first. But by the time the path became dirt and the grade gentler, I'd hit my stride.

I breathed in the familiar mix of musky florals and smog. I'd been in L.A. long enough for my body to read it as fresh air. My ears grew alert to the rustling foliage and small animals scurrying in the brush and the cries of birds, and from time to time, panoramic glimpses of the Valley would suddenly appear around a curve.

I absorbed the stillness and the strength of the hills, the trees, the earth. My mind seemed to empty of everything else. I began to feel the strong core inside me I had always relied on. As long as I could find my way back to it, the machine of the city below and the compulsions that drove the people in it could not touch me.

I had that. And I had the Baby.

Chapter 25

That night, the moon cast a soft haze through the fog and the willow leaves outside my window shimmered like slivers of silver.

I was awake but not restless, calmed I suppose by the sheer beauty of the night.

It was after two when I thought I heard a sound coming from the yard. I listened carefully. Nothing. Unable to shake the feeling that someone was out there, I got out of bed.

Shrouded moonlight shone into the living room. The street outside was still. Then, through the back window, something glinted and disappeared. It was so fast, it could have been a shifting leaf. I went back to the bedroom and got the Baby. Its cold weight in my hand grounded me but didn't slow my racing heart. I pulled back the slide.

Barely breathing, walking softly on bare feet, I turned the handle of the back door. It made a little click. I stopped and listened. A soft breeze breathed through the trees, a lone cricket chirped. I stepped outside.

Then someone whispered my name.

I spun around, gripping the Baby with both hands.

"It's me, Nikki."

She was sitting on the ground next to the geraniums, her back against the wooden fence, her face ghostly pale in the moonlight.

Darla.

Trembling, I lowered the Baby. Tears stung my eyes, the

release of weeks of tension and fear.

"My god, you're—"

With a panicked look, she shook her head to silence me. Then, slowly, as if she were listening with every pore for some sign of danger, she rose to her feet and we went inside.

As soon as I reached out to turn on a lamp, she grabbed my wrist.

"No lights," she whispered and slipped into the armchair by the window. She made sure her face was obscured in darkness, but the streetlamp cast a sheath of light across her hands resting calmly in her lap. There was dirt in the creases of her fingers and under the nails that used to be so carefully manicured.

Her platinum hair had been dyed a dull brown, and she wore loose jeans, a man's work shirt, no makeup. If it were me, it would have seemed natural, but it was disturbing to see her this way. Maybe because I sensed that more than her surface had changed.

I wanted to say so much, ask so many questions, but her attention was entirely focused on the window, which gave a clear view of the street.

"Darla, is someone out there?"

"I don't know."

As my eyes adjusted to the darkness, I saw she was blinking back tears. "Nikki," she said. "Oh, god, Nikki. Just being here, seeing you. It's like I've walked out of a nightmare."

Exhausted and without makeup, her face had the innocence of a child. If you didn't look at her eyes.

"What happened to you?" I said. "Where have you been?"

She put her hands over her face for a moment and shook her head. "Not now, please. I need to eat. I haven't had anything since yesterday." She managed a smile. "Tell me you've at least got leftover takeout."

"I can do better than that," I said. "There's a man in my life who keeps the fridge full."

"I have been gone a long time." She gave a soft laugh and for a moment seemed like the Darla I'd always known.

I fixed steak, threw some greens in a bowl and fried potatoes for her in a kitchen lit only by the moon and a flame on the stove. When I set the meal down on the table, she was so hungry, her hand shook as she began to eat. And when she finished, she resumed her watch at the window.

"Darla, talk to me," I said. "Tell me where you've been . . . who are you afraid of."

The question seemed to overwhelm her. It took her a long moment to answer.

"They killed Kyle," she said.

You could feel a lifetime of caring when she spoke her brother's name.

We had never been the kind of girlfriends who hugged or showed physical affection. It didn't come naturally to people like us, who had grown up without it. But I put my arms around her and held her close. Rigid at first, she gave into the warmth, and I felt her tears on my skin. Then she pulled away.

"No," she said. "I can't be weak now." And slowly, her strange calmness returned.

"Who killed him, Darla? Who are you afraid of?"

"There's a man . . . he drives an old hatchback."

It hit me like a raw current. "A heavy-set guy, around fifty, sandy hair?"

"You know him?"

"He's been following me," I said. "Who is he? What's going on?"

"There's no time to explain. You have to get me out of here."

"We need to call the police."

I reached for the phone. She grasped my hand.

"No! Don't call anyone."

"Darla, the man I told you about is a cop. He'll protect you."

"He can't. You don't understand. We have to go. Now!"

Her eyes were terrified, pleading.

"To where?"

"Anywhere. Out of the city. Far enough to be safe."

Chapter 26

I drove with my lights off and the roads were almost deserted. Once or twice, I saw headlights behind me, but never for more than a block or two. And there was no one behind me when I turned onto I-10.

We headed west, then north on Pacific Coast Highway, and by the time we hit Malibu, Darla had fallen asleep. There were creases between her brows, her cheeks sunken beneath the broad bones.

We crossed the county line and drove through empty streets that would have looked desolate even at midday. I'd hitchhiked all over the country and knew it was mostly made up of places like this, towns that hold people by force of inertia. I also knew too well how those who pull free, win or lose, are forever unmoored.

I turned on the radio and caught the middle of a saxophone riff, a long, cool, controlled wail. It ended prematurely, in static, as we drove out of range. I flicked off the radio. The sudden silence woke Darla. She was instantly alert.

"Where are we?"

"A couple of hours from San Luis Obispo. Then we've got another hour up the coast."

"No one's following us?"

"Not as far as I can tell."

The sky was still black, but a line of gold rimmed the tops of the mountains. She settled again into that catlike vigilance I had seen at the house. From time to time her eyes darted to the rearview mirror.

"We've got time to talk now," I said. "And I need to know what's going on."

She looked at me with eyes so soft, so helpless, that, were I a man, it might have broken my will. "Please," she said, "Don't make me relive it all. Not now. Not yet."

"Darla, my neighbor was shot, your brother was killed. You won't go to the police. I can't do this blind."

She turned away from me and stared at the flat fields outside her window. "I have to stay dead," she said. "It's the only thing keeping me alive."

"What about the man in the hatchback?"

"In a little while he won't matter. I'm going to become someone else."

"Are you out of your mind?"

"I'm out of everything."

The way she said it, I knew it was true.

"Whatever you've been through," I said, "you can get past it. You're strong, Darla."

"There is no more Darla. But I am strong. Strong enough to make myself into another person. I did it before."

"What are you talking about?"

"I created Darla from nothing. I was a skinny little kid in castoffs who wanted to be beautiful. Like a movie star. And I made everyone believe it. Even you. Look at me now, a poor little white girl. Not a single feature that isn't ordinary."

I did look at her. It was as if she had turned a light switch off. It was a pretty enough face, but the force that had made it so compelling was gone.

When she saw she had proven her point, she smiled and brought back the face I had always known.

"Beauty," she said, "is something you have to will. That little girl lying in her bed at night. She *willed* it, Nikki. To get what she was hungry for."

I thought about that little girl, alone in the house on Poinsettia with no father and a crazy mother. And I thought about my own childhood dreams. When I was very small, I would go to sleep thinking someday I would have blonde hair and wear satin gowns like the stars in old movies. But Darla had really done it.

"You found a way out," I said.

"No. Out is what *you* wanted. For me, it was exactly the opposite. To find a way *in*. To belong to someone who loved me so much that nothing could separate us. All my life, it's all I ever wanted."

She reached out and touched my arm. "Nikki," she said, "a few months ago, I found him. And what I imagined didn't even touch the reality. We were two halves of the same being. Do you know what he said once? He said that when we were apart, it was like something had been ripped out of him."

"Darla," I said, "are you talking about Johnny Rambla?"

A shock of a laugh burst from her. "Johnny? Johnny's the trash man. The one who picks you up when you're finished."

Ironic. Bitter. Aspects of Darla I had never seen before.

"It ended," she said. "A child's love. It couldn't survive the real world. He had to break it off, and it nearly killed us both."

I remembered the poisonous voice of the woman on Darla's voicemail. "He was married," I said.

"Yes. But it was more complicated than that."

It always is, I thought.

"The strange thing was," she said, "the pain burned out fast. Then there was nothing left inside me at all."

"Darla, I've been there. When everything in you feels dead. But I promise you, something new will take its place."

"No. You don't understand. It's beautiful in a way. At the very bottom of all that pain, everything becomes so calm, so clear. You walk through your days the same way you did before, only you don't give a damn about anything anymore."

"Who is he? The man you fell in love with."

"What difference does it make? He's got nothing to do with any of this. I only told you about him so you can understand the rest."

"Then tell me the rest."

"The rest is Johnny Rambla. And his magic white powder. Have you ever done speedballs, Nikki? Coke and heroin together."

I nodded, but even as a runaway, there were some things I never did twice.

"They tell you everything about dope except how beautiful it is. The first time Johnny got me high, I was lying on a filthy rug, but it felt like velvet against my skin, and the air was making love to me."

A room I'd seen through a pair of blinds came instantly to mind. "The rug on the floor at Ivarene?"

She snapped out of the reverie her story had woven and looked at me. "How did you—?"

"Go on."

"The first time Johnny took me up to Ivarene, two other girls were there. One blonde, one dark. Like us, Nikki. They were our age, but their faces looked old. The dark-haired one was missing a tooth and kept covering her mouth with her hand. I wanted to leave. But then Johnny made his magic and the whole world softened and it didn't matter . . . it didn't matter at all.

"Darla," I said, "were you there the night of the murders?"

She nodded. "I didn't want to go that night."

"You mean you knew? You *knew* what was going to happen?"

"No! All I knew was that Johnny had business up there. I didn't want to go because by then I was sick of him. But Johnny had a mean streak and I was always afraid if I said no to him, he'd make trouble for Kyle.

"I was trapped. I'd fooled myself into thinking that, because I was stronger than Kyle, I could handle everything. But that night I *saw* who they all were, saw the room thick with fear and suspicion, saw how the drug was eating away at their bodies, at their souls. I knew if I wasn't already as lost as they were, I would be soon enough."

Darla didn't look at me as she spoke. She had retreated into herself, into a memory more vivid than the present.

"Johnny had a gym bag full of dope they were going to sell for him. He brought some out and I turned down a taste. He didn't like that. He flashed me a look and when I walked outside to the backyard I could see he was furious.

"It was very warm that night, and I sat on the ground with my back against a tree, watching thin gray clouds glide across the moon and disappear. I started to feel that maybe I'd be okay again. That once I broke with it, this part of my life would drift into the past.

"Then I heard these pops, like firecrackers. I didn't even get it at first. I remember wondering, *what holiday falls at the end of August?* The girls started screaming, and there were more pops, a whole chain of them. Then nothing. I was too terrified to move.

"I heard a door open and close. Very quietly. I looked back toward the house. It was Johnny. He called out, 'Come on, sweetheart, let's get out of here.' But his voice sounded wrong, and he started looking all over the yard for me. After a while he said, 'Don't wait for me to find you, bitch.' He had a gun in his hand and I knew he meant to kill me.

"I had to get to the street, to a neighbor. As quietly as I could, I crawled along the ground in the shadow of the bushes, stopping every few feet to make sure he hadn't heard me. But when I made it to the side of the house, I realized that the front yard was completely open.

"I found an open window and climbed back into the house. It stank from blood. So much of it. All over the walls, all over the floor, and the three of them dead."

Her nostrils widened and her lips curled down as if the smells were still there. She took a ragged, involuntary breath and continued.

"I made my way to the kitchen. I found a knife. Once I had that knife in my hand, I started to think more clearly. I knew Johnny would be back. And if I couldn't take him by surprise, I'd be dead. An archway led to the dining room. I hid there, Nikki, and waited. He came in the back door. He moved slowly, cautiously, and that was good. It gave me time. But as soon as he walked through the arch, he sensed me behind him. Before he could turn around, I brought the knife down with both hands, with all the force I had. He bent forward, his head fell back, his mouth opened. I kept stabbing. I didn't stop. Until nothing fought back. Until there was no person left. Until all I could hear was the blood pounding in my ears."

She was breathing hard when she finished, then slowly relaxed as if her muscles were releasing the memory.

"When my heart quieted down," she said, "I was very calm. It was the strangest feeling. As if he had never been real."

Her face was smooth with the same sense of calm she had just described. But my fingers gripped the steering wheel and my stomach was a fist.

"You see, Nikki. You're the only one who can help me. The police would arrest me for murder."

"It was self-defense. The man I'm seeing is a detective. I'll call him and this whole ordeal will be over."

She took a long breath and her calm crumpled into helplessness.

"It won't be over," she said. "It will only be the beginning."

★ ★ ★ ★ ★

As we drove through a landscape parched from the long, dry summer, the sky turned light. At San Luis Obispo, I stopped for gas. Rush hour, every pump busy. Darla slumped down in her seat and as far as I could see, nobody paid much attention to us.

A few miles later we started up the serpentine mountain road that winds along the very edge of the continent. We stopped at a small grocery and I bought enough food to last awhile. Darla threw some sandwiches together. I was hungry, but too wired to taste what I ate.

A low fog hung over the coast and you could hear the surf crashing against the rocks below. Tall pines obscured the view, but as the fog lifted, sparkling patches of ocean flashed through the dark branches, while in my mind, I caught fleeting glimpses of something hidden between the threads of Darla's story.

Chapter 27

A scattering of motels and restaurants, rustic and unpainted, blended into the woods along the highway in Big Sur. I almost missed the Shadygrove Rest but managed to screech to a stop in front, my tires skittering gravel. Darla glanced around and I saw fear overcome her again.

"This is it?"

I nodded.

"It's safe?"

"I think so."

Adder had taken me here for our long weekend, and in that macho way of his, he handled everything. I had never even gone into the office. The cabins were down by the river, set far apart and separated by stands of redwood. Very private. Adder and I had seen no neighbors during our stay, which is why I chose it.

Darla pulled a roll of bills from her pocket. "Pay for a week," she said. "It may be more time than I need, but just in case."

The office was a wooden shack, its curtains, once calico, faded to a dingy gray. The girl behind the counter must have been about my age, but gravity had already slackened the muscles in her face.

"You and your old man?" she asked.

"Not my old man," I said, like there was a guy in the car who didn't mean that much to me, hoping she would not pull back the curtains to have a look. But she had no energy for curiosity and barely glanced at the fake name I wrote in her book.

We drove across the highway, down a bumpy dirt road to a cabin near the river. The sun through the branches felt warm on my face and I let it wash over me. I inhaled the fragrant redwood and heard the river.

Darla waited in the car until I had opened the cabin door, then quickly followed me in.

The room, which still held the night chill, had crude plank floors and two beds with mattresses no thicker than a fist. But what made up for it was a fireplace built from river rocks, a stack of logs beside it. Through a doorway was a small kitchen and a fridge that we filled with the groceries.

I crumpled some newspapers in the hearth and built a teepee of twigs over them. Everything was damp, but after a few tries, the kindling caught and flamed and I threw on some firewood.

When I looked up, Darla was holding one of the papers, staring at her picture on a yellowed front page. In anger and despair, she crumpled it and threw it into the flames. I tried to assure her that it was all right, that no one here had seen her.

We sat on a braided rug in front of the fireplace, watching the twigs become black figures leaping in the flames, dancing until, with one last flick of a limb or jerk of the head, they disappeared completely. Our faces grew warm, and after awhile she began to talk more easily.

She told me how she had walked under cover of night all the way to Kyle's and hidden there, how she had sent him back to her apartment before the sun came up to get the only money she had, the cash Gordy had given her.

"Then you had Kyle lie to me so I would go to the police and tell them the dead girl was you."

"Haven't you ever been desperate?" she said quietly.

For a while, we just sat there, watching the flames dart and flare, contained in the stone proscenium, yet unpredictable. After awhile I looked over at her. She was softly massaging the sleeve of her shirt and tears ran down her face.

"What is it?"

"His shirt . . . Kyle's."

Her face collapsed and she struggled to get the words out. "I waited all night for him to come home, and then I heard . . . on the radio."

I laid my hand on hers. She gripped it tightly.

"He was my baby brother. All I could think about was the way he used to sit on the porch on Sundays, his shoulders hunched, his skinny arms tight to his chest, waiting for his daddy to visit. Sometimes he'd wait till way past dark, till he'd be shivering from the chill, and mostly the man never showed up. My mother would be screaming how stupid Kyle was, and she'd start beating him, punching him, and I'd try to drag her off. It wasn't much better when that old drunk did come. Even sober he was mean. It got to be I was glad I didn't know my own father, so I could make him up however I wanted."

"Was your mother always—"

"Crazy?" Darla had an odd smile on her face, half ashamed, half amused. "You know what I used to think when I was a child? That she was broken. Like a toy. I thought my father broke her and that's why he ran away."

I saw that icy calm come over her again.

"Nothing is going to break me," she said.

She poked at the fire and said nothing more. A log collapsed, shooting sparks and hissing.

The stories she'd told were too vivid not to be true. But as I stared into the fire, my mind grew calm and I saw clearly what she had been holding back.

I said, "The dope you took from Ivarene—is that what you'll buy your new life with?"

She seemed only mildly surprised. "You knew?"

"Both our places were torn up. Someone was looking for

something."

She smiled. "Johnny's gym bag. He'd brought twelve plastic packets up to Ivarene. A kilo each. Pure heroin." Her green eyes burned with excitement. "Do you have any idea what that's worth, Nikki? About a million dollars, way more if I cut it myself and sell it off slowly, a little at a time. But that's too dangerous. I want to get rid of it fast. Then I'll be free."

"Free? You'll be running your whole life."

CHAPTER 28

With the curtains barely veiling the afternoon light, we lay down on the hard beds. I was awake for a long time, and even in my sleep I kept hearing Darla's voice and seeing the terrible scenes she had described.

The smell of cooking woke me. When I sat up, Darla was standing in the doorway, a spatula in her hand. Her hair, still wet, had been pulled into a ponytail. She looked like Ivarene had never happened.

We had dinner on a crude wooden table in the kitchen. From the canned stew and wilted vegetables I had bought, she'd made something that looked almost elegant on the chipped cabin dishes. Darla was relaxed now and didn't need coaxing. She couldn't stop talking.

"I tried to warn Kyle," she said. "I told him we had to get out of L.A. first, then repackage the dope. But all he could think of was all that money. It got too big inside of him. He'd never had anything, he'd never felt bigger than another human being in his life. It was such a stupid thing to do, Nikki. Because the packets were all marked."

"What do you mean marked?"

"Each one had a symbol on it, almost like the logo on a bag of sugar."

"Show me what it looked like."

She took a twig from the bundle of kindling and drew a rectangle about the size of the bag in the powdery ash on the hearth. Inside it, in the center, she drew a circle, the rim slightly thicker on the bottom, with a curved V inside. "Like that. And bright red."

"Where is it? Where's Johnny's gym bag now?"

"It's better if you don't know. Tomorrow, I'll give you money to buy a car. Then I can get around on my own. When things cool off, I'll go back for the packets."

"And build a new life by ruining other lives?"

"If I threw it all away, gave up a million dollars, would it save even one junkie?"

Beyond the soft control of Darla's voice, you could hear the cries of children at the campgrounds across the river.

"No," I said. "But it would save you."

"You don't understand, Nikki. It's too late. I can't *be* Darla Ward anymore. *I can't live in her skin.*"

"But that's exactly what you'll never be able to escape," I said.

"Just watch me."

She turned to the mirror and began arranging her hair in different ways, as I'd seen her do so many times, examining one profile, then the other, looking unhappy with the results.

"The color change isn't enough," she said. "I have to cut it, don't I?"

She rummaged through the kitchen looking for scissors and didn't find any, but on a shelf of the empty medicine cabinet was a water-stained packet of razor blades, and she began hacking away at her hair.

When she finished, her hair was short, the ends frayed. She looked strange, but it wasn't just the hair. You could really see her eyes now. You could see Ivarene in them.

"There's more you're running from, isn't there?" I said.

She pretended not to know what I was talking about.

"What happened to your ring, Darla. The ring you never took off."

Her color drained because she saw that I knew. I didn't want to hear it, but I needed to. And once she started to talk about it, I couldn't stop her.

"The garnet ring," she said. "You know, I'd worn it since I was a child. I found it in my mother's jewelry box and she gave it to me. 'Call it a gift from your father,' she told me. 'Except for you, it's the only thing he ever gave me.' " Darla's smile was as strange as her eyes. "That was the hardest part. Taking the ring off, slipping it on that dead girl's finger."

She told me what the dead girl's hand felt like. Cool. Rubbery. And about the weight of the head on her knee when she unclasped the girl's locket, a tiny gold heart someone must have given her when she was a child. Darla told me how safe she felt as she did this, and how powerful, because life's rules were for the weak.

The fire died down and the room grew chilly again. I wanted to be anywhere but here, yet I didn't move.

"Her eyes were open, staring like a doll's eyes," Darla said, "and they were green, like my eyes. In an ordinary pretty face, like mine. But, of course, it wasn't my face."

I told her I'd heard enough, but her words ran over mine. "I got Johnny's gun. I had to do it. I had to be strong. I slammed it down on her face. A rush of air came out of her mouth."

"Stop," I said.

Darla looked at me as if I'd woken her from a dream. "She was already dead," she cried when she saw the condemnation in my eyes.

I felt like I couldn't breathe. I was suffocating with Darla and Darla's story. I stepped outside to breathe the fresh sea air and hear the rustling trees.

When I went back in, she was sitting on the bed, holding a

match under a spoonful of liquid just beginning to bubble.

She looked up at me and said, "Poor Nikki. You still think there's some sort of right and wrong."

I'd been through all this before with another friend. A girl who was always a little out of step. A little too soft. I'd always looked after her. But then she started shooting up and I couldn't protect her from herself. I remembered driving with her in the middle of the night when she was desperate to find drugs. That was the last time I saw her, gripping the steering wheel of a car, hollow eyed, her soul shrunken to a single need. She would have sold me for a gram if she could have found one.

Darla put the needle in her arm and closed her eyes with the pleasure of the rush.

I picked up my car keys from the night table and her eyes opened at the sound.

"Nikki?" Her voice was soft and easy.

"What?"

"Before you go, I need one last favor."

"What's that?"

Her eyes were focused and she wasn't drifting now. "I'm all alone out here. I need your gun."

Something in me actually welcomed her request. I was sick of guns. Sick to death of all this death. I took the Baby Browning from my purse and put it on the night table.

Outside, the night air was fresh and the rich scent made you remember there was good in life. I started up the MG and took off out of there.

When exhaustion hit, I pulled into the parking lot of an all-night diner.

Bright fluorescent light bounced off Formica surfaces. There were maybe half a dozen people in the place. In the ruthless light, every face looked as if it had been mangled in the machine of life. A woman was reflected in the mirror behind the counter.

Her hair was wild and uncombed, and her eyes had the stunned look of someone who had witnessed an accident. It took a minute to realize I was looking at myself.

The waitress slid a cup of coffee in front of me. It was hot and I poured a lot of honey in, and it tasted good. But that woman in the mirror told me I was taking the easy way out. I had been wrong. Darla had been caught in the most extreme of circumstances. She'd been desperate to save her own life. What would I be capable of doing to save mine? I could not possibly know the answer. All I did know was that I had abandoned her.

By the time I returned to the Shadygrove, the stars were fading into a predawn sky and a few birds had begun chirping in the trees.

As I walked into the room, I heard a raggedy breath. A moan.

I flicked on the light.

Darla lay across the bed. Her eyes were closed and there was a neat black hole in the middle of her chest, a stream of blood running down her white skin.

I knelt and told her I'd get help, then ran up the hill and across the highway to the office. It was locked. I banged on the door and on the window and kept shouting until a long-haired man in a flannel bathrobe appeared.

"Call an ambulance!" I shouted. "My friend's been shot!"

He didn't look alarmed or concerned. He looked like this happened every damn night just to piss him off. But he opened the door to the office and picked up the phone.

I ran back to the room and did what I could to comfort Darla. I stroked her hair and told her to hang on, and when she opened her eyes I said, "Who did this to you?"

A gurgle came from her throat. It wasn't a word or anything like one. She was gone.

Chapter 29

I pulled up a chair and sat by the bed and waited for the people who take over after bad things happen in this world. I don't know how long I sat there with the noise of trucks from the highway as remote as spaceships in a distant galaxy.

It's funny, the tiny familiar details of someone you know well—details whose absence must have registered the day they showed me the girl on the gurney, though I wasn't conscious of what they were. The way Darla's hair grew around a cowlick and formed a wide part near her hairline, and the thumbnail with a slight dent across the middle that could never grow beyond the tip of her finger.

I thought, *She'd still be alive if I hadn't walked out on her,* and wondered how you live with something like that. I told myself that if I hadn't left, maybe I'd be dead, too. And I wondered how many times a day, for how many years, I'd have to quiet my guilt with the same thought.

It took me a while to notice that the dresser drawers and kitchen cupboards had been flung open, the furniture moved back from the wall. I knew now what they were looking for.

Then, beneath the edge of the bedding pooled on the floor, I saw a metallic glint. I toed back the blanket. It was the Baby. The gun I had no license for. The gun registered to Adder. If it was the gun that killed her, I would have to leave it here. But if it wasn't . . .

What did I know about guns except for one afternoon in

Palm Springs and a lifetime of watching TV cops? I knelt and touched the barrel. Cold. But maybe the chill night air had cooled it. I bent closer. It didn't smell like it had been fired. I picked up the Baby, went to my car, and tucked the gun into the spare tire well.

When the Sheriff and his crew arrived, I had to wait outside and leave Darla alone with the detached, slightly clumsy strangers to whom death was just a job. Through the window, I watched them search and sample and gather envelopes of detritus. They took pictures, then put her in a body bag and carried her out on a stretcher to the coroner's van.

When they were done, I followed the sheriff in my own car to a town that looked like it was built out of dust.

At the station house, someone brought me a paper cup with coffee and little globules of fake cream bobbing on top. I didn't care. I felt empty. Of everything. Of the shock and the grief and the brief sense of wisdom that death can bestow.

I told them everything I knew. I told them several times. When I was free to go, I asked what would be done with Darla's body. Because of the Ivarene connection, there was a tug-of-war over jurisdiction, and the case would probably be turned over to L.A.

I called Adder. He sounded upset. He offered to fly up and drive back with me, but I saw no point in it. I just wanted to get home.

Chapter 30

"Why'd you run with her?" Adder said. "Why didn't you call me when she showed up?"

He looked like hell. He'd had some kind of stomach bug and a fever and had spent the day alternately sleeping and wondering why he couldn't get hold of me. When he finally got back to work, to a roomful of detectives treating him like Swine Flu Mary, the sheriff from up north called. Now, in my living room, he was doing two things I'd never seen him do before: sipping weak tea and chewing me out.

"Because she begged me not to, Adder."

"You always do what people want?"

"She was in trouble. You don't say no when a friend asks for help."

"You realize if you had, she might still be alive."

It couldn't have hurt more if he'd hit me, though as soon as he realized what he'd said, he rushed to apologize.

"I'm sorry, baby." He softened his voice, though you could still feel the charge beneath it. "It was a battlefield call. You did what you thought was right."

I could see us in the mirror across the room, our faces drained and hollow.

Adder had read the sheriff's report but wanted to hear the story directly from me in my own words. So I told it all again, how Darla showed up at my house, how Johnny Rambla opened fire and killed three people at Ivarene, how Darla killed him in self-defense, then battered one of the victims, switched clothes, and ran with a gym bag full of heroin. A dozen kilos. Eleven left because Kyle had taken one the night he was killed. And I told Adder about the symbol she saw on the bags.

"A circle around a V?"

"Yeah."

"Did she mention anyone with that initial?"

"No. I don't think she had any idea what that V stood for."

"What about people she knew, people you might have met at those parties she took you to?"

I shook my head. V meant nothing to me.

"Think, Nikki, 'cause that's almost all we've got."

Adder patted his shirt pocket, pulled out a cigarette and lit it. After one drag, he made a face and extinguished it, then gave me an ironic little smile. It seemed the flu had killed his taste for everything.

"That's all I know," I said. "What about all the evidence the sheriff collected?"

"It's a goddamn hotel room. Your prints and hers, and a whole lot more from every sticky-fingered tourist who passed through that place."

"You mean there's nothing?"

"Well," he said, "they did find one interesting thing. Back in the trees between the cabin and the river, kind of half buried under a bunch of dried pine needles, they found a nice little collection of cigarette butts. The killer must have waited out there and watched, nervous enough to go through half a pack of Marlboros."

"Well, that narrows it down to you and a few hundred thousand others," I said.

"Yeah. But once we have a suspect, DNA will make or break the case."

Outside clouds swept across the setting sun and a bird took

off from the telephone wire, its silhouette cutting a black line in the sky. Then it hit me.

"That V, Adder. The sides were kind of curved. Maybe it's not a letter," I said. "Maybe it's wings."

He got it in an instant, said what I was thinking. The guy who hired Manny Roberson.

"Birdman."

That night Adder showed up at my door with an overnight bag and an extra jacket over his arm.

"Not one word," he said.

"You're moving in?"

"That was three."

"Adder, you know I'm not good with this kind of thing."

We'd talked about this once before when he had broached the subject of our future. I'd met a man when I was knocking around Europe. He'd opened my world, opened my mind to so many things. But the day we got married, the day we crossed the threshold of our new apartment, the door closed behind us and I felt trapped. I stayed for a year but it didn't work. Living with Dan Ackerman was another disaster. And I didn't want to kill what Adder and I had.

"Look," he said, "it's too dangerous for you to be alone. Whoever came looking for those drugs in Big Sur is gonna come after you next. And you're completely vulnerable here. You don't even have bars on the windows. As soon as you're out of danger, I promise I'll move right out again." He threw me one of those Adderesque grins. "If you still want me to."

He'd been standing at the threshold like a magazine salesman. I stepped back to let him in. "It's fine," I said. "It's a good idea."

Still, when he dropped that satchel on the floor in front of my closet and started to hang up his clothes next to mine, my little cottage suddenly seemed way too small.

Chapter 31

Living with Adder wasn't all bad.

It felt good falling asleep with him every night and waking every morning to the coffee he brewed, and the old-fashioned smell of his shaving cream, and his blue terry robe hanging on the back of the bathroom door. I liked it when he stood behind me with his arms around my waist while I did the dishes. I liked the curve of his shoulder ready and waiting for me when we watched TV.

My cottage had never been so immaculate. It was beautiful, but it wasn't my place anymore. He bleached the grout on the kitchen tiles to a pristine white, scrubbed the baseboards, waxed the wooden floors. The Marines really teach a man how to keep house. They just don't teach him how to clean out the memories.

He woke almost every night in a cold sweat. Sometimes he let me comfort him. Sometimes he would get out of bed, pour himself a glass of brandy, and sit in the living room in the dark. Sometimes he would go out to walk the empty streets.

Last night had been bad. We were spooned together when a dream woke him. His big arms were around me and he held on until the nightmare loosened its grip. As I was slipping back into my own dream, the breath of his whisper grazed my ear. "Are you with me?" he said. "I need to know you're with me."

I forced myself up from sleep to reassure him. "I'm right here, Adder," I said.

"Baby?"

"What?"

"I hate this sick old city. What it does to people. I don't want to see it ruin you, too. One day soon, you know what we're gonna do? Get on the road and keep driving. There's a whole world out there where a little American *dinero* can buy a nice piece of paradise."

I could feel the pull of the road again, the endless possibility of the unknown, the tremendous release that comes when you break free and leave everything behind. I understood how much Adder and I were alike, but I'd run enough to know that what I was running from was inside me.

"You and me," Adder said. "We both want the same thing, don't we?"

"Yes," I said, my eyes closing as I drifted back into sleep.

In the morning after Adder left for work, the brilliant sun and clear sky gave the illusion of a city without shadows. Except for the distant whoosh of traffic, it was quiet. Too quiet. I needed Billy Hoyle's music adding resonance to the flat bright colors.

At Cedars a nurse told me he wasn't allowed visitors. I said I'd seen him a couple of weeks ago and he was on the mend. She said there had been "complications" and I couldn't get another word out of her. My heart sank. I hadn't let myself think we might lose him.

The whole day stretched emptily out ahead of me, with no agent, no auditions, no work to fill it. I needed a job, any job. I figured I could always wait tables and spent the next couple of hours driving around to restaurants. No one was hiring, but some had waiting lists, which they promised to put me on if I sent in a resumé. "A resumé?! Do I need an MBA too?" I asked the first time I heard this. "As a matter of fact," I was told, "the waiter we just hired had one from Harvard. He was an investment banker before the crash."

It was only three when I got home, and I was surprised to see Adder's jacket on the chair and the back door open.

When I stepped outside the cottage, I heard rustling in the storage shed.

"Adder?"

"Hey, Nikki." He stepped out, his sleeves rolled up and a fine sheen of sweat on his skin.

"What are you looking for?" I said.

"You *could* sound a little happier to see me."

"You've been going through my stuff?"

He grinned at me. "You should see your face. Don't you trust me?"

"You don't seem the type to go hunting for old love letters."

"So that's what you keep in these boxes."

"Adder, what are you doing back here?"

He laid his hands on my shoulders. Those big solid hands that could calm a rattlesnake. "I had an idea is all. I've been running everything you told me through my head, trying to figure out where Darla might have hidden Rambla's bag. We've been everywhere between her brother's house and here, even the Greyhound lockers. Nothing. And I thought about how she was out here when you found her. "Come on, help me look. If we find the dope, you're out of danger. I can move out." He leaned in for a long, sweet kiss. "That's what you want, right?"

I didn't have a lot of stuff. Half a dozen cartons I'd crammed into the MG when I first drove down from San Francisco and some overflow from Billy's porch, boxes of old LPs, maimed knickknacks, and odd pieces of broken furniture.

As thorough as we were, it only took a half an hour for us to realize Darla hadn't stashed anything here. As hope plunged to disappointment, we prodded cartons with a foot, looked behind things we'd looked behind before. Adder picked up an old shoebox and opened it. Then a small grin broke the discouragement on his face.

He took a snapshot from the box, its colors washed out and yellowed.

"Who's this miserable kid?" he said.

It was me. In a starched pinafore. My hair in two braids so tight, I could still remember how they pulled at my hairline.

"Nicolette," I said, "The angriest little girl in the world."

"You never talk about it. Was it that bad?"

"Not really. Not compared to a lot of kids I met when I first left home. I knew one guy who had scars up and down his arms because when he was 'bad' his mother would put her cigarettes out on his skin. And this girl, she used to get locked in a closet under the stairs for days with the rats and roaches. Plenty of kids I knew had grown up homeless, too. Years of hunger and fear and parents who could barely function. Compared to them, my life was *The Wonder Years.*"

He lit his cigarette, sat down on the steps, and patted the stone beside him. He had the box of photographs on his lap, the only thing I'd taken from the house after my mother died.

"But you're the one I want to know."

"You want the story of my life? Like it was our first date?"

He granted me a little smile, but stayed right on track. "Nikki, why did you run away at fifteen?"

"I was hungry for life. Isn't that why you signed up to go to war?"

"Maybe. But we're talking about you."

He leaned back against the wall and I knew he was going to sit there in the afternoon sun, enjoying that cigarette and maybe another, until I was ready to talk to him.

He sifted through the photographs and handed me another. My father and mother leaning against a car, their faces close, their eyes closed, as if sharing the same dream.

"Your folks?"

"Yes. Both orphans raised mostly in foster homes. They knew each other a week, ran off to Las Vegas and got married."

"They look young and in love."

"They were," I said. "But whatever life they were imagining in that picture didn't happen. By the time I came on the scene, they could barely talk to each other. What was left of that dream was bitter disappointment caged inside the rigid respectability they'd achieved. Everything in that apartment matched. The furniture came in sets. A kitchen set, a bedroom set, a living room set with a sofa and chairs that were covered in custom-fitted plastic. They went to work every day and they came home. They were holding in so much hurt, they hardly spoke at all except to ask about dinner or what was on TV. We were bound together in three little rooms, with all that pent-up suffering permeating everything—except maybe those plastic slipcovers."

"Did they take all that pain out on each other, or on you, or all of the above?" He ran his finger along the bridge of my nose where it had been broken. His way of letting me know he already had the answer.

Chapter 32

The charges against the "Ivarene Cult Killers" were dropped, but the name stuck to those four lost souls even as the second cycle of the "Who Killed Darla Ward?" show began. The only real news in all the coverage, so far, was about the identity of the fourth Ivarene victim, the girl on the gurney. Callie told a reporter the girl was a hitchhiker they'd picked up on the Coast Highway. Smiling into the camera, Callie, oblivious to any normal sense of propriety, said cheerily, "She was looking to score, so we took her up to Ivarene."

"Why didn't you inform the police?" the reporter asked.

"The police are dark," Callie said. "Dark isn't bad. Dark balances the light, but you don't feed the dark."

"What was her name? She must have friends, family somewhere."

"We called her Apple," Callie said. "She was sweet."

The victim had a name of sorts now, but no one to mourn her. Except maybe me. And not unselfishly. Not so many years ago, I could have been a hitchhiker who no one had missed.

The news networks weren't the only ones helping themselves to a piece of the Darla pie. Hollywood wanted its share too, and her first feature film, *Hometown,* originally scheduled for the following spring, would be opening in a few weeks with the year-end rush of Oscar contenders. Already, there were billboards everywhere and nomination ads in the trades.

Gordy Hewitt had managed to get hold of a work print, the

final cut before sound effects and music were added. The screening was on a Sunday afternoon and Sari wore a dress barely long enough above and below the waist to be legal. I wore jeans, but good ones, and an obscenely priced T-shirt—a compromise between my usual style and not being shown the servant's entrance.

Under her bright makeup, I could see the same combination of shock and sadness in Sari's eyes as in my own. I don't know if it ever goes away completely when you lose a friend the way we did.

"Nikki," she said, "if I ask you something, will you answer honestly?"

That question always leads to disaster. "Be careful what you ask for."

"No, seriously. What do you think of Leo Auriole?"

It took me a moment to remember the little gnome we'd met at Gordy's the day of the funeral, the man who bragged about his deal with the devil. *Creep* came to mind, but I could see how much Sari had invested in my answer.

"Why are you asking about him?" I said.

"You didn't like him, did you?"

"There was something to like?" As soon as I saw her reaction, I wished I'd kept the thought to myself.

"I know he makes a poor first impression," she said, "but he's more sensitive than you think. When I told him we were friends with Darla, he wanted to know all about you."

"About me?" It struck me as more than a little odd. "Why? Was he trying to calculate the price my soul would bring?"

"Nikki, he was *kidding.* And he was asking about you because he likes me and he wanted to make sure you were, you know, a good influence. Gordy told him how close you and Darla were. So he was concerned. He was afraid maybe you were into drugs or weren't the most honest person in the world." She turned to me earnestly. "But I promise you, Nikki, by the time that conversation ended, I'd convinced him you were really, really sweet."

Everything about this conversation made me uncomfortable. Apart from wondering why Leo would be quizzing Sari about me, I worried about her utter vulnerability to a man who was as unrepentant a predator as I'd ever met.

"Are you seeing this guy?" I said.

"Well, nothing's really happened yet. We're taking it slow. But he really wants to help me, Nikki. He says there's no reason a beautiful woman has to live like a pauper."

Sari used that phrase, "beautiful woman," in a way I'd only heard in L.A.—not so much a description as an expensive brand name, which maybe in a way it was.

"What does 'help' mean?" I asked.

"He's very wealthy, Nikki. He knows a lot of important people."

"And you really like him?"

"I think I could. He's one of the most talented ad men on the West Coast. He wrote those car lot ads for Johnny Rambla."

"Speaking of the company people keep."

"Well, he also created that whole advertising campaign for Mike Ryle, the one that makes you feel so hopeful about life, 'Let's return to the America I grew up in.' Isn't Leo brilliant, Nikki?"

Like the shiny carapace of a well-fed tick.

An evening at Gordy's always comes with a sense of déjà vu—the crowded foyer, the butlers, the electric crackle of wealth and the promise of cool, slick sex.

Sari wandered off to "mingle with who's single," but wound up standing with two other girls, sipping white wine and laughing too loudly, aware that Leo Auriole would occasionally glance at her, or more precisely at the curve of her silk-swathed buttocks.

But most of Leo's attention was on a man who looked out of place among the spray tans, soft Italian loafers, and flashy veneered smiles. He wore a gray suit and a matching pallor perhaps one shade lighter. His even-featured face was unremarkable except for eyes the color of steel. They looked like they didn't miss much.

Auriole's voice was cajoling but his expression was anxious. "Just relax, Lyn. Enjoy. Whatever your pleasure, it's here for the taking."

"I'm here to do business, Leo. But you should have arranged it someplace more private."

"I told you, he only does deals here. That's just the way he is. But you coming here, a man of your prestige, makes all the difference."

Leo touched the man's lapel as if he were trying to reassure him, but succeeded only in producing a politely masked look of disgust.

"Nikki!" I turned to see Gordy and got a kiss on the cheek. "I'm so glad you could make it."

"I wouldn't have missed this screening for anything," I said.

"Wait till you see her. All that awards buzz. She earned it."

I was trying to find the words for what I was thinking—about the connection between the depth of her talent and what was broken inside her—when Lindsay, Gordy's girl of the moment, long and lean in satin jeans that fit like skin, took his arm and snaked her body into his. "Come and sit down, Gordy," she said. "Everyone's waiting." With the contented smile of a powerful man who enjoys pretending women control him, he let himself be led away.

Most of the seats in the screening room were already taken. I was searching for one when Anthony Scott looked up from a pad on which he might have been scribbling another poem, caught my eye, and patted the chair next to him. I had little choice but to take it.

The first time Darla appeared onscreen, talking to another girl on a dusty small-town street, the room went perfectly still. The camera moved in for a close-up. Darla was crying, her face given over to grief. Even without music, it was powerful.

There were soft gasps around the room.

The next scene took place in an alley glistening with rain, a boy in a leather jacket kissing her against a wall. I felt something scuttle sideways across my thigh. Anthony Scott's hand. I removed it. Twice. The third time, I stood up and left.

I walked out the back door, poured a glass of wine from a bottle on the now-unattended bar, and sipped it in the balmy evening air. I watched the sun turn the pool to liquid gold, and thought about platinum hair and white skin glowing on a rainy street. I thought about how some religions talk about God as light, and how maybe platinum blonde on celluloid was the closest we could get to it—Marilyn Monroe, gold chains flashing under dance club lights, jewels on the Pope's robe. Thoughts rolled on and on, my mind trying to pick up enough speed to leave feeling behind.

The patio doors opened and three men emerged. Leo, the man he'd called Lyn, and Gordy. Leo was talking to both of them like the anxious host of a party that was dying.

Everything about Leo felt wrong, from his pursuit of Sari and his questions about me to the acute discomfort the gray man displayed in his presence.

They headed toward a footpath at the edge of the lawn that disappeared into a stand of trees. When I could no longer see them, I started down the same path, which led to a charming wooden bridge over a pond. Swans glided past and, beneath the glamorous costume of sleek white feathers, their legs pedaled through the water, pink and raw like naked thighs. It reminded me of the exposed flesh of women I used to see at the beach as a kid, so different from Gordy's centerfolds, perfectly packaged in their own skin. Shrink-wrapped.

I heard them first and stepped off the path, moving quietly through the trees until I saw them in a clearing. They sat across from each other on weathered Adirondack chairs. Drinks and chips had been set out on a table, but no one had touched them.

"Gordy, you're not thinking this through." Leo's voice, shrill with anxiety, cut through the soft evening air.

Gordy seemed, in his mannerly way, somewhat disgusted. He gave a firm but polite shake of the head and said, "Thank you, gentleman, but I don't think so." He put his hands on his knees as if to get up. Leo, with an expression on his face that looked both cagey and desperate, kept talking like a salesman whose prospect was slipping away. From where I stood, I could almost smell the flop sweat. The third man seemed a distant, almost disinterested observer.

"What are you saying, Gordy?" Leo said, "You don't want to be on the committee? You don't want someone to call those anti-smut pit bulls off your back?"

"Leo," the gray man said in a soft cultured voice, "it is clearly time for you to shut the fuck up."

"Lyn, give me a minute here, okay?" He turned back to Gordy. "You don't want to make a contribution? Fine. Let's talk about a loan. Short term. Zero risk. Till we recover our assets. Which I'm telling you is imminent. Solid as a fucking short-term bond for Chrissakes. Fifteen percent! Where can you get that kind of interest these days?"

Gordy rolled his eyes like they'd been over this before.

"Okay. Make it twenty."

"Leo, I don't want any part of this deal or your committee or whatever your so-called assets are."

The gray man stood and extended a hand to Gordy. "A pleasure."

Gordy rose and shook the proffered hand. "I've got to get back to my guests. Mr. Fourray, please enjoy the rest of the party."

Before they could start up the path, I moved further back into the stand of trees and crouched down so I couldn't be seen. I heard their footsteps rustling the dried leaves as they made their way up the path. I waited until I couldn't hear them at all, then started back to the house.

Fourray, I thought, *Lyn Fourray.* I had heard that name before. But where?

I was about forty yards from where the path opened out into the expanse of Gordy's lawn when I heard someone behind me.

I spun around and saw Leo Auriole.

"Now why would a nice girl like you take such a keen interest in my business?" he said.

"I don't know what you're talking about. I was just out for a walk."

"Exercise isn't always healthy."

"Are you threatening me?"

He smiled. "Nothing turns me on more than a frightened woman."

As I walked back to the house, I heard him laughing behind me.

The foyer was empty except for a few butlers who cleared away empty wine glasses and crumpled napkins. Had Sari left without me?

I found Lindsay on a couch in the den, leaning over a mirror on the coffee table, doing a line with a rolled-up bill. She glanced up at me. "Want a toot?"

I shook my head. "Have you seen Sari?"

She got a nasty little smile on her face. "You look upstairs?"

"She's with someone?"

Lindsay shrugged. "It's just a little party, hon. Go on, join the fun."

The music wasn't loud, but you could feel the driving techno rhythms through the floor.

The smell of marijuana wafted into the hallway from a half-open door. I looked in at the little party. A girl held a long fingernail to Gordy's nose, while he took a deep snort of white powder. In a corner I saw Lyn Fourray, his head thrown back against the wall. In front of him, on his knees, was one of the butlers.

Several men stood with their backs to me. They were talking among themselves, occasionally glancing at something. At first, all I could see was an ornate gold headboard. Then one man laughed and stepped back, and I saw Sari on the bed. Leo Auriole, his pants around his ankles, was climbing off her and Anthony Scott was about to take his place.

As I pushed past the men, Sari turned her head. White powder rimmed her nose. I felt sick, wanted to grab her by the arm and drag her out of the room. Someone laughed. Sari's lips curled down in a coke-taut smile, but I could see the awful shame in her eyes.

"Sari, let's go home."

"Get out of here, Nikki," she said harshly and looked away.

Leo Auriole's gaze followed me as I walked out and closed the door behind me.

I called Adder and he picked me up outside the estate.

I stared out the car window at a starless sky, as dark and empty as I felt inside. I didn't say a word and Adder let me be.

At home, I slipped into bed, and when I settled in against the solid, undemanding bulk of him, I felt okay. We listened to the soft hum of cars cruising slowly up and down the street. After a while, he fell asleep.

Eventually, I did, too.

Chapter 33

The morning did its job. The coffee sweet and heavy. The Beach Boys' "Wouldn't It Be Nice" filling the sunny room. Adder singing along, reassuringly off key, boyishly biting the top off a Mallomar cookie, his favorite part, and handing me my favorite part, the chocolate-covered bottom. A new day swallowing up the dark, but traces of it still clinging like smoke to my insides.

"You thinking about that girl?" he said.

"She's so lost. She thought that man would *help* her."

"This town," he said. "You know, half the creeps we bust—you open a dresser drawer and there are pictures and resumés. But they wake up every morning and they're still nobody. It makes them do desperate things."

"Adder, something else happened last night."

"You want to talk about it?"

"This is something you need to know. Leo Auriole threatened me."

"Because you stumbled into their sick little party?"

"Because I stumbled onto a strange little meeting."

"Stumbled onto?" He took a sip of coffee and gave me a reluctant nod. "Go ahead."

"Auriole had this meeting with Gordy and another man, Lyn Fourray."

"Fourray? That's a familiar name."

"I know. I've been trying to remember it, too."

"So who's this pig Auriole?"

"He's in advertising. But the meeting was about getting money from Gordy for some kind of committee. That's why Fourray was there. He looks like a very buttoned-down guy, very East Coast. Gordy didn't want to contribute to this committee, so Leo asked for a loan until he recovered some assets. Gordy still wasn't interested."

"Okay, so you overheard a business meeting. Why would Auriole threaten you?"

"Because he's cocky and scared at the same time, and it makes him stupid," I said. "Auriole knew Johnny Rambla. He did those car ads for him. What if he did other kinds of business with Rambla, too? What if those missing assets are the drugs Darla stole?"

Adder let out a long, low whistle. "A lot of what ifs."

"It's something we have to look into."

"Not we, Nikki."

"What's that supposed to mean?"

"Listen to me. I didn't say anything after you found those weirdos in the hills, and I kept my mouth shut after you took off to Big Sur in the middle of the night and almost got yourself killed along with your friend. But you're still looking for trouble. So I'm going to say it now. First of all, you have a taste for risk. You like that pumped-up adrenaline rush. That's mother's milk to a marine, so I know what I'm talking about. Believe me, you don't want to feed that habit."

"Adder, don't lec—"

"Second, Nikki, solving this case is not your job."

"Someone has to do it."

It was a bitchy thing to say and the anger boiled up in him so quickly I saw his face color.

Before I could soften what I'd said, he strapped on his holster, threw on his sports jacket, and drained his cup of coffee.

His anger gave way to a wry smile. "Look," he said, "you

want to be a detective? Maybe *CSI* can use some help."

The apology I'd been about to make disappeared. "Adder, don't patronize me."

"You've got a life, baby. It's time to get back to it." He bent down and kissed me lightly on the lips. Then he walked over to the phone, picked up a scrap of paper, and handed it to me. "Your agent called. Call him back."

"The bad news," Phil said, "is that your friend got herself killed again. And I give you my re-condolences. Sincerely. But the good news is, you're hot. Well, not exactly hot, maybe hot-*ish.* Or at least not dead, excuse me if that's a bad choice of words. Anyway, you know the *Case Closed* thing? They're gonna squeeze you in at eleven with the final callbacks. Straight to producers."

"Eleven today? That's just an hour—"

"You still got the outfit? You know the song?"

" 'Boogie Woogie Bugle Boy.' "

He took that for a yes to both questions and I didn't correct him.

There was no time to get a costume, and the closest thing I could find was an old army shirt and a pair of khakis. Not exactly a WAC uniform, but close enough. Then I Googled the song lyrics and printed them out before I took off.

The call was at the Warner lot in Burbank. On the way I drove past Rambla Motors.

I pulled in at the curb. The plastic pennants that hung across the length of the lot were torn and streaked with dirt. A family of out-of-towners in Midwest pastels were snapping photos of themselves against a life-size poster of Johnny and his lion.

I thought about Leo Auriole, Johnny Rambla, and Lyn Fourray, a man in a gray suit, "an East Coast suit." Wasn't that how ZuZu described the money behind Rambla's drug operation? A picture was starting to form, but it was only a broken outline with blank white space where the details should be.

It took a lot of willpower to pull back out into traffic. But there was no way I could let Phil down again.

A few minutes later I drove up to the studio gate. My name was on the list, but I had to park on the street anyway. Looking for a space ate up fifteen minutes. By the time I walked onto the lot, I was hot and tired.

Still, there's a charge you get walking onto a film lot. This one was where they shot the great Warner Brothers films of the forties like *Casablanca* and *The Maltese Falcon* and *Mildred Pierce.* But the thrill wore off as I burned another fifteen minutes walking through the maze of streets and sound stages, looking for the right bungalow. Finally, a nice crew guy in one of those little golf carts offered me a ride.

I was a half hour late, but they hadn't begun to call people in yet, and I joined a group of girls wearing vintage WAC uniforms, bright red lipstick, pageboys and pompadours. It might have been the forties if they weren't all fiddling with iPhones.

I tried to study the lyrics, but every time I closed my eyes to go over them in my head, all I could see were the plastic pennants of Rambla Motors snapping in the wind. By some miracle I had the song memorized by the time they called me in and placed me between two other girls.

Three people at a long table were eating out of Styrofoam containers. One of them fussed with a ketchup packet, another picked olives out of his salad, and the third chatted on her cell while we mouthed the words to an Andrews Sisters CD. The girl on my right jabbed her heel into my foot and the other elbowed me in the ribs, trying to get out in front. But I was firmly planted, synching my heart out, and I didn't budge. They could have saved themselves the trouble. When we were done, the man who didn't like olives looked at me and said, "That's an interesting look, darling, but we're casting Patty Andrews, not Patti Smith."

I'd blown it. Just like the Boogie Woogie Bugle Boy.

At Rambla Motors, a lone salesman paced restlessly between the rows of cars, back hunched, hands in his pockets, looking anxiously out at the street. I drove in and the salesman walked quickly toward me. He wore pointy boots and his hair looked like a windbeaten artichoke. Even before he spoke, I knew he'd have bad teeth and a British accent.

"Four fucking hours? Fuck this shit." He pulled a handful of bills from his pocket and thrust it toward me.

"I don't mind the money," I said, "but I can live without the attitude."

"Don't fuck with me, luv. Just give it here." He held his worn leather jacket close against the balmy breeze, his hands raw and red, a man going through his own personal winter, waiting to warm up his veins.

"I'm afraid I'm not who you hoped I was." The theme of the day.

As he grasped his mistake, a few beads of sweat broke out on his pasty skin.

"It's okay," I said. "But you might scare away some other customers."

"What customers?" He glanced around at the empty lot.

"So all publicity isn't good publicity?"

"Business always sucks here. Look, I'll make you a good deal if you want to trade in that British piece of crap you're driving."

"It's all American under the hood. Wiring, too. And you know what happens when I turn on the ignition?"

"I'm dying of suspense."

"It starts."

He let out a low whistle. "No shit? So what are you doing here?" He ran one hand along the whip-stitched sleeve of his leather jacket, worn raw at the elbows and wrists. "Man, it's fucking freezing out here." He looked so miserable, I wished I had some dope for him.

A girl in dirty rubber flip-flops shuffled onto the lot. Except for skin the color of a rainy day, she looked barely out of her teens. From the look of relief on his face, I knew she was the dealer he'd been expecting. They went off together, and I was left to wander among the metal carcasses—rows and rows of sad old cars no one had even bothered to bang the dents out of. At the far end was a wooden shack that served as an office.

The woman at the desk must have been close to seventy, with dyed brown hair in a big teased pouf. I wondered if she looked in the mirror and still saw the pretty girl she must have been about fifty years ago.

She looked up from her laptop and said brightly, "Hi! May I help you?"

"Just looking around."

"That's all right. We get a lot of lookie-loos since the tragedy. Such a loss." The smile softened. "He was a wonderful man, Mr. Rambla. He took such good care of me. 'Millie,' he used to say, 'you're a jewel.' " She smiled up at me with the gratitude she must have shown every time Rambla threw her that bone. "You don't by any chance need a bookkeeper?"

"I'm afraid I don't even have a book to keep," I said.

"Oh, well, everything's going to be fine. I just have to pray real hard." She must have drawn her own conclusions about my dark hair and strong nose because she tilted her head to one side, examined me, and said, "My church is nondenominational. We even have some lovely Jewish people."

She beamed a hundred-watter at me, her eyes almost disappearing into her fleshy cheeks. There was no wedding ring on her plump finger, and she had all the eager friendliness of a woman with no one to talk to all day but a self-absorbed junkie and maybe a tabby at home.

"Millie," I said, "do you mind if I ask you something? It kind of surprised me what you said a minute ago, that Johnny Rambla was a wonderful man. They say he was a drug dealer and killed three people up at Ivarene."

"Oh, please," she said. "Don't believe a word of it. It doesn't make a bit of sense. Why would a man that rich have to sell drugs?" She leaned her pillowy bosom on the desk and whispered, "My dear, his dry-cleaning bills cost more than my whole wardrobe. Believe me, this business was a regular money machine."

"The salesman out there didn't seem to think business was so great."

"That poor fellow, he has his own problems." She mouthed her next words, "I think he drinks a bit," dismayed at a young man's bad habits. "Of course, walk-in sales don't amount to much these days."

"Then where did the money come from?"

"Oh, the big profits were in leasing. Corporate leasing. Thousands of cars. Business-wise it made so much sense. We didn't even have to store them here. They just got drop-shipped to these big firms. And not just in this country. All over the world. Do you know what rich people will pay over in Europe for American SUVs and convertibles—don't ask!"

"I guess the police have been looking at all his business records."

"The police," she said, with a surprising amount of disgust. "They barge in here, slam this, slam that, open my file cabinets, go into my *personal* desk drawer—you know how embarrassing *that* can be! Grab this, grab that. Cart away the computer. Oh, they got plenty all right." She smiled, a little girl with a secret.

"Millie," I said, as if conspiring with a naughty girl, "did you hold something back?"

"Those police could have had anything they wanted if they

had just asked *nicely.*" She lowered her voice and leaned toward me. "A woman my age . . . we're *invisible* to some men."

She patted the laptop with a plump hand.

"You hid that computer from them, didn't you?"

"I didn't hide it. It wasn't here when they made their search, and I wasn't about to extend myself when they were so rude!"

"Where was it?"

"At my house." She sighed. "Things were always so hectic in this office with Mr. Rambla always needing something, always running here and there, and Millie get me this and get me that. Well, when we only had the used cars, I could cope. But then the new business started, and I was so overworked, he went out and bought me my own laptop so I could do the books for corporate sales at home, with overtime of course. I keep it here now, at least until the police bring back the office computer."

"Lucky you had it then," I said with such unnatural cheeriness, her expression turned wary.

"Who did you say you were?"

For a moment I thought this bubbling fount of information was about to dry up. Then I saw my opportunity. "I'm sorry. I meant to tell you. Leo Auriole told me to come by. He said if you're going to look for a car, go down to Rambla Motors." I glanced down at the wooden name plaque on her desk, "He said be sure to see Millie Wyszkowski."

She beamed at me. "Oh, for Pete's sake. A friend of Mr. Auriole. Why didn't you say so? And here I've been bending your ear. The pastor always tells me I need to work on my listening skills. Anyway, you go find something you like and I'll make sure you get a good price."

"Do you know Mr. Auriole well?"

"Not as well as I knew Mr. Rambla, of course. He'd only come on board as a partner recently. But he brought in all that export business. And that was so wonderful for us."

A worried expression crossed her face and she leaned toward me. "I wonder if you could ask Mr. Auriole something for me. Do you think you could remind him about my check? I understand how difficult this has been for everyone, but I haven't been paid since poor Mr. Rambla passed away."

She blinked and smiled at me again from some long ago Beach Party film, where the worst a bad boy did was drink and gangsters were comic relief.

Chapter 34

Adder wasn't home yet and I wanted to tell him what I had discovered, but I was also dreading a rerun of this morning's argument. So it was good to have the place to myself. I got into the old sweats I hadn't worn since he'd shown up with his suitcase, popped in a CD, and lay back on the sofa.

Outside a bloodshot sunset streaked the sky red, and for a moment I saw Darla on the bed with a stream of brilliant red weaving down her skin. I listened to the Grateful Dead sing "Casey Jones," and thought about Sari. She was riding that cocaine train, too, and how long before it crashed?

I was still lying across the sofa when Adder walked in. He threw on the lights, looked at me, and said, "You didn't have to dress up just for me."

I said, "I learned something interesting today."

He bent down and kissed the top of my head. "No hello? Maybe if I patronize you a little. You like that, right?"

I said, "Rambla was laundering money through the car lot."

Adder grabbed a couple of beers from the fridge, handed me one, turned on the TV, then made a place for himself on the sofa by lifting my legs and, with a proprietary caress, setting them in his lap.

He said, "How was the audition?"

I turned off the TV. "Adder, I'm serious. We have to talk about this."

He said, "We've got a homicide squad and a narcotics division. They don't need your help."

"Apparently, they do. Because they pissed off Rambla's bookkeeper so much, she held back a few things."

"But you stroll in and she tells you they were laundering money?"

"She told me how the car business worked and where the profits came from. It wasn't from selling junkers."

For a few minutes, the only sound was the hum of the refrigerator and the electric buzz in the air. Adder took a long pull on his beer.

"So you're going to ignore it?" I said.

"No. I'll encourage you to keep taking crazy risks, interfering in a murder investigation, putting your life in danger."

"But I am in danger."

"That's why I'm here. That's why three other detectives and I are working on nothing but this case."

"Adder, the money laundering is at the heart of everything. Ivarene. Darla's murder."

"Money laundering is a federal issue, probably an international issue. The FBI and the DEA will take over the case. Foreign agencies will get involved."

"So what are you saying? You're not going to do anything at all?"

"No. I'm saying *you're* not going to do anything at all."

The room was so quiet I could hear the *whirp whirp* of someone's lawn sprinkler. Adder turned the TV back on. A sitcom where you could see the punch lines coming a mile way, the kind of show Adder couldn't stand. But he sat there with his arms crossed, staring at the screen.

I reheated Chinese takeout. We chewed, we swallowed, to the sound of forks ringing on plates and a laugh track. The music of my childhood.

"We have a good thing," he said, "you and me."

"I know."

"Do you? Do you know how good this is, and how rare?" His forearms rested on the table, his sleeves rolled up, his taut skin washed in the gold of the lamplight. I knew how good it was.

"It's a fierce world," he said. "When a chance comes, you've got to grab it. Or you wind up with nothing."

I cleared the table. He came up behind me and clasped his hands around my waist and said into my hair, "What do you want, Nikki? What do you really want?"

It was a question I'd never been able to answer. I just knew that all my life I'd kept moving, because there was a place inside me that was too sore to be touched.

I stepped back out of his grasp and turned to him. "I don't know the answer to that question, Adder. Do you? Do you know what you really want?"

I saw disillusion in his eyes, as if plans and dreams he hadn't had the chance to voice were already dying. "That's something for us to talk about," he said, "when I'm sure there really is an us."

He walked over to the cupboard where I kept the brandy. "I don't know about you," he said, "but I could use a drink."

He poured us each a glass and gently pulled me down next to him on the sofa. I took a sip, let the warmth spread. He put his arm around me, and I leaned into his shoulder. But we remained two separate people inside our own skins.

"Adder, maybe I need some breathing room. I mean, this living-together thing. I'm not good at it."

"It takes a little work."

"I have no idea what that means."

He laughed. "I don't, either. But everyone says it."

"Adder, I don't want it to be over."

"I know."

He gave out a long sigh that had enough sadness in it for both of us.

"I don't suppose it will do any good if I tell you again to stop taking risks," he said.

"I'm not made that way. It feels like a kind of paralysis when I do nothing."

"I know. But you've got to promise me one thing, Nikki. If anyone starts following you again, or if you sense any trouble at all, you call me. And I'll drive by a couple of times a night to make sure you're okay."

"You can stop in once in awhilc," I said.

"No," he said. "I can't."

We made love with a sad understanding that quickly became the fierce searching for what we had somehow lost.

Chapter 35

The cottage that had seemed too small with Adder there now seemed empty in a way it never had when I lived alone before. My own clothes didn't quite fill in holes left where his clothes had been. I missed seeing his shoes at the side of the bed. And my toothbrush was all alone on the bathroom sink, where the scent of his aftershave still lingered. It was time to clean away the past.

I put the radio on and dragged out a mop and bucket. A DJ was playing an unusual mix of really great songs, everything from Black Eyed Peas to the original soundtrack of *Gypsy.* I danced up a storm while Ethel Merman belted out "Everything's Coming Up Roses," and was beginning to believe her, too, when I saw Adder's blue terry robe still hanging on the bathroom door. A pang of longing shot through me.

Ethel's roses started to wilt. Tears choked my throat, but I couldn't cry.

I threw down the mop, got in my car, and drove. When I turned onto Sunset I realized where I was headed.

Class had already started. Two actors sat limply onstage like abandoned puppets while Derek gave his critique. He noticed me as I made my way toward the last row.

"Look who's doing a star turn today."

I mumbled an apology and slid into the nearest empty chair.

"You here to work?" he said.

"Yes," I said.

He turned to the class. "Anyone mind if we jump Nikki ahead?"

Lots of groans and protests. Everyone minded.

"Tough," said Derek. "This ain't a democracy. One of you finds your best friend dead, you can claim privilege, too. Nikki, get up there."

I stood onstage with the lights glaring in my eyes and my skin feverish, waiting for the moment when I could let loose everything churning inside me.

"What's going on?" Derek said.

I shrugged.

"What are you feeling right now?"

"Too much."

"Are you angry?"

"Angry. Mean. Sad. Crazy. Every damn thing!"

"Good," he said.

"No, Derek. It's not good. It sucks!"

"I feel weak. Go on, Nikki. Say it. I feel weak."

"I do NOT feel weak!"

"Sorry. I forgot. You're the street kid, the little toughie." He laughed. That mocking laugh that pushed you right where he wanted you. "What are you afraid of?" he said. "Life? Death?" He leaned forward and grinned up at me. "Love?"

I stood there staring out into the lights, the tears wanting to come, hurting my eyes, closing my throat.

"Who hurt you, kid? Who is it you need to talk to?"

I said, "I don't know." But in my mind I saw the photograph that always sat on top of our TV. An army portrait of my father, taken before he left for Vietnam. Lips as full and smooth as a boy's. Deep brown eyes, too opaque to show the fear that must have been there.

Things I had lost came back to me: the smell of the clothes in his closet, the army tin full of Vietnamese coins. I saw him washing dishes in an apron, living in silence year after year, and the three of us trapped together in those suffocating Brooklyn rooms. Then I felt that big hand across my face, heard the crack, felt the searing pain as if it was happening now all over again. My hand flew to my face and I bent over, fell to my knees.

"How old were you when he did it, Nikki? When he broke your nose?"

"Nine." I heard my own voice thin and expectant with a child's self-pity.

"A lot of pain," Derek said.

"Yes."

"You don't have to stay there, Nikki. Move forward in time."

And I did. To when he got sick, when the pain had taken over his body, and even the morphine the doctors gave him didn't kill it.

"Talk to him," Derek said softly.

I opened my mouth but I had no words. I opened my mouth and a rush of incoherent emotion forced its way out, breaking through layer upon layer that I had built around me from the time I was small until a moment I remember with perfect clarity—the moment I realized that there was nothing anyone could do to me that I couldn't endure, no slap or punch or blow I could not withstand. The moment I understood that, I thought I was free.

Only here I was now, onstage, making deep and terrible sounds, crying tears that hurt my eyes. Tears for my dead father, and for Darla who had no father; tears for all of us, for children who will one day make that final, terrifying trip alone. They were tears that came from the very core of me, where there was only love.

Chapter 36

On the way home I found myself thinking about the découpage box I'd found in Darla's apartment. When I got back to the cottage, I took the box from the drawer where I'd put it.

The illustration on the lid seemed to glow. A home warmed by the golden cast of lamplight. A man reading to his daughter in a claret armchair whose rounded arms embraced them. The girl, with her cherub face and blonde ringlets, nestled against his protective shoulder.

I thought about the conversation I had with Derek in the graveyard, when he told me Darla had been trying to find her father. And I thought about the love that broke her and sent her spinning down into Johnny Rambla's world. Would her life have collapsed without that fatherless emptiness inside her?

I went through the childhood pictures I'd looked at with Sari. And the *Bachelor Pad* shots. How did they fit with a box about fathers? Was it the only thing she had ever been proud of?

The tiny leather address book in the box must once have been the color of wine, and the gold embossing on the cover had mostly worn off. Darla's mother had written her name on the inside cover in a big, round girlish hand, and the entries, in blue ink, were faded—phone numbers from a quarter century ago and probably all useless now.

More promising was the scrap of paper, still crisp and white, with a number scribbled in Darla's handwriting. The name written next to the number was Lenore Lerner. The friend

Dottie had told me about. Maybe Darla had never completed her search. Maybe that was something I could do for her now.

I dialed the number and got her voicemail. An older woman, speaking carefully, as if she'd never quite gotten used to these new devices. I left my name and number but nothing more.

When I hung up I noticed my own message light blinking. Sari had called. I phoned her back and she sounded drugged, or drained, or maybe just empty and sad. She asked hesitatingly if we were still friends, and I said there was never any question about it. I'm not much for cheery small talk, but that's the kind of conversation I made until I was certain she knew I would never turn my back on her.

I turned on the computer. How long had it been since I checked my email? The in-box was full. I didn't need any Viagra but was happy to see I'd won a lottery in Africa. I checked "all" and hit "delete."

Then, out of curiosity, I Googled Lyn Fourray.

I didn't expect much and was astonished to find pages and pages of hits, and at the very top a Wikipedia entry.

> **Lyn Whitfield Fourray** (born Oct. 22, 1947), a minor figure in the Iran-Contra investigation of the nineteen eighties, is currently Chairman of the Board of Directors of the WorldWide Bank of Commerce.
>
> **Early Life**
>
> Fourray was born in Boston and attended Phillips Academy in Andover. He received a Bachelor of Arts degree from Yale University in 1968, where he was a member Skull and Bones [1][2][3], and earned a Juris Doctor from Harvard Law School in 1971.

Career

After building a successful career in corporate law, Fourray joined the staff of the Attorney General's office during the Carter administration and remained there through the Reagan presidency. During the Iran-Contra investigation (1986–87), allegations of Fourray's involvement were made [4][5]. He testified before the Tower Commission but no criminal charges resulted [6][7]. In 1990, Fourray left Washington and returned to the private sector.

I had only the fuzziest notion of Iran Contra from some long-ago school lesson, but I clicked the link to refresh my memory. Right. The secret arms-for-hostages deal that created a scandal during the Reagan era. Many of the people involved emerged unscathed, and time washed away the tarnish for even those convicted. I wondered what a man like Fourray was doing in the company of a lowlife like Leo Auriole. So I kept clicking links and wound up in the kingdom of the lunatic fringe, where all the fonts were huge and one exclamation point was never enough. They had a lot of obsessions, these pages, but there was one common thread running through them—a third leg of the arms-for-hostages deal. Drugs.

Then I remembered where I had first heard the name Lyn Fourray. Dan Ackerman, my ex-boyfriend, had been talking about him at Musso's the day I'd run into him after Manny Roberson's murder. The man who wanted to suppress Dan's research.

When I called him, he sounded so happy to hear from me. I immediately felt a pang of guilt for accepting the dinner invitation he nervously extended before I even had a chance to explain why I was calling.

★ ★ ★ ★ ★

The Japanese palace, nestled amidst carefully tended gardens, had been built by a couple of guys named Bernheimer. Early in the last century, they brought over hundreds of craftsmen from Japan to build this Asian fantasy in the Hollywood Hills. It had been many things since the Bernheimers' day, from a movie star hangout in the roaring twenties to a brothel during the Depression. But now it was Yamashiro, the dowager empress of tempura and tropical cocktails.

The restaurant was filled with art and antiques, and there was outdoor dining around a koi pond, but Dan and I had always liked the lounge with its sweeping view of the city below, blanketed in glittering lights and streaming neon freeways.

He was sitting across from me, his back to the nightscape. In the candlelight, his skin was still pink from a fresh shave, and when he leaned forward you could pick up the scent of Dial soap and department store cologne, a scent that always made him seem so completely decent.

As we sipped mango martinis and shared some amazing appetizers, I asked Dan how the battle over his research was going.

"Corporate corruption a perfect ten, Professor Ackerman, zero," he said.

"That guy who's trying to get you fired—"

"The head of my department?"

"No, the big donor who was pressuring him."

"You mean Lyn Fourray?"

"Yes," I said. "I met him."

You hear the expression a lot, but how often do you actually see a person's jaw drop?

"I know he was involved in Iran-Contra," I continued, "but what else do you know about him?"

"You met him? Where?"

"You first," I said.

He started to protest, then let out a sigh and gave in. "He's an East Coast blueblood. Comes from a long line of upper-crust crooks, and he isn't the only one in his family who slipped through a congressional investigation. His grandfather got a slap on the wrist from Congress for trading with Hitler. Didn't hurt business or their social standing. Fourray's kept a low profile since Iran-Contra, but he's still in the game."

"What do you know about that game?"

"Your turn, Nikki. Where did you meet him?"

"At the Bachelor Pad. He was with a horrible little man named Leo Auriole."

"Auriole!"

"You know him, too?"

"Just the name," he said. "An ad man. The 'genius' behind 'Let's return to the America I grew up in.' "

"Also the genius behind Johnny Rambla's car lot ads."

"Then he's come up in the world. He's the newest member of Fourray's committee."

"What committee? They were talking about a committee."

"The American Patriot Committee."

"You mean as in 'brought to you by . . .' That small print at the end of all those Mike Ryle ads?"

"That's the one."

The committee Gordy hadn't wanted any part of.

I felt seasick. Currents beginning to converge.

Auriole and Rambla and Fourray. ZuZu talking about the big money behind Rambla. Rambla flying heroin in from Afghanistan. And the twelve kilos Darla had taken—worth about a million dollars. Leo's lost "assets." The American Patriot Committee and the ads Auriole had done for Mike Ryle. I remembered something Leo had said to me the first time I'd met him. *Everything's for sale. People, pleasures, and every goddamn politician in Washington, D.C.* Was Ryle the dull eye at the center of this storm?

My pulse raced with my thoughts.

I said, "What exactly were they investigating Fourray for during Iran-Contra?"

"Well, nothing was ever proven against him. To this day no one really knows all the details of how the drugs and arms-for-hostages thing worked. But Fourray went yachting with a notorious Saudi arms dealer and also had some very good friends in Colombia."

"Cocaine."

He nodded

"Dan, I think I know how Leo got to play in Fourray's league. He was buying a piece of Ryle—on the installment plan. Only he missed his last payment. And I know why. Darla took it."

He looked at me like I had lost my mind.

"These dummy companies you were talking about—what do they use them for?"

"All kinds of hanky-panky. Tax loopholes, buyouts, concealing the source of lobby funding."

"Money laundering?"

"Probably, though I can't prove any of this yet."

"Would you like to?"

Chapter 37

The Valley side of Cahuenga was deserted. Not a single pedestrian or even a lost drunk, only the occasional car speeding down the boulevard on the way to somewhere else.

Dan turned onto a side street and parked. We got out of the car and closed the door quietly. I could smell the fear beneath his shave lotion. That was okay. His nerves made me calm.

At one time, Rambla Motors had been all lit up at night, but now half the bulbs were out and we followed the trail of shadows weaving between the cars.

We made our way around to the back to avoid the single beam of a security light glaring from above the office door. The rear of the building faced a hedge. On the other side was a house, dark and silent except for the flickering of a TV screen and the theme song from a *Monk* rerun.

The building wasn't much more than a wooden shack, and there were two windows in back, sealed tight. Even together, Dan and I couldn't budge one. Years of cheap paint jobs—better than a security lock.

Dan looked at me with a question in his eyes and I knew he was ready to use this setback as an excuse to leave. But I was focused on only one thing—getting Millie's files. I looked around and in the intermittent light from the TV, I saw a small chunk of cinderblock near the fence. I picked it up. Dan whispered "Wait!" as the block crashed through the window. We both dropped to the ground. My heart was trying to beat its way out of my chest and I held my breath, but all I heard were the tinny screeches of a TV car chase.

The night was chilly, but there was a moist sheen on his face. It had taken all the guts he had not to run.

Still crouched low, I went back to the window and carefully pulled free the large shard stuck in the bottom of the frame. The ones that remained were like a row of shark's teeth.

"I'm smaller," I said. "I'll do it."

"Nikki, no. Wait—"

But I was already halfway inside.

The glass tore my pants and the skin on my arm, but I didn't even feel it until later.

It was darker inside than out. I stayed still until my eyes adjusted, then made my way to the front door and opened it.

"Dan?" I whispered and heard the gravel crunch before I saw him coming toward me, each careful footfall crackling in the silence. When we closed the door behind us, he was breathing heavily, not from exertion but from nerves.

On Millie's desk were two baskets filled with papers and a coffee mug stuffed with pens. No laptop.

"Maybe it's in the desk," I said. But the drawer was locked. "We've got to get it open."

Dan found a letter opener in Millie's mug and wedged it into the top drawer.

His muscles weren't cut like Adder's, but he was strong and the lock gave with a tiny pop.

The laptop was right there. We set it on the desk, opened it, and as it was booting up, I heard something rustle behind us. We both stopped dead while the computer trilled a happy little *ta daaaa*.

Then we heard a groan. I glanced through the open door into the back room. In the dark, it had looked like a pile of clothes, but now I could make out the leather jacket. The salesman, the Brit, was curled into himself, his back to us, beginning to stir with the awareness of another presence. He turned over. His eyes opened, but if he saw us he had no reaction. He just closed his eyes again and turned his head away.

"It's okay," I said, "he's a junkie and totally out of it."

I could see Dan was torn, wanting to run, but wanting the information as badly as I did. Then he very quietly took his keys from his pocket.

"No," I said. "We can't leave yet."

"Who's leaving?" He held up the keychain. "Flash drive."

The screen of Millie's laptop was covered with loose documents. No folders, just everything willy-nilly. Dan didn't bother trying to figure out which document was which. He just dragged the whole mess of them onto his flash drive. I stopped and listened for a sign that the Brit was coming awake again. But he was dead to the world. Just to be sure we'd gotten it all, Dan opened the computer's "Documents" folder, but it was empty.

When he was done, he placed the laptop back in its drawer and closed it as well as you could with a twisted piece of metal that had once been a lock. Then I took the cardigan hanging from the back of Millie's chair and wiped our fingerprints off every surface we had touched.

We drove back to my place and I poured us both a good stiff drink. Then I booted up my computer, turned the chair over to Dan, and stood behind him looking over his shoulder.

"Damn!" he said.

"What?"

"These files are all in an accounting program. I can't open them. *Damn!*"

"Can't you download it from somewhere?"

"No. I just checked the website. You have to order a CD."

"Isn't there anything you can do?"

"I don't know. Let me see."

I watched from the couch while Dan sat with his back hunched over the screen, clicking the mouse so intensely, I thought he must have looked just like this as a kid playing Sonic the Hedgehog.

After a hell of a day and a long night and too many tropical drinks, I fought to keep my eyes open while he worked, but it was a fight I couldn't win.

The next thing I knew, Dan was gently trying to wake me.

"Nikki . . . Nikki," he said softly. "We've got it."

When he saw my eyes open, he said, "Get up and come look."

I'd slept at a weird angle and there was a kink in my neck. I yawned and rubbed my head. My hair was a rat's nest. I looked at Dan. His eyes were excited, but the lids were at half mast.

"You didn't sleep at all, did you?"

He waved away my concern and said, "I managed to extract the text. Took hours to clean up all the garbage and make sense out of it. But it was worth it. Listen to this."

He began to scroll down the screen. "Boradane Industries, Lysdell Ltd., the Kordan-Stelleck Group."

"You've heard of them?"

"I've been researching these companies for months. Registered in the Cayman Islands and owned by the WorldWide Bank of Commerce. Fourray is a major stockholder, along with a few friends from Europe and the Middle East. As far as I can tell, they provide no goods or services and have no employees."

"So Rambla and Auriole *were* laundering drug money through Lyn Fourray's companies."

"It certainly looks that way."

We sat there, stunned that our wild little escapade had produced this result.

Then the joy drained from Dan's face.

"What's wrong?" I said.

"The files. We can't show them to anyone. Not without winding up in jail ourselves."

We both sat there staring at each other for a couple of depressing minutes.

"We'd better wipe that stuff off your hard drive," he said.

"We have to keep it somewhere. It's all we have."

He copied the text files onto his flash and removed it from his keychain. Then we hid the tiny drive in the shed out back.

When we were done, I put up some coffee, while he took down mugs for us.

"This part isn't so bad," he said, "seeing you first thing in the morning again."

It was so comfortable, so familiar, the way he leaned against the fridge sipping his coffee. I realized I admired everything about him. His intelligence. His fidelity. His integrity. I did love him. But not the way I loved Adder. I knew that look in Dan's eyes and I had to be straight with him.

"Listen," I said, "I was seeing this guy—"

"Oh, great, Nikki. Thank you. That's just what I needed to hear."

"We're sort of not together right now, but I'm not sure it's over. The thing is—"

"Do I really need to hear this?"

"Yes. Because the thing is, he's a cop. He's investigating Ivarene and Darla's murder."

"Great. So the first thing he's gonna ask you is how you got all this information."

"Oh, he'll ask all right. But I don't have to tell."

I said it with enough attitude to convince Dan, if not myself.

Chapter 38

I found ways to put off calling Adder most of the day. Finally, I just bit the bullet and dialed his office. He wasn't there. I didn't leave a message, and I didn't quite get around to dialing his cell.

That night I dreamed about him. I dreamed about his skin and the feel of his hair under my hands. I dreamed about his long thighs tangled in mine, his heart beating against my chest. I dreamed about his face hovering above mine and felt his breath warm on my face. Only there was an odd odor. Sour. Salty.

Not Adder's scent. But something familiar about it.

Then I thought, *There are no smells in dreams,* and dreamed I should open my eyes. But before I could, a hand came down on my face, covering my mouth, crushing my nose so that I couldn't breathe. I flailed out at him, kneed him in the stomach, kicked at his legs.

He rammed his forearm into my neck. I began to choke. His face was close to mine. His sour breath carried a whisper: "Where is it? Where the fuck is the dope? And the stuff you stole last night!" He pulled his arm away so I could speak, and I started struggling again, both legs lashing out. I tore at his face, ripped skin. He cried out, indignant, grabbed my hand and pinned it above my head. My other hand felt under the pillow and my fist closed around the Baby. Then I hit him hard in the jaw.

He gave a cry and jumped back. There was enough light from

the streetlamp to make out the dark bulk of his form and enough of his face to know who it was. I pulled back the slide and saw a glint of metal in his hand. I pulled the trigger. He let out another yowl and grabbed his shoulder.

Then he turned and ran. His gait was uneven, heavy on one foot, light on the other. A man with a limp. He'd been sitting every other time I'd seen him—in the hatchback or bent over a pastrami sandwich at Jerry's Deli. Raymond. The man with the sour smell, the man who had killed Manny Roberson.

I leapt out of bed and ran to the door as the hatchback sped off toward the corner and turned right.

There was no time to call the police. By the time they got here, he'd be long gone.

Scared crazy and jacked up on adrenaline, wearing the sweats I'd slept in, I grabbed the Baby, started up the MG, screeched out of the driveway and followed him. I didn't see the hatchback at first. Then, as I neared Crescent Heights, he pulled into the left turn lane.

I ran three red lights and turned just in time to see him cross Sunset and head up into Laurel Canyon.

He veered left on Lookout Mountain and I followed. The narrow road snaked and twisted, and I kept one or two turns behind him. At every side street where he might have turned off, I slowed and listened for the sound of his car. After one blind curve, there was a long straight stretch. He made a right onto a side road with a yellow sign that said NO OUTLET. I took the Baby from the seat beside me, pulled the slide back, and waited till his taillights disappeared. Then I followed him, steering with my left hand, the gun in my right, my finger on the trigger.

It was a quiet street, a neighborhood asleep.

I heard a car door slam, heard the uneven rhythm of him running.

The road dead-ended at a cliff with a hurricane fence along its edge. In front of it was the hatchback. There was a tear in the fence, but beyond it was a sheer drop, impossible to negotiate.

A band of light glowed at the horizon, and the city began to emerge through a veil of gray.

He must have known I was following. Must have picked this street because there was someplace safe for him here. Maybe he lived in one of these houses.

I'd come this far on adrenaline, but it was time to call the police. I reached for my purse, but felt only the empty seat beside me. No purse. No cell.

I sat on a rock, shivering in the morning chill, trying to warm myself in the early sun. An old truck rumbled up the street, flinging the *Times* at doorways and gateposts. Someone turned on a radio; late-night jazz slid into rolling static, then the strident irony of an early-morning DJ cut through the dawn. Birds chirped and the new day seemed so innocent, until I noticed the damp spots, drops of blood that ran from his car to a wooded area.

Gun in hand, I followed the trail he'd left, making my way through the trees until the drops grew fainter and then disappeared completely. The hazy morning light shimmered through the leaves and made everything seem like it was moving, shifting. A crow landed on a branch and cried out shrilly.

In the stillness that followed, I heard him. Twigs breaking, leaves crunching under his feet. One step heavy, one step light. I quieted my breathing and turned slowly toward the sound. There were five bullets left in the magazine. Enough. But not enough to keep my heart still.

Then I saw him several yards away. He was bleeding from

one shoulder, but held the gun in his other hand, jittery, pointing this way and that, not knowing where I was.

Shoot to kill. Adder's daunting instruction. It made me hesitate, and in that fraction of a second I heard leaves rustling behind me. Something hard hit the back of my head, a blazing pain shot through me, and everything went black.

CHAPTER 39

I opened my eyes and it was still black.

The back of my head throbbed. I touched my fingers to it gingerly. It felt like a ripe papaya.

I was on a floor. Cold and hard. Concrete. There was a nauseating odor of furnace oil. The Baby was gone.

Even as my eyes adjusted to the dark, there was nothing to see but shades of black, and changes in the texture of black, and in one small area pinpoints of light like a handful of stars in a pitch black sky.

I struggled to my feet. My legs trembled. I was dizzy. I put my hands out in front of me, like a kid playing blind man's bluff, and moved slowly forward toward those tiny points of light until my hands touched a flat surface about as wide as the span of my fingers . . . and another. Windowpanes . . . smooth, but faintly ridged. Like they had been painted over, except for the tiny chips that let in specks of light.

Something crawled across my hand. I shook it off. It was big enough to make a small *whap* as it hit the floor. I let out a horrified yelp. But little crawly things couldn't hurt me as much as men with guns. I forced myself to put my hands back on the wall and began to feel my way around the room until I felt a light switch. I flicked it on. Nothing happened.

So I kept moving. The rough stone wall became smoother, warmer. Wood.

I found the knob. Turned it. Locked. Then the knob in my

hand started to turn—the other way. The door pushed open against me and I stumbled back, squinting into the sudden light.

His gun came into the room first. It was an awfully big gun for a man who was all skin and bone and worn leather jacket.

The Brit had a Coleman lantern that cast a dull yellow light around us but left the rest of the room almost black. I could make out the furnace and a ratty-looking armchair that he fell into the way a person does when it's just too damn much work to stand. He wasn't strung-out now, and he wasn't too high to aim and shoot. Still, it looked like that hefty gun was a bit much for him. He slouched back in the chair and let it dangle between his scrawny legs.

"All right, pet," he said, "No need to drag this out. We just want what you stole last night. Right out from under me. Made me look like a damn fool. Not to mention the white packets your friend took. Pretty pair of thieves, the two of you."

I felt less afraid now than when I had been alone, and despite the pulsing band of pain around my head, I could think clearly.

I said, "Why should I hand anything over to you?"

He flung one leg over the arm of the chair, an exaggerated show of ease. "Good question. Let me think about that. Hey, I've got it. Because you don't want to die."

He raised the gun and pointed it at me again. This time he slid back the release.

"You're involved in a high-stakes game," I said. My voice was shaky under the flip attitude, which was okay. The more scared I sounded, the more confident he'd feel. "How come Auriole isn't paying you enough for a new jacket?"

"Auriole? Who's he?" he said, not even bothering to hide his smirk. He figured I'd soon be too dead to talk.

"The next time you open your mouth, luv, I want an answer, not a question." He grinned. His teeth leaned into each other like a collapsing fence.

"You ought to think about caps," I said, "or porcelain veneers."

A flicker of light showed in his dead eyes. "I just might do that, actually. Add a bit of chin, too, take the bump out of me nose. Be quite dishy, don't you think?"

A cockroach made its way up his pant leg. He stared at it as if he didn't realize what it was, then swatted it off. He was more loaded than I'd thought. With a little luck, with a little timing, maybe I could take him.

Still woozy from the blow to my head, I wanted to exaggerate it. I began working on the sense memory of being delirious with fever as a child. The more I got the feeling, the more the room seemed to be spinning.

"How's a bloke to finance his extreme makeover," he said, "if you don't tell him where the goodies are?"

"I don't know where they are." My voice was weaker than it had been a few moments ago. I began to weave a little.

He looked at me and grinned. "Feeling a bit dicky, are we?"

"I think I'm going to be sick," I said.

"Tell someone who gives a flying fuck." He thought that was a clever thing to say and something like a laugh hissed out between his jagged teeth.

Unsteady on my feet, I took a few steps toward him.

"Get back," he said and gripped the gun tighter.

I retreated a little.

"Talk, sweetheart, or I'm afraid I'll have to hurt you."

"Please," I said, moving toward him again, reeling slightly. "Give me a little time to—"

My voice faded and I started to fall forward.

His hands flew up to stop me and I hurled myself into him full force.

He gave a cry of outrage, and I rammed my fist into his

stomach. He choked and doubled over. The gun clattered to the floor. I grabbed it.

He held his gut and glared up at me with a coward's hate in his eyes.

"Bitch," he said, "first good thing I ever get near, and you fuck it up for me. Like every other bloody bint I've ever known."

"Who else is in the house?" I said.

"Fuck you."

I pressed the gun between his watery eyes. A second later I was sorry I had done that. A dark stain began to spread across his pants.

"Who else is here?"

"No one. Fuck! There's no one!"

"Where's Raymond?"

"I said no one's here."

"Okay," I said, "show me the way out."

He got up and, still bent double, groaning like a child, led me up a rickety wooden staircase to a living room that was empty except for a sleeping bag on the floor. Nothing else there but his drug paraphernalia, some empty candy wrappers, and a few crushed soda cans.

"Where's the phone?"

"It's a fucking squat, not the bleeding Ritz."

"Then give me your cell."

He smiled and I didn't know why till he glanced at his pants pocket where the wet stain had spread.

Fine. Forget the damn cell. With the gun still trained on him, I made my way to the door. I didn't think he'd come after me. And I didn't think he'd be too eager to let Leo know he blew it. The way he eyed his works, I was pretty sure he'd just fix and drift off to dreamland.

★ ★ ★ ★ ★

The sun shone down on ramshackle hillside houses with driveways sporting spanking-new Beamers or rusted-out pick-up trucks. I was still in Laurel Canyon. If I kept going downhill, sooner or later I'd reach the boulevard that led back to Sunset. I must have gotten lost a couple of times because it took at least an hour to reach the Strip. The gas station on the corner had a phone booth and I cadged a couple of quarters from a guy filling his car.

"Baby . . ." Though it was late morning, Adder's voice was thick with sleep, and I realized I didn't know if he was alone.

"Look, I'm sorry to disturb you. But I need you—"

"Need you, too . . ." he said, his words fading like he'd closed his eyes and drifted back to sleep.

"Adder, I shot a guy."

That woke him up. "Where are you?"

I told him and he said he'd be right there.

Exhausted, I sank to the floor of the phone booth, my bruised head pounding.

I wasn't the only beat-up chick on this stretch of the Strip. Across the street, a woman in a wool overcoat, feet swathed in rags. She was having a loud, spirited conversation with herself about how Ol' Sammy Bin Laden was down under the sidewalk in hell, where he had built a network of space stations and was broadcasting lies, lies, lies about her. I thought about Darla's mother and her fear of the men who came out of the television. Maybe, like they say, it's the wrong chemicals shooting around in your body. Or maybe there's a breaking point, a single event so impossible to endure, it finishes you off with one fell blow, or maybe your mind sustains a million tiny fractures until it collapses.

It couldn't have been more than ten minutes before Adder pulled to a stop in front of me. At the sight of his big, tough face, a little shock of happiness cut through everything.

I slid in next to him. He still smelled of sleep. It was familiar and oddly comforting. I started to tell him what had happened. How a guy broke in. How I shot him, then took off after him. How someone hit me over the head. How I woke up in a cellar and got scared out of my wits by a bug. How I tricked the Brit and got away.

Adder listened and asked a few questions, but the unspoken personal stuff between us got so thick it was like trying to talk underwater.

"Oh for god sakes, Adder," I said and threw my arms around him and pressed my hand against the back of his head and brought his mouth to mine. He half groaned and held me so tight it almost hurt. Then we both fell back against the seat, like two boxers returned to their corners.

"Adder," I said.

"Yeah."

"I didn't tell you the worst thing about shooting a guy."

"You liked it."

"In a way."

"You're a good person, Nikki. You didn't hate it because it's the better end of a gun to be on."

He shifted into drive and pulled away from the curb.

"You didn't call the cops?" he said.

"You are the cops."

"It's a good thing I'm the one you called. Or the next couple of years of your life could be tied up in a criminal trial."

"For shooting a guy who broke into my house?"

"A while back, a burglar was up on a roof. There was a loose shake. He slipped and fell. Sued the guy whose house he was trying to rob."

"You're kidding."

"Nope. Not only did he sue him. He won."

Adder put the car in gear and we drove back up into the hills. After a few wrong turns, we found the dead end where I'd left my MG. It was still there. So was the hatchback.

Its door wasn't locked. On the floor were a few crushed coffee cups. I pulled open the glove compartment. An owner's manual, a half-eaten sandwich, and the registration. The car belonged to Rambla Motors. No surprise.

"Okay," said Adder, "you followed him up here. Then what?"

"He left a trail of blood."

"Show me."

I pointed to the dull brown drops in the dirt, and together we followed them into the woods. Adder was good at this. He spotted tiny flecks of blood in the brush and even shoulder high on the foliage. We passed the clearing where I'd been hit over the head. Then a few yards further, we saw another street. And the house I'd run from.

"Stay here," Adder said. "And wait for me."

With his gun drawn, he walked over and peered into the windows, then went around to the back. After a minute I heard the sound of cracking wood. Then silence.

I felt jumpy standing alone. It was too close to where I'd been ambushed the first time. The Brit's gun was in the waistband of my jeans. I kept my hand on it and crossed the street to the house. Adder had kicked in a door panel. I stepped inside.

In the room with the sleeping bag, Adder was down on one knee, sifting through the litter.

Before I could say his name, he heard the intake of my breath.

He jumped up and spun around with the gun aimed straight at me.

"Christ, baby! Fucking Christ! Don't *ever* come up on me like that!"

We stared at each other for a moment while the shock drained from us.

Then he said, "Nothing here. Let's go."

When we got back to the cars, Adder asked me if I was okay. I said not really. He put his arms around me and held me.

The day was as clear and bright as a children's book. One of the houses down the street had a bird feeder. A bird whose wings glowed electric turquoise swooped down, knocked a smaller bird off its perch, then ascended again with a large chunk of bread in its beak.

"Bluejay," Adder said. "Mean little suckers."

It made me smile. Adder came from a Michigan farm town. But growing up on the concrete streets of Brooklyn, there was only one bird you knew the name of: pigeon. Children loved them. Old people fed them. To everyone else they were one step up from roaches and rats.

Another bird, his chest a blaze of orange gold, lit down on the feeder ledge.

"That oriole better watch out for the jay."

"What did you say, Adder?"

"That oriole better eat fast, because the jay—"

"Omigod!"

"What?"

"*Oriole. Auriole.* Leo Auriole."

We stared at each other with the same word on our lips.

Birdman.

At home, I showered and dressed, then with Adder at the wheel of the MG and the top down, we took Sunset out to the Coast Highway and drove north toward Malibu.

We stopped at a restaurant with a perfect view of the four-lane highway and a parking lot. You could barely see the ocean, but you could hear the surf and the air was heavy with its scent.

I began to relax.

I stirred honey into my coffee, added milk, and that first taste was what brought me back to life. The sun was already low in the sky, but we both ordered breakfast, skipping the elaborate omelets and specialties for good, old fashioned eggs-over-easy, bacon, and English muffins with deep pools of butter.

Adder put his hand on mine and kept it there until the waitress slid hot plates in front of us and we dug in. I was starving.

"Those thugs are desperate for the dope, baby," he said, dousing his home fries with ketchup. "I know I've asked you this before, but you've got to think back. She must have given a hint, somehow, of where she hid it."

I shook my head.

"Nikki, sometimes things leak out in strange ways. A split-second gesture, something in the eye that doesn't jibe."

I'd been raking through my memories since her murder and came up empty every time. "Nothing."

The waitress poured more coffee. The sun began to disappear behind the houses. Time was slipping away. And I still hadn't told him.

"Look, there's some stuff you need to know," I said. "But don't give me a hard time about playing detective. Okay?"

"Okay." He bit his cheek. To keep, I suppose, from repeating the same mistake.

I didn't hold back anything. I told him about breaking into the car lot office and the files I'd taken and what Dan knew about the money-laundering operation.

"You're seeing the ex again, huh?"

I laughed. Because it was his way of not saying, *Dammit, what the hell were you doing at that car lot?*

"Adder, I know how it all hooks up."

"You know who killed Darla?"

"Not exactly. That is, I don't know who pulled the trigger. But I know who was pulling all the strings."

I told him everything I'd learned about Lyn Fourray and his connection to Rambla's drug operation and the American Patriot Committee.

"Oh, for Chrissakes, Nikki. Next thing you'll be telling me they killed Kennedy."

"Adder, we've seen Rambla's books. And the companies he was leasing cars to. None of them are real. Dan Ackerman knows all about Fourray and the companies that own those companies. And how the money was being funneled into the Ryle campaign."

"Give me a break, baby. Are you saying that Mike Ryle is behind all this?"

"Behind it? Mike Ryle? Have you ever heard him say a word someone else hasn't written? He's an *actor.* I think they cast the role and plunked him in front of the camera. *Mr. Smith Goes to Washington.*"

We were both struck dumb for a moment. It was the first time I had ever seen Adder truly stunned.

"My god," I said. Suddenly everything was breaking loose, coming clear. "Mr. Smith! It's Ryle. That's who Darla was in love with!"

Adder shook his head. "Damn, he's old enough to be her father. Hell, he's old enough to be *my* father."

"And she was a girl who never had one."

Adder lit a cigarette and stared out across the highway. "Ryle, huh? With that wife Dolly always glued to his side? He had a hell of a lot to lose if an affair ever got out."

"Fourray and Auriole had plenty to lose, too."

For once, there was no skeptical lift of the eyebrow. No lopsided grin.

"Politics and money laundering and international banking," he said. "This is way too big for you and me. It's not a local homicide anymore. We'll have no choice but to turn the case over to the Feds. And they'll have to work with agencies in other countries. It'll take years. Meantime, some dangerous men are still looking for their dope."

It was growing dark and we were the only customers in the place. The check must have been sitting on the table for some time, but we hadn't even noticed.

"Adder," I said, "there is one person within reach right now—without Rambla's books, without treading on fame and power. Leo Auriole. Because he thinks I have his dope."

"You're talking about being a decoy."

"Exactly."

He took my hand. His eyes were cold and direct.

"No," he said. "Period. It's way too dangerous."

"No more dangerous than waiting for him to kill me."

Adder saw the truth in that, so we laid out a plan. He would have to break a few rules and call in a few favors, but he didn't think he'd ever have a better reason to do both.

Chapter 40

It took three days for Adder to arrange everything. I spent half the time wondering if I had the courage for this job—and the other half wondering if I had the courage to live with him again.

When the afternoon of our operation finally arrived, I drove to the Hollywood Division and met with Adder and three other homicide cops. One was nice looking and had the soft eyes of a boy whose mama loves him. He held out his hand and introduced himself as Detective Chavez. The second, Shane, had a greased crewcut and looked like something newly cracked out of an egg. Third was Lefrak, Adder's partner. He was flipping a pack of Tums in his palm like it was an executive stress toy. I'd once mentioned to Adder that they seemed like an odd match. But he said they were perfect together. Adder didn't mind taking risks and the old guy didn't mind Adder taking risks, so everyone was happy.

The other guys congregated around Adder, who was clearly the alpha dog. They glanced at him frequently to see if their ideas, even their jokes, got an appreciative raised eyebrow or a pursing of the lips to suggest they could do better.

The plan was simple, but they went over it with me several times. Everyone was jittery because I was a civilian. And because it was a high-risk operation where everything that could go wrong might. After the third go-around, when I started to get impatient, Lefrak told me about a cop he'd looked up to when he was a rookie, Whitey Finn. "A damn fine detective," he said, "who got killed in a setup like this years ago." Shane began kneading his large hands, cracking his joints, saying, "Yeah, yeah, we heard all your stories, old man. Let's go get 'em."

The last thing we did was agree on the signals I could choose from if things turned bad. No secret codes. Only the obvious. *This isn't going to work. Hey, you can't do this to me. No guns! I'm not going anywhere!* I told them that if I happened to scream help, they should feel free to jump in any time.

When we were done, they turned me over to a matron who taped a body wire to the small of my back. It was about the size of an iPod, with an antenna that shot up between my shoulder blades. The cops would be able to hear everything from a half mile away. To help conceal it, I wore a snug top under a loose, bulky sweater.

Around noon, I left the police station with one-kilo of heroin in a bag that a police artist had made for us with Auriole's circle and wings in bright red. The unmarked police cars followed me out, then deliberately fell a few blocks behind. When I could no longer see them in my rearview mirror, I opened the glove compartment. The gun I had taken from the Brit was in there. On top of it, Adder had laid a pint of brandy. I put the gun into my bag and took a couple of swigs from the bottle. It helped. But I could still feel pinpricks swarming under my skin.

Camden Drive was lined with palm trees as slender and graceful as trophy wives. There were no people in the streets and no parked cars except for the occasional gardener's pickup truck. Not a scrap of paper blew in the gutters, not a browned blade of grass marred the landscape. Whatever mess these people made stayed behind their impressive double doors.

Leo's was the only house surrounded by a concrete wall. It was maybe eight feet high and the ivy that webbed thickly over it was a darker green than the bright lawns all around it. The vines were reassuring. They would make climbing over the wall easy for the cops, if it came to that. Above the wall, I could see the top story of a house, as big and as unadorned as an apartment building.

I rang a bell at the heavy wooden gate and after a minute or so, it opened slowly. As I pulled up the drive, I saw Leo at the door in terrycloth slippers, khaki shorts, and a golf shirt the color of pink bubblegum. He looked like a toad Walt Disney might have created, and I half expected his tongue to whip out and snag a fly.

"What's with the big sweater," he said as I got out of the car, and a cool wave of fear ran through me. Then he said, "Not even a peek of those perky little tits? You gotta learn to sweeten the pie a little."

"A million dollars should be sweet enough." The pressure had done something odd to my voice. I didn't sound like myself.

"You're a little uptight, doll. What are you worried about? I'm a nice guy. You know how nice? I won't hold it against you that you thought you could steal my goods. I won't even hold it against you that you hurt two friends of mine." He shook his head. "Bullets . . . fists . . . your mother ever teach you to act like a lady?"

"If I listened to her, Leo, I'd be a dead lady."

"You got a point. So why are we standing? Come in, come in. Let me show you around."

Leo put his arm around my waist and gave me a squeeze, as if I was part of the merchandise being offered. I pulled away before he could grope his way up to the wire.

An entry hall as grand as Leo's, with its black-and-white marble tile and wedding-cake ceiling, begged for a sweeping entrance by William Powell and Carole Lombard. But it was only us. Not even a table or an umbrella stand. And our voices pinged off the walls.

Leo led me down a hallway to the kitchen, which was not

exactly what you'd imagine in a house like this. The cabinets were white pasteboard, the kind you'd find in a basic rental, and there was nothing on the walls, not a print or even a calendar. The only touch of color came from a soiled terrycloth dish towel hanging from the refrigerator door.

On the table was a small plate with a half-eaten sandwich, a thin pink piece of bologna between two slices of white bread. Leo finished it off in three bites. He did not ask if I wanted anything. He filled a glass with tap water, swished it around in his mouth, and spit it out in the sink. Then he flashed his teeth at me.

"Clean?"

"Still look brand new."

My bravado didn't fool Leo. He said, "Relax, sweetheart. It's okay to blink once in awhile. No extra charge."

I followed him down another long hallway to the living room, a large room with no evidence of much living going on in it. No magazines on the coffee table, no books, no photographs or personal mementoes of any sort, nothing, in fact, but a multicolored, molten lump of an ashtray. The furniture was covered in a high-contrast brocade that made my skin hurt.

"Look at these statues," he said. "I got what they call a major collection here."

All around the room were bronze sculptures, the smaller ones on tables, the larger ones on the floor. They weren't Rodins, but maybe wanted to be.

"Whadya think?"

I searched for something to say and finally noticed, tucked away in a corner, a gracefully wrought woman holding a child.

"That one is beautiful," I said.

"What are you talking about?" he said with a dismissive wave of his hand. "That little thing? Weighs almost nothing. Came as part of a lot. Lookit this, that's the one you shoulda picked."

He pointed to a life-size statue of a man, nude except for his bronze Speedo.

"Eight hundred and fifty-seven pounds of solid bronze," he said. "Plus look at that detail, the toenails, the eyelashes. That's what you call art."

"Amazing," I said, which was true.

"All right, already, enough chit-chat. You have what's mine. I want it back."

"That's why I'm here. Like I said on the phone, I want a finder's fee."

"I don't see where you got the balls to bargain for anything."

"It's just business. We make a good deal, everybody's happy."

"Show me what you got."

I pulled the packet out of my bag and laid it on the coffee table. Leo picked it up and studied the symbol the police artist had drawn. A shock of panic bolted through me. Was this rendering of my crude sketch good enough to fool Leo?

He slapped the bag with the back of his hand. "Look at that!" he said.

I steeled myself for the worst. Mentally flipped through the prearranged signals.

"Is that a logo, or what?" He had a big smile on his face. "Designed it myself."

"Lovely," I said, not so much a word as a huge sigh of relief.

He tore open the plastic, dipped in a moistened pinky, took a little taste and nodded.

"I lost twelve kilos in that Ivarene mess," he said.

That was it! We had it on tape. The dope was on his table. Time to wrap things up and get my butt out of there.

"You got one bag back," I said. "From Kyle."

He didn't deny it. "Where's the rest?"

"I have two safe deposit boxes at the B of A on Beverly. We go to the bank, you put ten thousand cash in one box. The dope's in the other, and when I have your money, I'll give you the key."

"What? I'm supposed to give you ten grand on faith?"

"I'm not stupid enough to try and screw you."

He seemed to like that. He crossed his legs and breathed a satisfied sigh. Then his eyes traveled to something behind me.

I turned around.

The Brit, in his ratty leather jacket, slouched against the archway. He had cleaned up, the slack muscles of his face were exhausting themselves in an effort at arrogance, and he'd found another gun. It drooped toward the floor. Still too much weapon for him.

"Hey! No guns, Leo!" I said it loud. The signal. I pictured the four cops suddenly alert, slamming car doors, running, guns drawn, to the rescue.

"Halbert," Leo said, "put the pistol away."

Nerves pushed me to laugh. "Halbert?"

The Brit looked offended. A man who had never been in on a joke. "Clever little tart you are, always mocking. Well, you're gonna be very sorry you ever fucked with me."

"Oh, for Chrissakes," Leo said, "cut the crap. Just go with her and get the dope. And don't screw up this time."

"Crap, is it? What if she fucks us over and there's no dope in the locker?" His voice sounded shaky.

"What are you, a moron? How's she gonna fuck us over? Just get the damn key from her."

A voice behind me said, "I'll take care of it."

"That's right," said Leo. "This big genius will take care of it."

Raymond took it as a compliment and smiled. With his one short leg, he listed a bit as he pushed past the Brit into the living room. His jaw was still bruised and his shoulder was bulky under his shirt where I'd shot him. He had to use his left hand to grab my arm. "Let's go," he said.

"I'm not going anywhere!" How long had it been since the first signal. It seemed a lifetime, but it was only a minute or two. Not enough time for the cops to get here. And my gun was in my purse on the table.

I jerked free from Raymond's grip and reached for my bag, but Leo leaned forward and pulled it into his lap. The effort made him grunt.

"I love these things," he said. "Love to see what the little ladies carry."

He reached his hand in, felt around, and pulled out the gun.

"What's this?" he said. "A cigarette lighter?" He wheezed out something like a laugh. "No guns, she says. Trust me, she says."

"You can't do this, Leo!" Where were the cops? I looked out the window and saw nothing but trees and an early autumn sky growing darker. Sweat streamed down my back, and I wondered if it had shorted out the wire.

"Get her out of here," Leo said.

"You can't do anything to me, Leo. People know I'm here. I stopped next door to ask if this was your address." My heart sounded louder in my ears than the voice that came out of me. "How does a member of the American Patriot Committee explain that he was the last person to see me?"

"I'm an ad man, sweetheart. Explanations are my business."

The Brit slouched toward me and stood so close I could smell his rotting teeth. He pushed the muzzle of his gun into my solar plexus. I had never felt such naked terror. He saw it in my eyes and smiled.

"I owe you," he said, "a little pain, a little humiliation."

"Halbert, stop dicking around," Leo said. "Raymond, get her out of here already. If she won't go easy, you can hurt her, but just a little bit."

Out of the corner of my eye I saw Raymond lift his weapon. He held it in his bad hand and steadied it with his left.

With a force driven by pure fear, I slammed into the Brit. He staggered back and reeled smack into Raymond, just as he fired. The bullet blasted the nose off a cherub on the ceiling. I grabbed the Brit's gun and fired at Raymond. He went down with a cry of surprise.

Leo's face turned red. "Goddammit! Goddammit! That's a fifteen-thousand-dollar Persian rug he's bleeding all over." He waved his gun hand wildly and I thought he might shoot me for ruining his carpet.

Then I heard glass smashing. Leo spun around as Adder crashed through the window with a wild cry and a gun in each fist, like a goddamn cowboy. Blood ran down his face where the glass had torn his skin, and there were cuts all over his hands.

Leo jackrabbited down the hallway and Adder took off after him.

Raymond pulled himself to his feet, blood spurting from his belly as he ran toward Adder, an open switchblade in his fist.

"Adder!" I shouted. "Behind you!"

Adder spun around and fired at Raymond, who went down like he'd been hit by a wrecking ball.

"Where are the other cops!?" I felt like I was screaming. I may have been.

Leo came back down the hallway, the gun clutched in both his hands, and aimed at Adder's back.

I fired. The bullet hit Leo in the chest. He stood there, a look of disbelief in his wide-open eyes, even as he fell.

Then I saw the Brit. He had another gun. The one he'd taken from me. The Baby.

Adder blasted it out of his hand. The Brit began to whimper, "It hurts, it hurts." Blood dripped off his hand, water ran from his eyes and nose.

I felt as torn up as those bodies around us. Only without the pain. Without any feeling at all. Except a kind of nausea.

Adder touched my shoulder, asked if I was all right. I had no words.

"Holy shit, Jack." Chavez gaped through the broken window as Shane carefully cleared away some of the jagged glass. One by one, the three cops, Lefrak slightly winded, climbed into the room.

"Where the hell were you?" Adder said.

"It was a hostage scenario," Shane said, "but you're such a goddamn showboat—"

"Easy, Shane." Chavez looked ashamed that they had hesitated while Adder took it on all alone. He said to me, "We were afraid if we moved in too fast, it would go bad for you."

I stared at Leo Auriole. I remembered Adder saying he knew marines in Iraq who got hard-ons when they killed. But that had nothing to do with how I felt. I felt cold. I felt as empty as a corpse.

CHAPTER 41

We didn't have all the answers. But I was ready to pick up the threads of my life and move on. Maybe I would have if I hadn't seen that interview with Mike Ryle and his wife. If I hadn't heard her voice again. That precise pronunciation. And suddenly remembered where I'd heard it before.

The press was getting a solid run with yet another resurrection of the Darla Ward story. For a few days I had to unplug my phone, and there were news trucks in front of my house and pretty girls with microphones waiting to ambush me every time I went out. But I didn't want that kind of spotlight and didn't give them much and eventually they faded away.

Still, like everyone else, I flipped from channel to channel watching the coverage. Only this time, in addition to endless pictures of Darla and recaps of Ivarene and her murder, there was my headshot and a scene from *Law & Order SVU,* where I played a crazed rape victim wildly waving a gun at a detective. Then newscasters would gaze searchingly into the big eye of the camera and called for an investigation into the reckless use of a civilian decoy in a police action. It might have been worse, but Adder's report said he was the one who'd killed Leo, not the decoy. If there's a heaven, it won't be filled with saints.

The bullets that killed Manny had come from Raymond's gun and he would be tried for that murder. The Brit would probably spend the rest of his life in prison. The police had little doubt Darla's murder had been ordered by Leo and carried out by Raymond or the Brit. But they couldn't find the gun that killed her. Or the dope she had stolen.

As for the political side of the case, Adder ordered a second search of the Rambla Motors office so that his colleagues could discover Millie's laptop with the records that would link Leo Auriole and Lyn Fourray to Rambla and the money laundering.

Dan tied it all together and got all the credit he deserved—as well as his tenure. Book offers came in from major publishers and CNN featured him in a special about drugs, money laundering, and the Ryle campaign.

On *60 Minutes,* the public got their first glimpse in decades of Lyn Fourray when Leslie Stahl and her cameras cornered him as he stepped into a limo on the way to the airport. I'd never seen anyone cooler. He said, "Leslie, I want you to know, I've severed all connection to the WorldWide Bank of Commerce, and I'll be cooperating fully with the justice department investigation. Gonna give 'em all the help they need. Got my own reputation on the line here. But I have to catch a plane." Fourray quietly closed the limo door and sped away—a lot slicker about media now than in the grainy Iran-Contra clips they ran, where he hunched his shoulders and blocked his face with his hands.

Once it came out that Mike Ryle's run for the senate had been financed by drug money, his campaign was pretty much dead. You couldn't turn on the TV without pundits of every persuasion demanding that he withdraw from the race.

The police quietly looked into the question of his involvement with Darla, but Manny Roberson's journal and *Mr. Smith Goes to Washington* wasn't concrete evidence, and they couldn't prove Ryle's link to her or her murder.

Despite the pressure, Mike Ryle had not yet stepped down from the race and image rehabilitation was in full swing. His charming smile and earnest eyes were everywhere. All the media exposure didn't cost them a cent now.

Diane Sawyer interviewed Ryle and his wife Dolly for an ABC special. She asked what they were going to do about the drug money that had been funneled into his campaign. Ryle's soothing voice assured the public that any money determined to have come from illegal sources would be donated to charity. Diane asked about the American Patriot Committee and Lyn Fourray and foreign interests with tentacles in the American political system. Ryle said Fourray personally assured him he had no involvement in any criminal wrongdoing. Then Diane asked Ryle if he could give her audience the same assurance about himself—that he had absolutely no knowledge of the money-laundering scheme.

With a single line, Ryle put himself back in the race. His eyes twinkled and he said, "The only laundered money I've ever seen was up at the house, when Dolly did a wash and left a dollar bill in the pocket of my old blue jeans."

Dolly looked up at him. She smiled like a schoolgirl. The camera went in for a close-up. "Diane," she said, "thank you so much for giving us this opportunity. There are always people out to ruin a good man who speaks the truth."

Ru-in, she pronounced it. Two syllables. Her voice sounded proper, even a bit sugary, but still imperious. Like a voice I had heard before: *If you're under the illusion that I will allow you to ru-in my husband's life, then you're not just a cheap little whore, but a terribly stupid one.*

The woman on Darla's voicemail.

Chapter 42

There was a wealth of material online about the Ryles, and I couldn't take my eyes off a picture of Mike and Dolly that must have been taken back in the early eighties. He had sideburns and sported a pinstriped jacket with wide lapels, a vest, and a fat satin tie. She wore a suit with enormous shoulder pads and a blouse with a chiffon bow at the neck. For once she was looking not at him, but directly into the camera. Her eyes were wide open and clear and, above the feminine and quite fetching smile, she looked like someone to be reckoned with. She stood demurely in the crook of Mike Ryle's broad shoulders, and his cheery grin made his eyes crinkle so that they were almost slits. It made you want to grin back, until you really looked at those eyes, glassy and withdrawn.

I was wondering when we had all begun to read bared teeth as happiness, when the most beautiful sounds floated into the room. The deep, sad sweetness of a cello solo wrapped around me and wound through me. Jacqueline DuPré. It had been a long time since Billy Hoyle's music had poured out onto our street.

I walked over to his house. Through the screen door I could see him lying on his sofa. His injured leg was still bandaged. His eyes were closed, but I could tell by the gentle arcs of his head to the music that he wasn't sleeping. I waited for the piece to end before I knocked.

He opened his eyes and with one hand motioned me to come in.

"Billy! I've missed you," I said, not even realizing how much until I saw him. "Are you doing okay?"

"Been . . . better," he said, his voice thready.

"I'm sorry I didn't visit more. I kept trying to see you, but they wouldn't let me."

Like all excuses, it sounded hollow, even to me.

Billy waved away my attempt at an apology. "Didn't want visitors . . . tubes and needles . . . looked like hell."

He had aged a decade since I'd last seen him. His face was gaunt, and when he raised his hand the skin of his forearm hung away from the bone.

"Billy, what happened? I thought it was only your leg."

"Old . . . old is what happened." He managed a laugh. "And old is . . . boring. How's the career? All publicity's good publicity, no?"

I laughed and told him the news I'd gotten that morning. *Street,* the homeless pilot I'd shot, had been picked up for a full season, and my character, nose and all, had been beefed up from semi-regular to lead.

I could see he was happy for me. A month ago, I would have been excited too. But everything I'd been through had made it all seem paper thin. It was like what Adder had said once about war—as terrible as it was, nothing else would ever be as vivid.

"Billy," I said, "are you all alone here? Isn't there someone to take care of you?"

"Old broad comes with meals . . . helps me out."

"If you need *anything,* you call me. You understand?"

"Get that look off your face," he said. "I'm not dead yet, kid."

For a minute that wicked glint was back in his eye, and I knew he still had some fight left in him.

"Nikki?"

"Yes?"

"Sorry about your friend," he said. "I liked that girl. Chatty little thing. Chirp in your ear all day." He started to chuckle. Hoarse and weak. But he was smiling.

I shot him a grin back, one that said, you're gonna be fine, Billy, you're gonna make it.

As I walked back across the street, I thought about what Billy had said, about the way Darla used to be before she showed up that night at my house, traumatized and twisted into something else. I pictured her making her smoothies and chatting away the whole time. Or calling me three or four times a day to talk about everything or nothing. Talking to cover secrets, as Derek had so accurately pointed out, but also for company, or to work out a problem on her mind—anything from whether skinny jeans were on the way out to the meaning of a disturbing dream.

So it was almost impossible to imagine her falling in love and not talking to someone about it. But who had she trusted enough to confide in about Ryle, a married man running for senator? Obviously, not me. Sari could not hold back a secret. Darla's brother? Completely unreliable. And Derek had his own agenda with her.

When I asked myself who I had ever really trusted, I remembered someone I hadn't thought of for years. One of the few friends my mother ever had, a woman who wore bright clothes and big tinkly earrings, a woman who radiated kindness. Sometimes she'd watch me when my mother ran an errand, and I would talk her ear off. In the safety of her company, everything inside me came bubbling out.

It was almost like the relationship Dottie Ward had described when she told me about her friend Lenore Lerner: *She was the one my little girl confided in instead of me.*

I found the paper in Darla's box with Lenore Lerner's

number. It was crisp and white, though it seemed to have been unfolded and refolded several times. If Darla had gotten in touch with her, maybe those locked-in feelings had come rushing out.

Lenore had never returned my first call. I tried the number again. She picked up on the second ring.

"Hi," I said. "This is Nikki Easton. I called you the other day."

"Oh, yes. I'm terribly sorry to have taken so long getting back, but I just returned from Palm Springs." She had the careful diction of an actress trained the old-fashioned way, the Hollywood idea of an upper-class accent that you sometimes heard in old movies.

"That's okay," I said.

"You mentioned something in your message about Darla Ward?"

"Yes, she was my friend."

"Ah, I knew your name was familiar. You're the girl who's been in the papers, aren't you? And aren't you the one was with her when—"

"Yes."

"I'm so sorry. That poor child. What a terrible tragedy."

"It must have been hard for you, too," I said. "You knew her when she was a little girl, didn't you?"

A pause. "I did."

"I wonder if we could talk."

The line went so quiet, I thought maybe she'd hung up. Then she told me to stop by that afternoon.

In West Hollywood, old women come out in daylight and disappear at night. They have platinum hair, faces crumbling under face powder and blush, and polyester pant suits with stains a hundred launderings in basement washing machines can't remove. You see them in dinosaur sedans, driving in the same hesitant and careful way they count out pennies at the supermarket, as if that could stop life from short-changing them. That's what I expected to find when I went to see Lenore Lerner. But I couldn't have been more wrong.

She lived in a condo on Kings Road. A slim woman in gray slacks and a sleeveless beige blouse answered the door. She was well over sixty, but her arms were still firm. Her hair was cut in a neat silver bob, and around her neck she wore a string of what looked like real pearls.

The apartment was an air-conditioned sea of beige. From a phonograph somewhere, Mantovani poured syrup from a violin. If décor were a drug, this place would have been Valium.

"Can I get you something? There's iced tea in the refrigerator."

"Thanks," I said.

"Good." She smiled. "Please make yourself comfortable."

The firm cushions and shallow seat of the sofa were built for etiquette, not slouching. I sat straight-backed and looked at the framed photographs placed in groups on every polished wood surface. An eight-by-ten publicity still of a young, raven-haired Lenore in a satin evening gown. A wedding portrait posed in a photographer's studio. Dozens of snapshots of Lenore and her husband, his hairline receding progressively through the decades.

There were no pictures of kids or grandkids, and the happiness Lenore and her husband displayed in those photos struck me as the ageless romanticism of a childless couple.

A few minutes later, she was back with tall frosted glasses on a silver tray that she set on the coffee table.

"What a lovely place." My classy posture talking.

"Thank you." She took a chair and crossed her legs neatly at the ankles. "My husband and I chose everything together. He was really wonderful that way. He died . . . it'll be two years in January."

"I'm so sorry."

She looked me squarely in the eye so I would know she did not need sympathy. "I try to keep busy. When you're young, life rushes at you so fast you have to hold it back. But at my age, you have to work harder at it. I do a little volunteer work, have a few friends over for dinner from time to time. That doesn't mean I don't miss George. I do. Every day. But at my age, time disappears so quickly and is so very precious."

Then she laughed. "Like every old lady who lives alone, I'm chatting far too much. I do apologize. You wanted to talk to me about Darla."

"Yes," I said, not sure how to begin. "You knew her as a child."

"We were very close when she was small." Lenore looked stricken. "It's so heartbreaking what happened. I can't help thinking that maybe I did the wrong thing all those years ago, maybe I could have been, you know, an influence on her. But we lost touch when she was about four."

"Why was that?"

"Because of her mother. Do you know Dottie?"

"Yes, I met her."

"Then you understand."

"Was she always like that? Always a little . . . uh . . ."

"Nuts?" Lenore smiled at my overly polite caution. "No, not when I first knew her. Just a little . . . different. Very sweet. But she lived in a bit of a dream world. All feeling, not a practical bone in her body. And when she fell for a man, that's what she did. She fell. It was like watching someone get hit by a car. I tried to tell her, you can't let life just happen to you, like an accident."

"Lenore," I said, "was Darla's father the accident that happened to Dottie?"

The question made her pause. "I'd never thought about it that way, but yes, now that you mention it, she was never really the same after him."

She stirred some sugar into her tea and took a sip, then gave the smallest smile of pleasure, something sweet in the present to replace an unfortunate memory.

I said, "It must have been quite a surprise when Darla called you out of the blue."

"Oh, it certainly was."

"Did you get to spend some time together?"

"She came over once. We'd meant to see each other more, but then . . ." Her voice trailed off.

"That must have been something, to connect again after so many years."

"Oh, it was. I'd never forgotten her. But I was quite surprised that she remembered me. She even talked about the time I took her to a hot dog stand shaped like a giant frankfurter on a bun." Lenore's eyes grew moist and she patted them with the corner of a cloth napkin from the tray. She took a sip of the cool tea and recovered her composure.

I tried to steer the discussion to what Darla might have shared with her. "It's good you had some time together. I bet you must have packed a lot of catching up into that visit."

"Well, she did tell me she'd broken off a long relationship with a . . . Jim?"

"Jimmy. And did she mention her new boyfriend?"

"No. I don't recall her mentioning anyone like that."

Lenore looked at me a bit warily. I could tell she didn't like to gossip, and I knew I had to stop asking such direct questions. I took a sip of tea then told her about the découpage box.

Lenore nodded as I spoke. "Yes. She never knew her father. In fact, that's really why she called me."

"You knew who he was? You told her?"

"I told her no good was going to come of it. But she had a strong will—which certainly didn't come from either of her parents."

"Lenore, who was Darla's father?"

A wariness came into her eyes. "I don't mean to be rude, but why dig into her life now?"

I searched for a way to explain it, but all I could say was, "Something seems incomplete."

She rose with the grace of lifelong habit, picked up the glasses, and went into the kitchen. I thought she was letting me know it was time to leave, but when she came back she'd refilled them.

"I don't know why I'm being so protective of him," she said, setting the tray down and taking her seat across from me. "He's a man with no sense at all of others' suffering. People called him sensitive, but what they really meant was thin-skinned. Sensitive only about himself. Do you know what he did when Dottie told him she was pregnant? Came over, handed her five hundred dollars for an abortion, and walked out the door without even taking off his coat."

"Pure rat," I said.

"Oh, you know it. But I'll tell you what Dottie did with that money. We went down to Rodeo Drive and she bought herself a present, a beautiful garnet ring. She wore it only once though, then put it away. It was too painful a reminder. I never saw it again until the day Darla came to visit."

"She loved that ring." I pushed away the image of what, finally, she had done with it.

Lenore looked somehow smaller under the weight of sadness, but she pulled herself together quickly, sat up even straighter, and took a sip of her tea.

"Dottie did see that man one more time," she said. "A couple of months after she'd gotten pregnant. She'd been so depressed, I talked her into having lunch at Chasen's. It's what we used to do when we wanted to feel special. Hobbing and nobbing with the stars, she'd call it. Of course, all we could afford was the chili, but the place was famous for it.

"Anyway, we were having lunch and in he walks. Well, Dottie's eyes lit up. She smiled at him like a child and said so brightly, so expectantly, 'Hi!' Well, that man looked straight at her like he didn't even know her! The humiliation was so deep. Have you ever seen a person shatter right in front of your eyes? She never mentioned his name again. That's why Darla had no idea who he was. What made it even worse for Dottie was that horrible, skinny creature hanging on his arm. With that smile made of ice. Let me tell you, more than twenty-five years later, nothing's changed. Dolly still has him on a string, even today."

"Dolly?" I said. "You mean Dolly Ryle?"

She sat back in her chair and nodded. "A dumb lug like Mike Ryle needed someone with spine to steer him around."

It took a minute for me to realize I had gotten what I'd come here for. But I'd only been half right. Ryle wasn't Darla's lover. He was her father.

Chapter 43

In other countries, you pass bullet-pocked buildings and bronze plaques and remember old wars. In L.A., you drive past the Beverly Hilton and remember Lucy and Ethel stalking Cornel Wilde at the pool. Or you go up to the planetarium and see the ghost of Sal Mineo in *Rebel Without a Cause.* I drove through the stately East Gate of Bel-Air, then snaked my way past the house where Clark Gable and Carole Lombard once lived, to the address that had been easy enough to find on the Web.

The Ryles' house was surrounded by hedges, maybe six feet high. Behind a wrought-iron gate, the driveway sloped downhill to a terrace where several cars were parked—a Mercedes S600 sedan, a Range Rover, and a Rolls Phantom convertible, which cost about the same as a nice little cottage down in my neighborhood. A pair of hired cops slouched against the front door. Even from here, they didn't look like the sharpest razors in the pack. Maybe I could pretend I was lost, schmooze with them a little. Coax out some tales about their employers. The problem was, if that didn't work, I couldn't show up here again.

As I drove slowly past the tall shrubbery, something caught my eye, something that disrupted the perfectly clipped wall of hedge. I parked a few yards up and walked back. One section of hedge was a brighter green than the rest, scraggly and not quite as tall, a recent replacement, the branches not yet hardened into wood.

I stood still and listened but heard nothing, not even a car in the distance. Heart racing, I pushed myself through the branches. Twigs scraped at my bare arms but were too green to break the skin, and in a few seconds, I found myself on the other side, in a grove that sloped downhill to the estate.

Except for the gentle rustle of leaves, it was very quiet. The late-afternoon light made the new skin of the eucalyptus trunks glow like living nudes. At the bottom of the hill, the low sun glinted orange on the surface of a pool. Slowly, I made my way through the trees to a place where I had a clear view of Ryle's home.

It was an overgrown tract house, gussied up with French windows and columns like the palace of Versailles—the bastard child of Ward Cleaver and Marie Antoinette. From where I stood, I could see into the living room, where a man in a Louis something-or-other chair was tapping his tasseled loafer with impatient reserve. Lyn Fourray.

I could hear the guards at the front door chatting aimlessly, unaware of my presence but far too close. As quietly as I could, I edged my way through the woods toward the rear of the property. From behind the trees, I found myself looking straight into a guest house that could have been a cowboy cabin, if cowboys made a cool million a year. Hand-hewn beams, a stag-horn chandelier, Navajo rugs.

In the center of a long rawhide sofa, wearing jeans and western boots and a shirt with tooled-silver collar clips, sat Mike Ryle, so still he could have been made of wax. He appeared lost in thought, and even from a distance, I could feel the weight of his depression. Maybe he was mourning Darla's death. Maybe it was guilt. Maybe he only came to life when someone said "action."

Yet his physical presence was imposing—broad shoulders and thighs so long they jutted beyond the depth of the ample couch. His full head of hair was flecked with silver, and his face, though slack, still had an architectural perfection.

I searched for a resemblance to Darla. He had a fine straight nose, broad cheekbones, and eyes that, though brown, were wide set. Similarities, yes, but you wouldn't notice unless you were looking for them.

A few moments later the door opened and Dolly came in. Mike looked up but his face remained dull. I couldn't hear what she said, but she spoke without pauses, the way a mother does when she comforts a distressed child. She sat down next to him and pressed his face to the bony cushion of her bosom. She stroked his hair and kept talking, talking, while her eyes, annoyed, impatient, looked everywhere but at him.

After a while, she gave him a pat of dismissal. He lifted his head and she smoothed the front of his shirt and brushed a few stray hairs from his forehead. With each little thing she did, his face took on more life.

She led him over to a mirror, and when he saw himself, he stood up straighter, seemed to fill up more of his own body. She beamed over his shoulder into the glass. Then he smiled. *The* smile. I could feel the magnetic warmth of it and I remembered when I was no more than eight or nine, watching *Homesteaders* on Thursday nights, how that smile and his low, honey-smooth voice could make me flush with pleasure. As he transformed in front of the mirror, I began to understand what Darla meant when she said she had willed her beauty—that she had learned to inhabit it, as Ryle was doing now.

Dolly took his arm and led him toward the door, then stood back so that he could open it for her. As he did, she glanced out the window and saw me.

I fought the instinct to run. Instead, I grinned and waved at her like I was some goofy tourist. She hesitated for a split second, then hurried her husband out of the room.

I ran.

Halfway up the hill, I could hear the rent-a-cops shouting at me to stop. They took off after me, but they were big and slow. I reached the hedges before they made it past the pool, only I couldn't find the young green plant that had made entry so easy. I wasted precious seconds looking for it, while the sound of dried leaves crunching beneath their feet grew closer. I made a dash for the gate, thinking maybe there was enough space between the hedge and the granite pillars to squeeze through.

But before I could get there, one of the cops grabbed my arm. I tried to wrench free, and he twisted it back hard. I let out a yowl. His partner caught up and gripped my other arm.

I struggled against them as they dragged me back from the hedge, but when I saw they were taking me to the house, I knew this was my chance.

In the entry hall, the bigger of the two guards picked up the phone to call the police.

I said, "Before you do that, tell Mr. Ryle a friend of his daughter's is here."

"Lady," he said, "they got no kids." He started to dial.

I said, "You want to bet your job on that?"

The lower you are on the food chain, the fewer risks you can afford. He hesitated, then put the receiver back and knocked—delicately for such a big man—on the double doors of the living room. When no one answered, he looked at me and shrugged as if he were off the hook.

"Knock harder," I said.

Reluctantly, he did.

Dolly Ryle opened the door a crack and slipped through like a wisp of chill breeze. Before she closed it behind her, I glimpsed her husband and Lyn Fourray.

"What's wrong with you," she said to the guard, "interrupting us like this?"

"Sorry, Mrs. Ryle. But we got a little problem with the girl."

"What are you, a child? Handle it."

"She says she's a friend of your daughter."

"Ridiculous. I have no children."

I said, "Not *your* daughter. Your husband's."

She deigned to notice me then. "I beg your pardon?"

"Your husband's daughter. The one who was murdered."

Her face was without expression, except for an almost imperceptible twitch of annoyance at the corner of her mouth.

"Have her wait," she said.

Then she turned her back to us, cocked her head coquettishly to one side, and walked back into the living room.

It was almost dark when Fourray drove off in the Mercedes. I was afraid he might recognize me, but he didn't even glance my way.

About ten minutes later Dolly sent for me and dismissed the guards, who trotted off like a pair of arthritic Rottweilers.

She was alone, seated in an armchair, her back finishing-school straight. She did not invite me to sit.

"Now, what is this nonsense about a daughter?" she said.

"Mike's daughter. Darla Ward."

"My dear, you must be out of your mind."

Her face was smooth and her lips were the shiny red of a new toy fire engine. When she smiled, just slightly, to show me that nothing I said was of much concern to her, the lines that appeared under her eyes were almost horizontal, radiating toward the fine scars that formed a seam between ear and cheek. But her eyes were ageless and alive. Her hands rested in her lap, There was something about the curve of her fingers, scaled by age, that resembled a creature lying in wait to grip its prey.

"My husband," she said, "has no daughter and never did. The only reason we haven't called the police about you is that once the media get hold of a rumor, they can do terrible damage, even after it's proven false. I suppose you want—"

Her gaze traveled past me and saw something that made her mouth grow so tight, dozens of tiny lines cracked through the paint. I turned to see what had displeased her.

Mike Ryle was closing the double doors behind him. He looked as he had in the guest house, the flesh over his perfect bone structure a curtain of defeat.

"Dolly," he said, "you know I don't want to be alone."

She went straight to his side and those fingers curled around his arm.

"Darling," she said, "I'll just be a few minutes."

For the first time, he noticed me. "I'm sorry. I—"

"Why don't you wait for me upstairs, Mike?"

She tried to pilot him out the door, but before she could I said, "I wanted to talk to you about Darla."

Awareness slowly penetrated the fog of Ryle's depression, and he quickly tried to cover it. "Darla?" he said, like a man awakening from sleep.

"Darling, this girl is a trespasser. Those incompetent guards can't handle anything."

I ignored her and addressed Mike directly. "I'm Nikki Easton. I was a friend of hers."

"Darla? The girl who was murdered?" Now he was acting. His eyes went directly to his wife for direction.

"You don't have to pretend," I said. "I know how much finding you meant to her."

My words made a direct hit. His mouth went slack and he stared at me.

"Mike," Dolly said sharply, "I'll take care of this." The claw tightened around his arm.

"You're the girl who was with her when she was killed, aren't you?" he said.

"Yes."

He broke from Dolly's grasp and sat down on the sofa. She sat beside him. Her hand curved around his thigh, but as hard as she gripped him, it made no impression. "Mike, stop," she said fiercely.

He focused so intently on me, he didn't seem to hear her. Pain burned through his glazed-over eyes. "Did Darla tell you about me, about how much we loved each other?"

"Darling, get control of yourself." Dolly tried to cut him off with her sharp clear voice. But he was riding emotions too powerful to halt.

He looked at me, his eyes pleading. "You have to understand. I didn't want to hurt her. There was too much at stake. I did the right thing!"

He turned to his wife, palms out, pleading. "Dolly, you understood. You know how hard it was for me. But I did the right thing in the end, didn't I, Pudding?"

"The right thing?" I said. "You abandoned her before she was born and then abandoned her again because you wanted to win an election."

"Before she was born? What are you talking about?" Mike looked at me as if I'd betrayed him. "I thought you knew how it was with us."

"Mike!" Dolly's voice pierced the air like an alarm.

"Dolly, you know I never meant to hurt you. But it was so powerful. She would just touch my hand—*touch my hand*—and take my breath away. I'm a man. I was weak."

What was he talking about?

Dolly had a look on her face like someone speeding headlong into an accident.

"You can't imagine," he said, lost in memory and beyond all caution, "the joy of making love to her. That beautiful face. It was like a . . . a mirror."

I was so stunned that for a moment I couldn't speak.

"Your lover's face was like a mirror," I said, "because she was your daughter."

In the first shock of those words, he looked at me without seeing. Then he lowered his head and stared down at his fingers, at the long nail beds with a sliver of moon, exactly like Darla's. He clenched his eyes shut. His face went gray. He shook his head, still refusing to understand.

It was all coming clear to me—the découpage box with its strange mix of childhood photos and provocative nudes. "She spent her life longing for her father," I said, "longing for you. She thought the only way she could have you was to seduce you."

No one had drawn the curtains. Outside was black sky and brilliant stars.

"Now you have really gone too far," Dolly said to me, her body rigid with anger.

"Do you remember Dottie Ward?" I said.

There was no recognition in his eyes. But Dolly was ready for it. "Dottie Ward was a cheap trollop who fell into bed with anyone."

"Mike," I said, "you gave her five hundred dollars. To get rid of the baby."

The money. That he remembered. Then he saw it too clearly, could barely breathe under the weight of it.

"Darla was my . . . my child?"

He looked at his wife, searching for the shock in her face. But there was none. Only a slight tremor in her pinched mouth.

"Dolly . . . you knew?"

"I didn't want you to find out this way," she said. "You see, when that black man, the detective, told Leo about your affair, the girl and I had a little talk. That's when she started to make all these desperate insinuations. But for heaven's sake, Dottie Ward? Who's to say who the father was?"

"You never *told* me!"

Dolly remained stone, but her voice was soft, almost coy. "There was no point upsetting you, darling. I discussed it with Leo and he promised to take care of the situation."

There it was. Ninety pounds of cold ambition behind all that death.

I looked directly at Dolly. "That's what happened at Ivarene, isn't it? Leo tried to take care of it. But Darla couldn't be the only victim. People might ask the wrong questions and wind up at your doorstep. So Leo told Johnny Rambla to kill the other three along with her. Just another drug deal gone bad. But things didn't go according to plan, did they? The detective had to be killed, too, because he was the only one who could link Darla to your husband. 'That black man' had a name, by the way. It was Manny Roberson. He also had a wife. And a little boy."

"What ludicrous accusations." Dolly's voice was controlled. But I could see the panic in her eyes.

So could Mike. I'd never seen such a look of raw pain on someone's face. His eyes were moist and his lips trembled. It was hard to watch an old hero crumbling.

"Darla survived Ivarene," I said. "She must have phoned you from Big Sur, Mike." I remembered waking up in the cabin, Darla with makeup on, cooking in the kitchen like she'd been up for a long time. "You told your little Pudding about the call, and that time Leo didn't bungle it."

"Phone call? What phone call?" He looked at Dolly with childlike helplessness.

Dolly was smiling. Some shred of confidence had returned. "That woman never phoned here," she said. "We've listened to your filth long enough."

Then, calm and sure, she walked to the desk and opened the drawer. When she turned back, she had a gun in her hand, a western revolver with a long barrel, the kind Mike Ryle had carried on TV. It looked strangely out of place in this room. And she handled it awkwardly. I could see that she'd never used a gun before.

"We really can't have you talking this nonsense everywhere," she said.

For the first time, Mike did not seem lost. He approached her slowly, confidently. A cowboy hero. This was a role he knew how to play. She gazed up at him and the adoration in her eyes was real. Her steely slimness appeared frail. Her body curved into the shelter of his chest and she released the gun into his hands.

He held it in his open palm, feeling the weight of it. Then he opened his mouth and tilted his head back as if he were about to howl like a wounded animal.

But he didn't.

He put the pistol between his lips and pulled the trigger.

CHAPTER 44

It was over but it wasn't.

I still woke up every morning with my gut in a knot. In part, it was my share of the guilt. I had killed one man and pushed another to suicide. There had been no choice with Leo, and Mike Ryle would have had to face the truth sooner or later, but both deaths had changed me in ways I could not yet fully understand. And there were still unanswered questions. The drugs Darla stole had never been found, and though it seemed clear that Dolly Ryle had been responsible for Darla's murder, there was no proof.

As for Adder and me, that definitely wasn't over. I wanted him, and I wanted us to work. He hadn't officially moved back in, but his clothes were slowly filling up my closet again. He was here now, his rumpled face on my pillow, my head resting on his shoulder. He was still sleeping, and I floated along the blurred line between thought and dream.

I thought about yesterday, when Adder and I had gone downtown to pick up Darla's ashes. The Coroner's office had called her mother several times, but Dottie never showed up, so the body was sent to the County Morgue where it was cremated. Only then did someone notice my name on the paperwork. We picked up a brown plastic box and drove out to Malibu to scatter the ashes. But standing on the cliff, looking out at the dark, choppy ocean under a gray sky, I had been overcome by an enormous sense of loneliness. And I couldn't do it, couldn't abandon her to that huge, impersonal sea where she would still be so alone.

She had always been alone. A hollow-eyed child smiling at the camera with her arm around her brother's shoulders. Smiling from the pages of *Bachelor Pad.* Smiling, eerily peaceful, out in back of my house the night we drove to Big Sur.

I thought about burying the ashes in my yard, remembering how she had looked out there in the moonlight, sitting beside the geraniums, the flowers she loved because they were so indestructible, because even if you severed the stems, you could stick them back in the ground and they would just keep growing. I remembered the dirt on her hands that night, the broken fingernails.

Suddenly, I was wide awake.

I threw on my sweats and got the shovel from the tool shed. We'd had no rain for awhile, but the ground was soft and the roots of the geraniums gave too easily. I pulled out a cluster of them. Fine new root hairs were emerging from the stems. I had just begun to dig up the rest when the shovel struck something hard, but not like a rock. I got down on my knees and began scooping the dirt out until my fingers touched cloth, then a weathered leather handle.

I lifted out the gym bag. It was stuffed with plastic packets of heroin, eleven of them, with Leo Auriole's logo.

"Baby." Adder's voice was still fogged with sleep. He was leaning in the doorway in jeans and a shirt, with one eye still half closed. "You gonna come on in and have coffee with me?"

I held up the bag. "Look what I found."

He stared at it and scratched his head. I could see the fog slowly lift and both eyes open wide.

"Holy shit," he said softly.

We took the bag into the house and set it on the coffee table.

"You know what you're looking at?" Adder said.

I thought of all the people who had been murdered for the contents of this bag. And all the people the dope would kill a little more slowly.

"A million dollars, baby." A glint of excitement flashed in his eyes.

"No," I said. "Don't even go there."

"Yeah, you're right. We'll let it rot in a police locker." He got that amused grin on his face, the grin I knew so well.

"Adder, you're not serious."

He looked directly into my eyes, as if the brightness in his could ignite mine. It had the opposite effect.

"No," I said, "I don't want any part of this."

He laughed. Big. Open. Happy. "Of course you don't. What would we do with a million dollars?"

He threw his arms around me, and the closer he held me, the farther away he seemed to get.

I stepped back, and he laid the weight of his big hands on my shoulders. "Listen to me," he said. "You've spent your whole life running toward freedom. Well, you finally made it, baby. Here's your freedom, right here in this bag."

"No," I said, "there's nothing in that bag but misery and death."

Neither of us told the whole truth. I could see the fear in him. And I could feel the greed in me.

You get so close to someone, you know the feel, the taste of every inch of them, you know how to ignite them with the slightest touch, with a warm rush of breath, with a hand hovering inches above their skin. From this, you imagine you are learning their truest places.

But now I was looking at a man I didn't know at all. His eyes burned with excitement, but beneath was something leaden, something desperate, something finished.

He watched me cautiously as the space between us widened

into a cool, steep chasm. He took the box of cigarettes from his shirt pocket and flipped open the top.

You can spend a lot of time chasing down answers, finding the pieces, working the logic, yet the truth escapes you. Then, when you're looking the other way, it assaults you. It comes in a sudden shock of understanding. And you know it's true because the pain shoots so deep.

I couldn't look at him. Because he would see that I knew.

"Maybe you're right," I said. "I just need a little space to think."

I got up and went into the bedroom and closed the door. The Baby was tucked away in its box, high up on a shelf in the closet, but his holstered Baretta hung from the chair. Every inch of my skin listened for his movements in the living room as I slipped the gun out of its sheath.

When I came back out, he was zipping the bag shut.

I pulled back the slide. At the sound he spun around, reflexively reaching to where his holster would have been if he had it on. When he saw it was me, he laughed and put his hands up as if it was a joke.

I said, "You killed her, Adder, didn't you?"

The hands dropped to his sides, the grin dropped from his face. The pain in his eyes told me all I needed to know.

Everything made sense now. Darla had never called Ryle or anyone else from Big Sur. *I'll drive by a couple of times a night. Just to make sure you're okay,* Adder had said when we'd broken up.

He must have driven by the night she showed up. Or maybe he guessed Kyle's death would flush her out. Maybe he'd seen her in the moonlight through the window or seen us drive off. He was no dumb lug like Raymond. He would have known how to follow us without being seen. Once we started north up the coast, he would have had a good idea where we were headed.

He and I had spent a weekend together in those cabins. And he hadn't been sick when Darla and I were in Big Sur. It was a way to cover his absence from work.

"I can't believe it, Adder. I can't believe you killed her in cold blood."

His eyes were as wet as mine. It was no act.

"I didn't mean to. I didn't mean to hurt her at all. She pulled a gun on me and I reacted. I never meant to kill her."

"But you did. And if I'd been in that cabin, I'd be dead, too."

Inside I was all quicksand.

"I waited out there a long time," Adder said. "I watched the two of you. I know you, Nikki. I saw your face while you listened to her. The more you heard, the more you wanted to run. I waited until you drove away."

"And if I hadn't."

His eyes were pleading, desperate. "I could never do anything to harm you."

"From day one, all you ever wanted was the dope."

He looked at me as if I didn't understand him, as if I was the one who had betrayed him.

"I wanted it, but I *needed* you."

It sounded real. His voice was heavy with emotion. But the quicksand in me had turned to ice and nothing he said could touch me.

"Christ, baby," he said, "I told you I had a dream for us. What did you think it was? Life in a fucking rented apartment with a guy on a paycheck?"

I kept my eyes on him, kept the gun steady. But I was thinking about him and me and how it had all begun with death and the hunger for life it imparts. Behind his eyes I had always seen his battlefields, the smoke, the noise, the filth, the fireworks, the blood, the ferocity, the bravery; and with him I had embraced a strange mixture of my imagination and the war that he had lived. Yet even now, diminished by his greed and his guilt, the smooth skin of his forearm beneath the rolled-up sleeve and the hair falling lank across his forehead still pulled me as if our cells were attached by invisible threads.

"It's a sack of powder, Nikki," he said. "I don't give a shit about it." He kicked the bag of dope and it fell at my feet with a thud. "Do what you want with it. But don't throw away you and me and how we are together. I've lived with death and killing for a long time. Long enough to know that's all there is. Death and killing and whatever sweetness you can find in between. We found the sweet, baby."

Then he said softly, "It's your call."

He reached out to me, palms open. But it was his eyes that killed me. They were completely unguarded. The way they sometimes were in bed. He looked like he was ready to die, almost seemed to be longing for it.

I kept the gun on him until his hands fell to his sides. Then he slowly bent down, his eyes on me, calibrating my reaction, and picked up the bag.

The terrible thing was that I still loved him. Only there was a rent down the middle of that love, bright red and the exact shape of the stream of blood that ran down Darla's skin.

He walked to the door.

I still held the gun. But I was thinking about the way I used to lay my head across his chest and feel his heart beating and be frightened at our fragility.

I didn't shoot him.

I didn't call the police.

And I do not regret it.

ABOUT THE AUTHOR

Maxine Nunes is a New Yorker who's spent most of her life in Los Angeles. She has written and produced for television, and currently writes for several publications including the *Los Angeles Times.* Her satiric parody of a White House scandal won the Pen USA West International Imitation Hemingway Competition.